The Game of Gods

~The Beginning~

Joshua Kern

Other Books by Joshua Kern

Refton & Thomas

Forgotten Spies

Forgotten Child

The Game of Gods

Arc 1 – Human

The Beginning

The Death of Champions

Arc 2 – Demi-God

Fragments

A Tower Novella

Pieces of Divinity

Arc 3 – God

The Dungeon Alaria

Arc 1 – Integration

Contents

Prologue

"I have grown tired of watching over these foolish humans!" Zeus roared in annoyance. Many of his fellow gods that were gathered around the circular table nodded in agreement.

"What would you have us do? They have all but forgotten us!" Odin replied, one hand stroking Muninn while Huginn rested on the opposite shoulder.

"Speak for yourself, some of us still have worshippers and followers." One of the gods clinging to the wall of the room shouted.

"Bah," Odin snorted in derision. "Those worshippers you're so proud of are nothing more than sheep following the people around them. They don't truly believe in us anymore." He finished angrily.

"No, they don't, but there is something we can do. We can reset the board, we can change everything before we truly are forgotten." Zeus told them wearily. The long intervening years had not been kind to any of them. Many of them were one comic book or movie away from being forgotten by the masses.

"How? None of us have the strength to do something of that magnitude anymore. Even at the height of our powers it would have proven difficult!" Brigit of the Tuatha Dé Danann, said angrily as she finally rolled the dice waiting breathlessly for it to finish rolling. She got an eleven.

The man at the head of the table was garbed in a large cloak and hood that kept his face in shadow. "You needed at least a thirteen to avoid the attack from the crazed Dark Elf. His strike hits for one hundred twelve damage taking the rest of your health. You have died." The games Dungeon Master told her with a barely hidden smirk.

Brigit stood in a huff and kicked over her chair. That was the third character she had lost in as many weeks.

"If you worked together with everyone else, you would not die as often!" He told the beautiful and angry goddess. His words doubtlessly falling on deaf ears, playing nice with other people had never been her strong suit.

"Well, there's an idea!" Shiva interjected in a deep smooth voice. "We could all work together to make it happen. Combine all our remaining powers."

"Hmm, it could work," Odin said thoughtfully, his fingers still stroking the silky black feathers of the raven Muninn.

Arinna the Sun-goddess's softly glowing hands reached across the table and snagged the dice. It was her turn to roll them. "What do we do then? How would we change things?" She asked as she tossed the dice across the table.

Zeus reached out and caught the dice before they could hit the table, ignoring Arinna's squawk of displeasure. "That's obvious we turn the entire world into this!" He told them all in a powerful voice as he waved his arm at the table.

Slowly, all the gathered gods began laughing as they caught onto what he was suggesting.

It was unnoticed by the rest when the face of the Dungeon Master upturned into a gleeful grin. Finally, things were about to get interesting. The game of gods was about to begin.

Chapter 1

Charles woke with a groan already able to feel his head pounding in anger at him having stayed up as long as he had. It wasn't his fault that the episode of his favorite TV show had been particularly good, nor did it matter that he had watched the entire series at least five times already.

He had pulled three all-nighters in a row at work, in an effort to complete the project on time. When he had finally gotten home, the night before he had flicked on the TV to his favorite show instead of going to sleep. The high of being awake for so long had slowly faded away as he watched the show from his bed. A deep sleep had claimed soon afterwards.

His eyes felt like they were glued shut as he forced the palms of his hands to scrub at them with another groan. His dreams had been odd and disturbing forcing him to ignore them all night long.

"Oh, quit your whining, you pathetic weakling!" An uncompromisingly hard voice said to him.

With a hitch of his throat, Charles shot off his bed and to his feet, his eyes pulling themselves open with a wrench. His sandy and dry feeling eyes revealed a blurred and hazy looking room with a red-haired woman standing in front of his desk. As he blinked furiously, she slowly came into focus, revealing her long curly red hair that cascaded down the middle of her back. Her large green eyes were hard, and her sharp nose upturned haughtily as she looked at him. A sword was strapped to the thigh of her dark red leather pants. A soft green blouse tried to hide her womanly form only barely succeeding. She was an exceedingly beautiful woman, but none of that so much as hinted to the reason that she was standing in the bedroom of his apartment.

Then he felt his mind stutter and grind to a halt as he saw the long-tapered ears that peaked through her hair.

"Who... who are you?" He stuttered weakly as he tried to cover his overly skinny chest. His dark blue boxers highlighting his pale legs.

A hazy black transparent box flickered into being in the corner of his vision.

You have been cursed by the gods!
Your refusal to acknowledge their announcement has
earned their ire!

The curse 'Sleepless' has been placed upon you by the gods,
as such only the gods may remove this curse.

As Zeus is one of the gods involved in this curse, it was
decided that you will need to complete twelve challenges to
have this curse removed. Details of the
challenges you will need to complete will be revealed in
time.

For now, enjoy not being able to sleep.

Charles felt his legs grow weak at what he was seeing. The soft edges of the box stayed in his vision no matter how much he blinked.

"You have to will it closed like you would a window on your computer, you dimwitted fool!"

Charles extended his hand and tried pressing the corner as she had said. A harsh laugh filled the air at his actions.

"You have to do it with your mind, not your hand. Just think about it closing." At the direction of her words, he pushed with his mind and the box closed leaving nothing behind.

"What is going on?" Charles asked weakly as he sank back onto his bed.

"If you had woken like everyone else in the world, you would already know the answer to that question. The world has changed. My fellow gods and I decided that we had grown bored looking over the world. You all had but forgotten us, leaving us with nothing to occupy our time. Can you really blame us for growing bored and needing to find other things to occupy our time with? We decided that we no longer wanted humanity to continue down the path they had been treading. So, we combined all our powers and changed the very fabric of reality and the world." The red-haired elfin eared goddess pushed away from his cluttered desk to stand at her full angry five-foot height.

"The world is now modeled after the fashion of your table-top role-playing games. People can now gain levels by completing tasks or killing monsters. And yes, there are monsters in the world. We have brought back the monsters of legend and awakened them from their slumber. As time passes, more will be introduced when the time is right. You will be happy to note that when we made these changes, we decided to include a helpful guide to the way the new system works. All you have to do is think 'Help' and the guide will pop into being in the center of your vision." She continued speaking, but Charles felt his attention drift at the fantastical change that she was talking about. Nothing was the same. The entire world had been changed overnight.

"What happened to the power?" He asked numbly as he noticed that his alarm clock was no longer working.

"About that," She answered with an audible smirk. "You see something interesting happened when we changed the world. It created something akin to an Electro-Magnetic Pulse, consequently, the entire world no longer has power. All the technology humanity has created over the years is now worthless."

"What about pacemakers and life-support machines?" He asked, trying to wrap his head around everything.

"What about them? They're all dead!" Was the cold reply. "Do you even know how many people have died in the hours since our announcement? The shock alone killed a full tenth of humanity, since then roving monsters and accidents of all kind have taken another thirty percent. Of the nearly eight billion people that were alive yesterday just under five billion remains."

"Who are you?" Charles finally managed to ask as the shock of what she was saying broke him from his stupor.

"My name is Brigit of the Tuatha Dé Danann, and I am a goddess you mortal worm." As she spoke her voice grew deeper, and she seemed to grow in height.

"My family," Charles asked, choosing to ignore what she had just announced a second before. The Fae weren't real, then again neither were the other gods. He would have to ask her about them all later if he had the chance.

"Hmm?" Brigit asked, seeming unable to follow what he was asking.

"What about my family? Are they alive or dead?" He clarified for her. Last night, both his parents and his older sister had all been alive.

"Your parents are dead, they were in their car when it happened. As for your sister, it seems that she is still alive and has formed a party of survivors on her school campus." She paused for a second before refocusing her large eyes on him. "Enough about other people, I must leave soon, and we have a lot to cover. Pray that we have time to finish the list."

Charles forced himself to push aside the feelings he felt concerning the death of his parents and the situation his sister was in. For now, at least he had other things to worry about, and by the sound of it, his sister was doing better than he was. Besides, she was on the opposite side of the country at MIT. There was nothing he could for her from Denver. He would make his way to her though, he would make sure of it.

"Pull up your 'Status' page by thinking about it. This page will be very helpful to your future, so don't forget that it exists. It will be where you manage your various abilities." She told him, once more getting down to business.

Charles thought 'Status' and saw a page with three simple lines in it and nothing more.

Name: Charles Byrne

Level 1 - Exp to next level: 40

Cursed by the gods with 'Sleepless'

"Umm, isn't there usually more than three lines of information on a status page?" He dared to ask the goddess who was suddenly looking at him strangely.

"Yes, there are supposed to be lines for Strength, Dexterity, Agility, Intelligence and more. For some reason, you don't have any of those listed." She crept closer to him until he could see that her eyes were unfocused and slightly glazed.

He watched as her mouth began to move softly whispering to herself in a language he didn't understand. The more she whispered, the brighter her green eyes became until they were glowing brightly. Finally, the glow in her eyes began to fade as she finished whatever it was she had been doing, no longer whispering.

"It is because of our curse on you!" She said at length. "To level-up properly you need to fall asleep for the various changes to take effect. Since you cannot sleep, those changes are unable to be applied. It is good we discovered this now before we curse anyone else."

"If I can't level-up and grow stronger, then how am I supposed to survive?" Charles asked weakly as he pulled his still warm blanket over his bare legs.

"Yes, that may prove to be difficult for you. Oh, well." She said nonchalantly as her eyes fully refocused on him.

"Oh, well?" Charles sputtered. "I'm going to die because of what you people did and all you can do is say oh well?" The sunlight in the room dimmed as clouds passed over it.

Brigit's hair took on an otherworldly glow blazing red at his question. "You dare to question the gods?" The anger was palpable in her voice as it lowered to a deep bass that he felt in his bones.

"Yes, yes, I do." He said indignantly, glad that he was already sitting. He didn't think his legs would have held him otherwise. Just sitting in front, she was almost too much for him. His mouth and throat were dry, and his heart was beating faster than it had before causing everything to take on a reddish tinge.

"Do you understand that I could kill you without a thought and not feel anything more regarding the act than I would for stepping on an ant?" Her eyes had begun to glow again, flashing dangerously.

"What is your point?" He returned, acting far braver than he actually felt. "From what you have told me, it sounds like I am going to die, anyway. So why exactly should I fear the wrath of the gods?"

The goddess's eyes flashed one last time and then the light illuminating them began to fade taking the blazing red of her hair with it. She stood there in front of him looking down at him a gleam replacing the anger in her eyes.

"Hmm, you surprise me, human. You drew our attention by your lack of action during our announcement. Now you have drawn my personal attention by your actions." She stepped back and leaned her hip against his desk in the corner of the room her eyes fixed on him thoughtfully.

A small grin slowly crept across her face as she continued to look at him. "I think that I am going to enjoy this new world that we have created!" She said softly to herself unaware that Charles still heard her words. Her eyes slid out of focus as her attention drifted from him to somewhere else.

Charles struggled to keep his face even as he sat in his bed. The goddess put out a palpable and near stifling aura of pressure, even while she was just standing there calmly.

"Very well," She said, finally drawing his attention back to her and away from his inner musings. "I have discussed it with the other ruling gods, and we have decided that there may be something we can do for you. The gods have decided to gift you with a weapon and an item that will help you survive if used correctly." The air in front of her blurred as she held out her hand with her palm open and fingers pointed upwards.

"How will a weapon be useful to me?" Charles managed to force out, his tongue feeling increasingly thick and unresponsive the longer she was in front of him. "I've never even been in a fight before. I don't know how to use any weapons!"

Brigit's face tightened at his interruption. "If you would remain quiet, I will explain!" She enunciated each word carefully through clenched teeth. "As I was saying. Both items will possess certain enchantments that you should find useful in remaining alive." The air above her hand solidified into a small black flask with an attached strap to allow it to hang from a belt. "This flask contains a health potion that will heal you back to full health as long as you remain alive to use it. It will not bring you back from the dead in other words."

Great, a single use item! That will only be useful one time, Charles thought carefully keeping his inner thoughts from showing on his face.

"This flask is more than what it appears, however," She continued with a smirk on her face clearly having guessed what he was thinking. "There are a number of enchantments on it. The first binds it to your person so that it cannot be sold, stolen, or given away. The second, refills it over time, every twelve hours it can be used one time. Bear in mind that it doesn't matter how much you drink, it will still count as using it a single time. Also, the potion inside cannot be stored inside any other container, so don't even try. Finally, the flask can only be used on yourself or a member of your party." She passed the flask over to him watching as he looked at it closely.

Those limitations on it, he knew would ensure it remained useable over time while keeping it out of other people's hands. It was definitely a good item as long as he could find a way to remain alive, with any luck the weapon she had mentioned would have equally useful enchantments on them.

The air above her hand once more blurred as a long black sword that seemed to absorb light settled into her open hand. It was what was known as a hand and a half sword allowing it to be used with one hand or two depending on the situation. The blade was thin and appeared to be suitable more for piercing than slashing. Above her hand, a simple unadorned leather scabbard and belt appeared and then settled limply in her grasp hanging over the edge of her hand.

"This sword also possesses a number of enchantments that you will find useful in helping you to remain alive. The first is the same as what is on your flask. The sword is bound to your person, it cannot be sold, stolen or given away, it also cannot be lost as it will reappear on your person should such an event take place. The second enchantment allows it to increase your strength and speed during a battle, it will also scale with your levels. This will help to lower the gap between you and everyone else but will not eliminate it entirely. There are two more enchantments on it, as you have no doubt already guessed by its appearance normally this sword would have to be used along the lines of a rapier where it is used for piercing attacks instead of slashing. That is not the case with this particular weapon, it is unbreakable so feel free to use it as you would any other sword. The final enchantment is one that I think you will find particularly useful. It will allow the sword to help guide your movements when you use it for practice. In other words, it will teach you how to use it properly in a fight, so make sure that you spend some time each night practicing with it." Carefully she placed her free hand on the flat of the blade and extended the hilt and scabbard to him.

Charles took the scabbard first and set it to the side on his bed next to the flask. Reaching for the hilt of the sword he braced his arm expecting it to be heavy, instead, it was surprisingly light. He brought the sword closer as his eyes ran over the black blade, hard to see runes ran over the surface of the blade blending in with whatever the sword was made of.

Without thinking, he lightly tested the edge of the blade with the pad of his thumb finding it razor sharp as it cut his skin effortlessly. Bringing his thumb to his mouth he sucked the blood from it as he eyed the blade wearily. If, it could truly teach him how to use it properly then this sword was truly going to save his life. He just needed to make sure that he put in the time to practice with it.

"Thank you for these!" He began as he kept his eyes on the blade. "I know it won't be easy, but with these, I think I can at least have a fighting chance."

Brigit looked at him her lips curling into a smile as she started laughing. "Do you have any idea how stupid you sound? You are going to die right away!" Her eyes drifted off of him as she scanned everything in his room, stopping when she saw the box set in front of his TV. "How about this, I can't put a computer in your head, but I can make it so you can learn certain abilities or skills easier."

Charles felt his face go blank at her reaction and answer. "Uh, why would you do that for me?" He finally managed to ask her.

She cocked her head to the side as she answered. "Because you surprised me. It doesn't happen as often as you might think. I want you to remain alive long enough to entertain me some more. This will help that to happen!" She stepped right up to his bed as she finished speaking and put her hand on his head covering his eyes.

A bright flash lit the room as the pressure from her hand left his head, and he opened his eyes on reflex.

Charles began to gasp for breath as the pressure in the room seemed to explosively lighten. Brigit had disappeared and with her the pressure her very presence caused. Three notifications popped into his vision as he struggled for breath. He closed two of them right away as they were about the items he had been given. The third one, however, pertained to the ability he had just been given.

The goddess Brigit has generously gifted you with the ability 'Quick Learning'. This ability allows you to quickly learn certain abilities and skills that otherwise would take a large time commitment.

Charles closed the last window thoughtfully, his mind still struggling to process everything that had happened since he woke. The goddess, his parents, the world, there was so much that he needed to wrap his head around but that would take time. Something that he did not think he had very much of, as the sound of the world outside his apartment began to trickle in and reach his ears.

Really it was the lack of noise, there were no sirens in the distance or the sound of angry drivers honking constantly. There was none of the normal noise that he had come to expect no matter the hour of the day. Denver was like any other city, it never slept. Or at least it never had until now.

Tilting his head in apprehension, he flung the blankets from his legs and hopped off the bed. His sword went over the side of the bed as it tangled with his blanket and was ripped from his grasp. Crossing the room in a rush, he stopped next to the window in shock. Everything looked like it was on fire.

All the buildings surrounding him and, in the distance, had flames either climbing the sides or shooting from windows. Movement in the streets below drew his wide eyes from the burning buildings and onto the endless line of wreckage that filled the streets. Vehicle after vehicle filled the street clogging it completely, leaving little room on the sidewalk for walking. A number of the cars and trucks were nothing but still smoking husks of burned out metal. Others were still on fire, making it clear where at least some of the fires around the city had originated from.

Movement below and to the right allowed his eyes to narrow in on what had drawn his attention initially. A roving pack of dogs was dragging something from a car that had yet to catch fire. He smashed his head against the glass of his window as he struggled to focus his eyes on what they were dragging from the car.

His apartment was on the sixth floor of his building, making everything happening on the street appear small and indistinct. Something shifted in his eyes and suddenly everything zoomed in and came into focus. To the side of his vision, a notification popped into being.

Due to intense focus, you have learned the ability 'Far-Seeing'. This ability allows you to see things far in the distance with intense clarity.

With a thought, he closed the transparent window and refocused his eyes on the street below. The dogs zoomed in close enough for him to see the drool that dripped from their mouths and the blood that had matted their fur in various places. Two dogs at the front of the pack gave a great heave, and he was finally able to see what they had dragged from the car. A single leg torn at the knee with a red strappy high-heel filled their snarling mouths.

Charles looked away, his eyes moving over the wrecked silver sedan and stopping on a large green monster with a club in its hands that was jumping from car to car. From the corner of his eye, he saw the dogs grab the leg and drag it into an alley away from view. Each jump of the monsters' huge legs and feet brought it crashing down on another car, crumpling part of it each time.

The monsters' tusked mouth bent towards the sky, its large snout-like nose flaring as it smelled something. Its head swiveled towards the alley the dogs had disappeared down and a malicious tooth filled grin crept over its face. With a single great bound it leaped from the car crumpling it in the middle and landed in front of the entrance to the alley.

It vanished from view as a series of howls and animalistic screams softly reached Charles's ears. Stepping away from the window, he felt a wave of terror wash over him that had been long in coming. He wasn't angry for some fictional injustice that had been committed against him or the world. He knew enough about the world and the way life worked to understand that it was always the strong that ruled. The gods who had done this were simply the strongest beings around, there was no point in getting mad over something he could do nothing about. Maybe someday, if he ever got strong enough, he could do something to the gods if that was even possible.

In the meantime, he had more important things to occupy his time with; he needed to go east to his sister. She was the only family that he had left now, and there was no way he was going to let her die. With the gifts from the gods and some luck, he might be able to at least help her stay alive. She was smart, far smarter than him. Physical exercise had been sacrificed more times than he could count for studying; he was worried about her.

Taking another step back away from the window, his feet tangled in his blanket, causing him to lose his balance and fall heavily to the floor. He remained on the ground as he struggled to push aside his emotions for the time being. He knew his sister was safe for now, and there was nothing he could do for her from his current location. She was on the east coast, and he was in Colorado, it would take him some time to make his way to her.

The news that his parents were dead was something else entirely. He had spoken to them the night before. They had been healthy and doing well at their home in California. It would take some time for him to work through his emotions properly, and he knew that. For now, though he had to ensure that he survived long enough to make that happen.

A violent rumble filled the air as the floor beneath him shook and the building groaned. Pulling his feet free, he climbed to his feet with one hand on his bed to steady himself against the moving floor. He looked around his room as what he needed to do next became obvious.

He needed to quickly get dressed and grab some supplies and then leave. The city was on fire and something was wrong with the building. He couldn't stay where he was for much longer. He began to rush around the room as he grabbed some suitable clothes. A pair of thick tan cargo pants and a heavy dark blue waffle knit long sleeve shirt went on his body as he dug out a pair of black boots that were in good condition and his leather bomber jacket. He would need the heavy clothes for warmth and protection. It was really too bad that he had never gotten into camping, he could use the sleeping bag. If he was lucky, he might be able to find one in a store somewhere along the way. Looting in these circumstances was natural.

He threaded the belt for his sword through the loops on his pants, cinching it tight. Carefully he slipped the sword into the leather scabbard on his hip and secured the health flask to the belt on the opposite hip. A large backpack sat beside his desk, currently full of items from work, such as his laptop, which was now useless.

He pulled everything from the bag and tossed it on his bed, it would only be a dead weight now. There was no reason to keep any of it with him, it no longer worked and served no purpose. He needed the room for other things, like another heavy shirt and food. He pulled a clean shirt that matched the one he was currently wearing from his dresser and stuffed it into the bottom of the bag.

Moving from his room he entered his kitchen and began rifling through all the cupboards in his kitchen. An unopened box of pop tarts and a package of beef jerky went into the bag alongside a box of matches that he had found. A couple of apples and all the bottles of water that he could carry took up the rest of the space.

The building groaned again as he finished putting everything into the backpack. His eyes roved over his small apartment one last time as he hurried to finish. The full import of what he was about to try to do hit him as he stood in front of the door with his hand stretched towards the doorknob.

His life would never be the same again, from here on out everything would be a struggle to survive. He would be constantly fighting for his life using weapons and tools that humanity mostly stopped using years ago.

It could take months to make his way back east, he would have to walk at least part of the way. If he got lucky, he might find a bicycle or a horse to ride some of the way.

In all likelihood, this would be the last time he ever laid eyes on his small apartment and the contents therein. With those thoughts firmly in mind and dragging his mood even further down, he opened the door and entered the darkened hallway. A window at the far end of the hall allowed a small amount of smoky light to dimly illuminate the area.

In the darkest corner of the hall, a set of closed metal doors led to the powerless elevator. Charles glanced briefly in that direction before heading the opposite direction. To the side of the sole window lay the door leading to the stairwell and his way down to the ground floor.

He crept down the hall keeping his feet light as he walked. The apartments were quiet and deathly still as he passed them. The entire building was silent in fact, outside he could hear screams and see the flicker of flames in the distance. Inside, however, there was nothing, no voices from people panicking or looters looting.

With every step Charles felt himself growing more on edge and leery of what he was going to find as he made his way down. His heart beat faster and his palms grew slick with sweat as his nerves began to get the better of him. He paused to wipe them on his tan pants, staining them with moisture before opening the door for the stairwell.

His skin began to prickle as the door swung inwards revealing a well-lit stairwell, windows appeared over every landing letting natural light fill the area. The prickling on his skin grew worse as he took a single step through the door.

Your apprehension has gotten the best of you and allowed a new ability to spawn. The ability 'Detect Bloodthirst' has been learned. This ability allows you to know when a monster or enemy is near.

Charles felt his senses heighten with this ability and then focus at the certainty that there was a malicious presence somewhere below him. A shaking hand filled his vision as his focus narrowed to the hand he clasped over his heart. His knees grew weak at what was to come, he wasn't ready yet. He hadn't practiced with the sword at all. He didn't know how to use it! Could he even kill a monster? How strong was it? If it was already inside the building, then it had probably already killed people. Could monsters level up? What was he going to do when he saw a body for the first time?

All of these thoughts flashed through his mind as he fought for control of his own body, desperately trying to ignore the fear that threatened to overwhelm him. The beat of his heart pulsed violently inside his chest, thumping against his hand as he sank to his knees. His head bent forward, the weight of his backpack seeming to grow heavier with every second.

He was a programmer, a desk jockey, a nerd! He had no business holding a sword and trying to fight monsters. He had no experience with something like this; he had no idea what he needed to do. Did he just rush down the stairs with the sword outstretched and hope for the best? Should he try to sneak up on it? Was it possible to bypass it? Would it be better to just go back inside his apartment and wait for the end?

No, he needed to fight! He needed to survive! His sister was fighting to live on, and she didn't even have the luxury of knowing the fate of the rest of her family. How could he expect her to do more than he was willing to do himself?

The simple answer was that he couldn't!

His resolve sharpened as his thoughts and the options laid before him became clear. The harsh rapid in and out of his breathing gradually slowed and evened into deeper and more filling lungfuls of air. The shaking of his hands eased as he focused on what he could do.

The world had changed, and with-it certain morals had to be forgotten. Killing was now a way of life, protecting those close to you was the purpose of living. People would change, many of them for the worse. The evils of society and humanity would doubtlessly become more prevalent in the days to come.

The world had gone back to being a lawless anything goes place. Might would rule the day, he could only hope that he had the strength to be among those that would rule.

The death-grip his hand had on his shirt over his heart weakened and released. The eyes he hadn't realized he'd closed opened as he pulled himself back to his feet. His legs trembling lightly beneath him. He had made up his mind, but that didn't make what he was about to do any easier. He hadn't even run into any people yet, what he could be thinking might not even be accurate.

If that was the case, then he could live with that. Unfortunately, he had never had much faith in humanity as a whole. They were emotional beings that tended to be ruled by their baser desires. The loss of laws and people that could punish them would only serve to accelerate the process of people becoming the worst version of themselves.

His booted feet carried him to the edge of the stairs, and he looked over the side, three floors below he saw the monster. A red swath of blood covered the landing where the monster sat. Long flabby arms connected to its large grey hands that cradled a red meaty blob as it brought it to its face. Large pointy yellow teeth flashed into view as it opened its lipless mouth.

Two slits occupied the middle of its face just above its teeth where its nose should have been. Bony ridges jutted out above its small beady black eyes covering them in shadow. Flecks of blood mixed with sweat created a frothy shine atop its bald head.

Charles backed away from the edge and put a sweat slickened hand on the pommel of his sheathed sword. This was something that he needed to do, he couldn't get to the first floor without passing the monster. More than that if he wanted to survive in this new world, then he had to fight. He may not know how to use the sword properly but if he snuck up behind it, then it wouldn't matter. A backstab through the neck would hopefully be enough to finish it off regardless.

The world had just barely changed after all, how high of a level could any of them be already?

With that thought firmly in his mind and giving him a small amount of courage, he dropped his backpack on the floor and began to slink down the stairs. Moving from one step to the next, he tried to keep as quiet as possible as he moved into position and drew his sword.

He stopped on the landing above the grey ugly monster, the impossibly sharp sword firmly in hand.

The sound of pieces of flesh and drool hitting the ground occupied the still air as its sharp pointed teeth tore through the lump of flesh in its hands.

Charles felt his gorge rise as the nauseating sound of a person being eaten reached his ears. His feet shifted unsteadily as he fought to regain control of his stomach. His eyes were wide and wild as each beat of his heart caused a pulse of pressure in them.

In front of him the words 'Troll Lv. 3' appeared floating gently above its grey head. It shifted in place, tilting its full bloody mouth on its short neck to look back at him. A grin stretched across its face as it saw him standing there on the landing above. The chunk of bloody meat fell from its grasp as it climbed to its feet with a grunt.

It stooped over and picked up a large white scarred thigh bone as a makeshift club.

Charles couldn't move as the large troll stood before him and raised the bone club high above its head. He stumbled backward as the club came down, with him falling to the floor just out of the trolls reach.

The sword fell from his hands as he scuttled backward until his back hit the wall. All thought had fled his mind, replaced with an all-consuming terror at what was happening.

A low growling laugh came from the troll at his actions bubbling up from its no-lipped mouth.

The sound of it laughing at him shook him from his daze as a wave of anger rushed through his body and filled his muscles with a strength that refused to be put down. He would not let this monster, this thing, decide how he died! More than that, he would not die like a coward without putting up a fight. When it came time for him to die, he would do it fighting!

Pushing away from the wall he slid forward and picked up his fallen sword holding it out in front of him as calmly as possible.

Before he could think twice and begin to doubt what he was about to do, he rushed forward and pushed off with his leading foot. He leaped through the air landing with both feet flat on the ground with his knees bent, just to the side and behind the massive troll. Spinning on his right foot he held the sword in both hands and plunged it into the monsters back, burying a couple of inches of the blade into it.

With an ear-shattering roar, the troll whirled around and buried the thigh-bone club into Charles side with a rib smashing crash. Charles was flung away from the troll and through the air, his body impacting the far wall at high speed abruptly stopping his body. A rush of blood ejecting from his mouth as his head cracked against the wall.

Charles slowly slid from the wall and to the floor, a dent in the wall holding his body upright for a moment before releasing him with a wet sounding plop. His legs were unresponsive, and each breath was painful and wet sounding to his ringing ears. He fell to the side and over the edge onto the stairs leading down.

His back impacted the edge of the stairs, forcing what little air he had in his lungs painfully from his body as he began sliding down them. Each step he slid down sent a fresh wave of pain through his body as above him the troll let out another earth-shaking roar. With huge ponderous steps, the troll ran down the stairs and picked up Charles' body from the bottom of the stairs as it passed him. Charles was swung around by one arm, his body flopping in front of the troll as his other arm was grabbed.

Charles was slammed against the wall as the troll began pulling his arms from their sockets. His arms stretched to the side as his body was held in the air by the pressure on them. The sudden surge of fresh pain cleared his mind enough for him to think. Gasping for air he set his feet against the wall and pushed, wrenching his arms from their sockets as he did so.

His vision went red at the pain as the troll stumbled backward and fell onto its back. The sword that he had stuck into its back was thrust fully through its body as it fell backward releasing Charles as it died. Charles fell on his stomach with a bone-breaking crunch, his arms flopping uselessly at his side.

Troll lv. 3 has died.

Congratulations, you have leveled up. You are now level 2; you have gained 5 status points for distribution.

The ability 'Pain Resistance' has been learned, this ability allows you to ignore a small amount of pain.

Appeared in his red-tinged vision as he struggled for breath everything growing hazy as spots began to dance over his vision.

Chapter 2

"You are more trouble than we thought, although I admit it was at least partially our fault for giving you a weapon that you are clearly unsuited for!" Brigit told Charles firmly, her words barely registering in his pain-addled mind. She plucked the health flask from his side and tipped the contents into his mouth as she noticed how unfocused and glazed his eyes were.

A river of burning fire shot through his body followed closely by an endless flow of ice that soothed and calmed the ravaged nerves inside his body healing him as it went. With a wrench, he felt his arms pop back into place and the shattered ribs in his chest extract and then reset themselves.

With a great heaving gasp, his chest expanded and filled with air bringing the world back into focus. Brigit was leaning over him, her red hair falling in waves around her head.

"Feeling better?" She asked in her mocking lilting voice.

"Much!" Charles managed to grind out, still fighting to regain his breath. "What happened?"

"Hmm? Oh, we were watching you. We wanted to see how you would do in your first battle. Needless to say, we were all vastly underwhelmed by your performance!" She explained as her hair tickled the sides of his face.

"What did you all expect? I've never used a sword before, heck I'd never even been in a real fight before this." He rolled off his back and looked to the side where the body of the troll lay still in a pool of its own cooling blood. "I think I did alright all told, I killed it after-all!" He said feeling oddly disconnected from what he had done.

"Yes, you did well, killing a weak monster and almost dying in the process. Wonderful job, I've never seen better, you're destined to be the mightiest person on the planet!" The sarcasm in her voice was so heavy it practically dripped from her tongue.

Standing, she walked over to the troll and kicked it in the side, flipping it onto its stomach the sword in its back buried to the hilt and barely visible. Reaching over she pulled the blade from the body and flicked it to the side scattering the blood that had clung to the blade. With a flash, the sword vanished along with the scabbard from his belt.

"Wait, what? Where did it go?" Charles asked, puzzled as to what was going on. He had won, right? Why were the gods even paying such close attention to him?

"We decided to take it back from you!" She announced with a smirk. "The general consensus among the gods after watching you try to fight is that you are not suited for the sword and that it was a mistake giving you one. As a result, we have taken it back."

"How am I supposed to fight then?" Charles asked, daring to interrupt the goddess.

"I was getting to that, now remain quiet." An invisible pressure held his tongue in place at her words, preventing him from saying anything. "We have looked over your life and decided on something that we believe will suit you perfectly this time. I must warn you though, use it with caution. If you overuse it, it will begin to damage you in turn. Other than that, it has similar enchantments to the sword in place." A black fingerless glove with thin silver runes inscribed all along the back blurred into being above her hand.

"This glove will allow you to use Lightning magic, furthermore, it will aid you during periods of meditation and help you learn how to use magic." She tossed the glove to Charles with a careless flick of her hand. "Also, this is the last time I will interfere, so make sure you act more carefully in the future. To quote and paraphrase the games that inhabit your world, the tutorial portion of your life has now ended!" Her body began to glow softly and fade from view. "Oh, one more thing, don't forget to use your inventory!" With those parting words, she disappeared and left him alone with the cooling corpse of the dead troll.

Charles tilted his head to the side at her abrupt departure and parting words. "What inventory?" He asked aloud. A ten by ten box opened in his vision offset to the side, it was currently empty. He stared blankly at the box for a minute before his mind started working again. With this, he would be able to store his backpack and not worry about losing anything. More than that if they had really designed everything off of games, then the odds that similar items would stack was high, he might even be able to store a bag full of items in a single slot. He really needed to take the time to read the manual.

With a thought he closed the inventory and slipped his right hand into the glove, he felt the glove grabbing the outside of his hand sending little barbs into his skin as it settled in place. The silver runes on the back of the glove flared with light and then dimmed as the barbs dug deeper into his hand. His hand should have been in pain, but it felt more like the inside of his hand was being gently massaged. A short description of how to properly use the glove and its meditation ability popped into view. He quickly read through it before dismissing it for now. He would properly read through it later.

Getting to his feet he stomped over to the troll deciding to see just how game like they had made the world. Putting a hand firmly on the troll he thought 'loot' only a little surprised when a new window popped into being with three items in it. There were several pieces of copper, the stained piece of fabric it had used to cover itself along with the thigh bone club it had been using. Without another thought, he accepted the items watching as they vanished into his own inventory and the window closed. The massive body of the slain troll shimmered and then faded from view after it had been looted.

That was good to know, bodies of monsters disappeared after they had been looted. That meant if the bodies were still there, then they were free game. He might be able to pick up some easy items until everyone figured out that the bodies could be looted for items.

He felt a smile pulling at his face for the first time since he had woken that morning. He knew things were serious, and that people were dying but a part of him felt more alive than ever before. His eyes were drawn to the black glove on his hand, that was especially true if he could learn how to use magic.

He had dreamt of being able to use magic more than a few times as he grew up. That was one good thing about the new world at least, and it was important that he focused on the positives. Focusing on the negatives would be counterproductive at this point in time.

He pulled up his status and felt his smile grow; it had changed and grown since he had looked at it earlier. His level had increased to two, and additionally two new lines had been added to the screen as well. The new information would be very helpful in the future. The first displayed his available mana or how much magic he could use and the last let him know that he had five status points available for distribution. The only problem with that was there was nothing he could place them into just yet.

He closed the screen and started up the stairs; he needed to fetch his bag and see if he could truly put the entire thing in his inventory. The bag and all its contents went into his inventory without a problem occupying a single slot. Charles was debating whether to go back to his apartment and grab more items when he felt the building shake again. Deciding not to risk it he hurried down the stairs, taking care to avoid the puddles of blood and gore that were scattered throughout the stairwell.

The entrance to his building had been smashed open and was missing, undoubtedly done by the troll to gain entrance. Quickly he stepped through the rubble and into the outside air finding it thick with smoke. The sun had taken on a hazy quality, making everything appear orange and indistinct.

A new notification filled his vision as he stepped from the building.

The gods have issued you a challenge, join your sister in Massachusetts!

He knew where he needed to go and knew just how long it was going to take him. It would be a long, difficult journey, at the end of which his feet and legs would probably hate him.

Dodging cars and keeping to the sidewalk as much as possible he began walking, making his way through the vast city. In the distance, he could see monsters and packs of animals walking the crowded streets scavenging for survivors and other forms of food.

Charles placed his left hand over his right, with his thumb finding the meditation point on the back of the glove. If he could walk and meditate at the same time, then he would be able to properly use magic that much faster. He knew he would need it soon enough; monsters, animals, and people would all be drawn to the roads. He would need to be ready to fight his way through them all. He couldn't afford to freeze up again.

The gods had given him gifts, and he needed to use them to stay alive. The glove was on his hand and the health potion was affixed to his hip displaying a small countdown timer until he could use it again.

He felt a part of his mind separate and focus on other things as he pressed on the meditation point. He kept his eyes open and focused on his surroundings as his mind delved into the mysteries of magic and the flows of mana.

Bodies filled the cars, offering a grim reminder of the cost the whim of the gods had already extracted on the world. People were noticeably absent from the roads as he walked by them, making him wonder just how many more people had died since he had talked to Brigit earlier. Fewer and fewer screams sounded distantly in the air as more and more people died.

Charles continued down the road, part of his mind meditating on his magic while the rest of him concentrated on opening the manual the gods had written. It was time that he learned how the world now worked and just what he was capable of.

The smoke in the air was thick and burned his lungs as he tried to breathe through his mouth. The manual was interesting, although a lot of it was common sense for games. Part of the virtual document described the process of leveling up and how it worked. The useful part, however, was located near the end of it, it was a listing of all the various commands he could use. Status, inventory, loot, and more were all there.

The sound of tortured animal screams rent the air, shocking him from his reading and meditation. The sheer agony and feeling in that heart-wrenching wail were enough to make his knees feel weak. It had come from the left somewhere, although he couldn't place the exact location because of the buildings distorting the sound.

Running toward where he thought the sound had come from, he prepared himself for what he was about to do. Even if it was just an animal that was being attacked and not a human, the odds were good that it was still a monster doing the attacking. This would be a good chance to practice his lightning attack without the monster actively coming for him.

The meaty sound of flesh being struck followed by a pained whimper came from just ahead of him and to the side down an alley.

He turned the corner, and the alley stretched in front of him dead-ending at the back of a building with a large burnished aluminum sectional door blocking entrance into the building. A large silver growling husky was on the ground its back legs were bloody and its large teeth were showing in a frightening snarl.

A large green monster similar to the one he had seen from his apartment window earlier loomed over the injured dog with a massive wooden club in its hand. From behind, Charles could see the sharp tapered point of a tusk jutting up from its jaw. Straggly strands of thin grey hair hung limply from its head shining with a greasy sheen in the overly orange light.

This was the chance that he had been looking for, a single monster that was unaware of his presence. This was the perfect opportunity to test out the attack from his glove. Charles focused his eyes on the monster and willed the information into being. Over its head, the words 'Orc Lv. 4' appeared followed by a notification in the center of his vision.

The ability 'Analysis' has been learned. This ability is passive and automatically displays the type and level of monsters and enemies.

Charles closed the window with a small grin, that ability would be very helpful, especially if it worked the way he hoped it did. Shaking his head, he focused on what was to come and extended his gloved hand towards the unaware monster as it raised the wooden club into the air.

Aiming his hand, he activated the lightning attack with a thought. A shaft of white-hot plasma extended in front of him in an arcing forked tongue of heat and energy, piercing the level four orc like it was paper. A gaping black smoking hole appeared where its abdomen had been seconds before. The wooden club fell to the ground with a clatter as the orc fell to its knees and then onto its filthy stomach. Its tusked mouth was open in a silent snarl that would never produce sound while its big black eyes had already glazed over in death.

A large hole had appeared in the aluminum door where the lightning had gone through it and into the building beyond.

Charles had enough time to absorb this sight before he felt the barbs embedded in his hand flex painfully followed by a red-hot pain on the upper thigh of his left leg. He slumped to the ground in pain as another notification flashed into being. He pushed it to the side and minimized it. He could take the time to read it over later, right now he needed to focus.

He lay on the ground, gasping in pain as his leg spasmed and his hand shook from the pain. At the end of the alley, the injured husky used its front paws to drag itself around the smoking corpse of the orc and towards him with a whimper.

Charles tried to straighten his leg, flexing the tight muscles in it as he did so. The pain was fading as quickly as it had come it seemed.

The dog whimpered again as it pulled itself closer to him by its front paws.

He pulled his straightened leg in and under himself levering his body into a kneeling position as he focused on the whimpering husky. The information appeared above its head like he was hoping it would, although it was different than he was expecting. The words 'Husky Lv. ??' followed by the symbol for female appeared, giving him more information than he thought he would get.

The information it gave on monsters had never provided a gender before, it also let him know that animals could gain levels now as well. For the first time as he looked into the dog's multi-colored eyes, he saw the hints of intelligence in them. He wondered how he had missed that gleam in them before.

"Stop right there girl don't force yourself!" He said warmly as he climbed to his feet, thankful that they were steady.

He calmly walked over to her, keeping his movements slow and steady so as not to frighten her. Even injured she was a beautiful animal. Her silver coat was smooth and sleek except where her rear leg had been crushed by the orcs club and was bloody. Her eyes were separate colors with one of them bright green and the other a dark blue, the two opposing qualities of bright and dark giving her a mysterious look.

Her head twisted as he crept closer her muzzle opening with a quiet whimper as she licked her ruined hind leg. The leg hung limply as she dragged it along behind her, dragging it over the rough asphalt and gravel of the alleyway.

Charles knelt next to her, resting a hand on the top her watery eyes. He felt her neck with his free hand but couldn't find a collar.

"Do you have a name girl?" He asked gently as he shifted his hand to her rear leg carefully.

Her tongue lolled out as her eyes tracked the movements of his hand warily.

"I'll try not to hurt you too much, but I need to see how badly you are hurt, so stay calm for me. Ok girl?" His voice remained calm as he felt the area beneath her fur, her ears twitching in acknowledgement of his words.

She inhaled sharply as he prodded at her, feeling rough and sharp edges where only smooth bone should have existed. Her entire rear leg had been crushed by the club, the bone shattered where it had been hit.

He didn't think that there was anything he could do for her, except maybe give her a comfortable place to die. His eyes flicked to the gaping hole his attack earlier had created in the door. Inside the building, it would at least be warm if they were lucky, he might be able to even find a couch in an employee workroom. Beneath the door was the green body of the orc that he had yet to loot.

"Hold on girl, I'll be right back. I need to find a way inside the building for us!" Her pointed ears twitched in response as he stood and walked over to the hole in the door looting the orc without a thought as he passed it.

Chapter 3

A dark abyss loomed past the hole, the interior dark without running electricity. There was a small whimper behind him as he climbed through the door and entered the dark within. He moved to the left of the hole getting out of the light as he waited for his eyes to adjust to the dim lighting. Wooden crates and boxes filled the area, leading him to believe that it was some kind of warehouse or storage area for the rest of the building.

Across the crowded floor and against the wall he saw a set of metal stairs that led up to a door with a bunch of windows next to it that looked over the floor. It was probably an office or employee lounge, either way, it would be his best bet to find a couch or something comfortable to lay on.

On the far side of the door from where he was standing, he spotted a couple of chains that hung from the ceiling. It looked like he had found the way to open the door if he pulled the chains then the door would roll into the ceiling. Not wanting to waste any more time he moved over to the chains and heaved. With a low grinding noise that he felt in his hands, the door crept into the ceiling with each fresh pull on the chain.

Deciding that the door was high enough he ducked under it and hurried over to the injured animal. He kept his voice soft and gentle as he approached her. "I'm going to pick you up and carry you inside, we'll see if we can find a comfortable place for us to rest." His arms slipped under her sleek fur as he carefully picked her up and hugged her to his body.

She remained still even as a pained whimper escaped from her bloody muzzle.

The orange, smoky light made it impossible to tell what time it was by the position of the sun. Everything was hazy and blurred, and the smoky smell was quickly giving him a migraine. The sooner he got inside out of the light and away from the smoke, the better.

Keeping her steady, he ducked under the partially opened door and moved over to a wooden box that came up to his hips. He set the husky on the box for a moment as he moved back over to the chains next to the door and began pulling on them. The grinding noise filled the air as he pulled on the chain, lowering the door and blocking any large monsters from getting inside. Anything that wanted to get in would have to crawl through the door like he had the first time.

The orange light reflected the different colored eyes of the husky, making them glow in the low light. Charles felt his feet hesitate as he saw her eyes start to glow with what seemed like an unearthly light. Picking her up again he walked over to the stairs and held her steady as he climbed to the second floor. She was quiet though her eyes were wide and slightly watery as she kept the pain inside.

Hugging her warm body in front of him he steadied her as he reached out a hand towards the closed door at the top of the stairs. The weathered off-color knob felt cool under his hand as he turned it uncertainly, not sure if the door would be locked. It turned easily, and the door opened on well-oiled hinges. The interior was dark with the only light coming through the now opened door and the heavily smudged windows. In the far corner, he saw a long low shape that he thought might be a couch.

Stepping into the room he nudged the door closed with his foot, the sudden darkness forcing his eyes to adjust painfully. His feet remained close to the ground as he walked, searching for anything that might have otherwise tripped him in the dark room. Keeping his body steady and his back straight he lowered himself into a crouch and carefully laid the injured dog on a cushion of the couch.

He pulled his arms from underneath her as gently as possible, her eyes flickering open revealing a soft inner glow that remained even in the dim lighting. Her breathing had grown ragged and strained during the time he had held her, the jostling still there no matter how hard he had tried. He patted her head and then stood to move to the other end of the couch to give her room.

The cushion sagged beneath him as he sank onto the couch, his eyes shut as he relaxed into the comfortable cushions. His mind began to wander as he thought about what he was going to do now. The day wasn't over yet. In fact, he didn't think it could have been more than four or so in the afternoon. There were still hours of light left, time that he could spend walking, or time that he could spend with an injured dog that seemed to like his company.

To the side, at the end of the couch, she straightened her neck extending it until her head rested on his thigh. With a pained whimper, her eyes closed, and she let out a huff of air relaxing as much as she could.

Charles felt the beginnings of a small pull at the corners of his mouth as he gazed down at the pretty silver husky. Curiously enough his eyes grew watery as he thought of her dying, she should have meant nothing to him. He had only known her for maybe half an hour. Her mismatched eyes had made a profound impact on him during that time, however.

The thought of losing her, felt wrong like there was something more that he could do for her. The roads had been mysteriously empty of people all day, truth be told he was only now beginning to think on just how quiet the world had become. The ever-present sounds that accompanied civilization and people had vanished. Distant screams and roars sounded alongside the flames that engulfed buildings and cars alike. It all provided a background noise that was vastly different from any that he had ever known before.

He shifted slightly feeling something digging painfully into his side, his hand dropped as he pulled the flask from his hip. Along the top of the flask, were white numbers counting down the time he had left until he could use it again. In a little under five hours, he could use it again. His eyes drifted from the flask to his lap, if she could just hang on for five hours then he would be able to use it to heal her. He could save her if she could just hang on for that long.

It was a big if... Her breathing sounded off, and he could feel tremors wracking her body with every breath she took. Dipping his head to her ear he blew on it gently before speaking; her eyes were open and fixed on his as he spoke. That gleam that spoke of intelligence shining brightly within.

"If you can just hang on for five more hours, then I can use my potion to heal you. Can you do that? Do you think that you can hang on for that long?" His voice was soft as he pleaded with her.

She gave a pain-filled whimper before shifting her head and licking his face with what he could only describe as a slightly bloody doggy grin. He knew then that she truly did understand what he was saying; it wasn't just his imagination. This dog really was intelligent, and as such, she deserved a name.

"I'm glad to hear that, but I think you need a name!" She nudged the center of his head with her wet nose before turning to look at the door they had come through.

"I'm not going to call you door!" He said sarcastically, not quite understanding what she was hinting at.

The lids of her eyes lowered, and she growled softly at him before shifting her head slightly to the side. No longer was it pointing to the door at the top of the stairs but more towards the large door to the warehouse and the alley beyond.

"You want me to call you Alli?" He asked his head tilted to the side.

She gave him a long lick of his face and then settled back onto his lap. "Alright, Alli it is. Just hang on, and then we'll get you fixed up good as new!"

With that decided he settled back into the couch and pulled up all the notifications, he had pushed to the side earlier.

Orc lv. 4 has died.

Congratulations, you have leveled up. You are now level 3; you have gained 5 status points for distribution.

Apparently, he had gained another level from this last fight; he knew that couldn't continue though. People always gained levels quickly when they were low leveled, that, and he had been fighting enemies whose level were greater than his own.

Grinning at the increase in level that he couldn't use, he closed the window and opened the next one.

Congratulations, 'Unnamed Dog' has been added to your party under the Animal Companion Slot.

He closed that with a thought and moved onto the last one.

Congratulations, your animal companion Alli has leveled up. She is now level 2; her status points have been automatically distributed.

Closing that message, he looked down at the silver head in his lap. He was glad that she could level up as well. If she could just hold on long enough for him to use the potion on her, then the chance of her staying alive and continuing to level with him would be great. It would be nice to have someone to talk to, even if she couldn't talk back. A companion of any kind would be nice, she would help him to remain sane during the long road ahead.

His mind drifted from the messages and to what had already occurred. The battle had been easy, but the pain the glove had caused was going to be a problem. If it was going to do that to him every time, then it would prove too prohibitive to be used in most fights. If he wasn't able to take out the enemy in a single shot, then he would be left wide open to attacks. The opposite was also true, however. The glove seemed powerful enough that he could probably one-shot any enemy he might meet.

It was just the backlash from the glove that was the problem. Unfortunately, there was nothing that he could do regarding that matter. The only thing he could do was continue to meditate and hope that he could learn some kind of attack magic soon. If, he could learn healing magic that could prove helpful as well. Really any kind of magic could be useful, at this point learning everything he could, would be his best bet towards remaining alive. He could specialize later on after he had learned more about this new world.

His gloved hand drifted to Alli's head petting it lightly as she dozed through her pain, then using his other hand to press on the meditation spot he began. Using all of his mind instead of just a part of it as he had before was an entirely different experience. His mind expanded in all directions as the wonders of magic and something else began to be revealed to him. There was something there on the edge of everything hanging back, subtly guiding the meditation and the direction it needed to take.

Time seemed to flow around him as he sat there deep in his meditation, barely aware of the passage of time. It was only when he received a notification that he was pulled from that state and back into the real world. Everything was dark, and Alli was whimpering in pain. Her breathing had grown progressively more labored as time had worn on. Each breath pained her, and her eyes were wide and focused on him as she felt him stir at last.

His hand shot to his side, pulling the flask in front of him. The white numbers on top of the lid glowed with a dim light, letting him see that he had fifteen minutes left even in the dark room. Putting it to the side for the moment he concentrated on Alli.

"I'm sorry girl. It needs another fifteen minutes before we can use it on you. Hold on, alright? Just a little longer and then I promise you everything will get better." He dipped his head to hers as he spoke, finding that tears had crept into his eyes.

Pulling away from her, he pulled up the notifications he had ignored.

Congratulations, you are the first human in over a millennium to learn the basics of mana usage. You now have access to learning basic spells. As a result of being the first to learn magic, the restriction on types of spells you can learn has been lifted.

Congratulations, you can now learn all types of magic. Basic spells have now been unlocked, more advanced spell types may be unlocked at a later time.

To learn a specific spell, concentrate on the type you desire to learn during meditation.

The message continued by listing the variety of basic spells he could learn, fire, water, air, and even a type of healing magic were all listed. All of them would be useful in the future, especially the healing magic. He had the potion, but he was already feeling how restrictive the limits imposed on it were. The side effects from using the glove were nothing to scoff off at either. The other spell types would probably give him some more attack options as well.

Charles looked down as his lap became wet. Alli had her face buried in his thigh, her tongue hung limply from her mouth as blood flecked drool poured from her open mouth. Her eyes were slightly glassy, and her breaths were coming in short sharp gasps. He ran his hand over her head, trying to provide as much comfort as he could for her.

His eyes went to the flask, praying that it was almost time. He didn't want to let her go, certainly like this. He was being selfish, and he knew it, he didn't want to be alone. Keeping her alive had more to do with him than with her. He needed something to keep him grounded and sane in the coming months. He could see the time spent alone, fighting monsters constantly changing him. Changing him into someone or something that he would no longer recognize, that had forgotten what it meant to be human.

The last few glowing seconds counted down as he held the flask in his trembling hand. He was ready to rip the top off and dump the contents down Alli's throat as soon as it reached zero.

He knew she was in pain, even in the dim light that was more than obvious. Her eyes flickered weakly as his hand gently ruffled the hair around her ears. Closing her eyes, she nudged his hand and let out a soft pain filled sigh.

The last few seconds flickered down on the flask as he readied his hand to pull off the top. The glowing numbers reached zero and then vanished, hurriedly he pulled off the top and tilted Alli's head back to open her throat. Forcing her jaws open he tipped the flask over her mouth. He held his breath as he watched it trickle down her throat. Finally, he saw her swallow once, then twice as he continued to pour the magical liquid into her mouth.

Her body seized and went rigid as he emptied the rest of the flask down her throat. He knew what she was going through. That first wave of pure fire and pain that rushed through the body, and then the second wave of ice that cooled everything and healed in its wake. The stiffness left her body as quickly as it had come, leaving her limp and breathing easier.

Charles felt her legs shift on the end of the couch as they set into position and healed with soft popping sounds. In the wake of the healing, Alli lay limp on his lap, seeming to enjoy the lack of pain as her tongue lolled out in a relieved doggy grin.

"Is that better girl? Sorry, you had to wait so long for the potion! It has a time limit on how often it can be used though." Alli seemed to perk up at his words, nodding her head as if she understood what he was saying.

Sitting up, she put her face next to his and licked his cheek before nudging her nose against his. "Alright Alli, I'm glad you're doing better. Now, do you feel up to moving on or are you too tired after all that?" He asked her with a laugh. It was good to see her feeling so much better, the problem now was how to manage their activities. Since he could no longer sleep, he was unsure if he needed rest or got tired. If he did, then he figured he would just spend the time meditating instead of sleeping.

Alli tilted her head to the side before looking to the door and then back to him. With a giant yawn, she shook her head and settled back onto his lap. Her eyes closed and her breathing evening out as she rapidly fell into what must have been an exhausted sleep.

A small smile spread across his face as he looked at her. Everything had turned out all right, he had been able to heal her, and he was no longer alone. Everything had happened so quickly though that he hadn't been able to spend the time to think over everything. All day he had been mainly reacting with no thought to the future. He knew he needed to sort through his emotions, it wouldn't do to just ignore them. Brushing them to the side wouldn't do him any good, and in the long run, would change him in unhealthy ways.

Pushing himself back into the couch he settled in for the night, he'd try to get some meditation done while he sorted through everything. For now, he was going to focus on healing, no matter what he needed to be able to heal injuries in a short amount of time. The flask was great, and it would undoubtedly save their lives on the big injuries. Unfortunately, they needed to save it for those times, otherwise, it wouldn't be there when they needed it most.

Charles pressed his finger onto the meditation point and closed his eyes as he felt his mind separate. He focused the meditating portion of his mind on learning how to heal, while the rest of his mind focused on healing his emotional issues.

Time seemed to disappear and fade away as he maintained the meditation through the night. His body remained still, his breathing slow and even. Every once in a while, Alli's ears would twitch as she heard something in the otherwise silent night. The end of the world had truly come, not with a bang, but with a shocking speech made by the gods of old. Everything had ended with a shocked whimper and the seizing of hearts around the world.

Chapter 4

Charles had pushed aside the notifications he had received during the night, choosing instead to focus on maintaining his meditation for as long as possible. He noticed though that the longer he held onto it the worse his head began to hurt. He was forcing himself to learn things in a way that people had not used for a very long time.

The constant influx of information built up a pressure that would normally be released at the end of the day through sleep. He no longer had that luxury, he had found the limit on the time he could spend meditating each day, at least for now.

When Charles could handle it no longer, he opened his eyes and released the meditation point on the back of his glove. A splitting headache made everything appear brighter, and noises sound louder, sending his empty stomach into a roiling spasm. It was a good thing he had forgotten to eat the night before, otherwise, it was likely that anything he had eaten would be coming back up to visit right then.

Alli stirred from his lap where her drooling mouth had left a damp pool of slime on his tan cargo pants. She appeared larger in the soft morning light that had trickled in from below. The intelligent gleam in her eyes had grown brighter during the night, all traces of the injury from the day before had vanished completely. A good night's sleep and the potion had fixed her up as good as new.

"I'm starving, how about you?" He asked as he reached into his inventory for his bag. Opening it he withdrew some bottles of water, a bag of jerky and his first aid kit that had some Tylenol. Laughing lightly as her head perked up at the mention of food and water. Popping the top on the medicine, he shook out a couple of tablets and threw them into his mouth before taking a deep swig of his water.

He opened the second bottle of water and put it in Alli's mouth, only a little surprised when she clamped it in her teeth and tilted her head back. He split half the bag of jerky with her pulling out the meat for her before he started to look through the messages that had accumulated during the night.

He quickly scanned through them and then dismissed them. During the night he had learned two basic healing spells. One was useful for injuries and the other was used for basic poisons. Pressing his hand to his head he activated his basic healing and sighed with relief as he felt the headache dissipate a second later.

The feeling he got from the healing spell was vastly different than what he got from the potion. With the potion it felt like it was scouring his entire body looking for any and all imperfections to heal. The spell was more localized, focused on healing the one thing he was trying to fix. He would have to think about it more later, it might just be that the potion was doing more for those it healed than he had realized.

Looking down into his lap he noticed a fresh pile of drool and two small pieces of beef jerky. Alli had devoured all of hers and then went after his it seemed, rolling his eyes at her he tossed the last two pieces to her and stood. He could eat something later, right now his stomach was in knots at the thought of what he might find when they left the building. His earlier hunger had fled, leaving an uncomfortable roiling sensation in its place.

Picking up his empty bottle of water he placed it into his inventory as he watched her devour the last few pieces of meat. Licking her lips, Alli stood next to him and stretched her forelegs out with an enormous yawn. It was only when she had finished her stretch and was standing next to him that he noticed how tall and large she was. Granted yesterday he had never seen her standing, but he had held her in his arms. Now seeing her next to him he didn't think he could hold her anymore, she had somehow grown much larger overnight.

Charles walked over to the closed door and opened it, letting in more of the dim light that filtered in from below. Stepping away from the doorway and out of the light, he looked around the newly illuminated room. There was a small stove in one corner with cupboards above it and a full-size silent refrigerator standing against the wall pressed against the end of the cupboards.

On top of the fridge was an unopened package of twenty-four water bottles that he took and shoved into his inventory, smiling when he saw that it only took a single slot. Opening all the cupboards, he found a few glasses and mugs alongside a couple of boxes of cereal that he also stored in his inventory. Any food he managed to find would be helpful to them in the future.

From the corner of his eye, he saw Alli watching and waiting for him at the open door. "Alright girl, I think that is everything in here, let us see what we can find in the warehouse below, and then we'll leave." He told her as he walked towards her and looked down into the wooden crate filled warehouse below.

She nudged his legs with her side as he joined her before leaping down the stairs and began sniffing at each of the sides of the crates in turn.

Following her down the stairs he peeked into the first crate he came to and saw it filled with old broken cell-phones. Moving onto the next crate he found it full of broken VCR's, with each wooden crate he came to after that full of old broken electronics. With a sigh of disgust, he moved away from the crates and to the large closed door.

Electronics, broken or otherwise held no value to him anymore. Even when people found ways to generate electricity again, anything electronic would have to be fixed before they would be able to use it. That would take years, there was no point in even thinking about it at this point in time.

He passed in front of the circular hole he had blasted through the door the day before as he walked over to the chains that would lift the door. Pulling on them he ignored the loud grinding clang that filled the warehouse as the chains ground noisily on each other. With each jerk of the chain, the door lifted a little higher, disappearing into the ceiling above them. He stopped when there was enough of a gap for Alli to squeeze herself under.

Brushing against his legs, she rubbed her side against him before belly crawling underneath the door and waiting for him to join her outside. Flinging the chain in the opposite direction, the door closed with a clang as it slammed into the ground. Charles glanced around the darkened warehouse one last time before climbing through the hole and joining his silver-haired companion on the outside.

Alli nudged his hand as he stood next to her, licking the tips of his fingers with a slobbery tongue. His hand absentmindedly went to her ears as he scratched them without looking. His eyes were fixed down the alley and to the buildings beyond, overnight the landscape had changed.

Fires and monsters had decimated the buildings all across the vast city. Smoke and ash hung thick in the air, coating his tongue and clogging his nose. Lifting his shirt, he covered his mouth and nose before looking down to see that Alli was in even worse shape. Her silky-smooth silver coat was already covered in clumps of ash, making it look like she had mange.

He could hear her breathing grow labored as she fought for breath, her head sinking low to the ground. Wide pitiful looking eyes gazed up at him as she shook her head, ridding it of the thick flakes of ash that had accumulated on her.

He pulled his backpack from his inventory and pulled out his spare shirt determined to do something for her. Kneeling down in front of her, he brushed her face with his hand before wrapping the shirt around her muzzle and tying the ends around her neck. The end of the shirt hung over her soft nose, letting her breathe freely and keeping her from getting clogged again.

Putting the backpack back into his inventory he blew his nose heavily to the side, getting rid of his own clogging issues. As soon as they saw a store, he needed to find something to wrap around his own face. Walking down the alley he stopped at the entrance and felt his mouth drop in shock, what he had seen from the end of the alley had been only the beginning. Trails of smoke lined the skyline, where tall buildings had stood the day before. Broken spires of twisted metal and concrete leaned heavily to the sides where they had fallen during the night.

In the distance, he could see the orange of fires backlighting the smoke and giving the world an unhealthy tinge. The thick cloying smoke and ash limited the distance he could see clearly and prevented even his enhanced eyesight from piercing it.

Beside him, Alli growled softly as she looked into the distance as well. The comforting presence of her beside him shook him from his revelry and back to his present circumstances, first he needed to find something to cover his face with, then he could continue on his journey.

His mind decided he stepped from the mouth of the alley and onto the road with Alli running in front of him, dodging in and out of the cars that filled the otherwise deserted road. He could see maybe the length of a block down the road, any monsters or people that might be about were hidden from view.

Ahead of him, he noticed that Alli had stopped in front of a building and was looking inside it. Hurrying to her side he looked inside the building and saw that it was full of clothes.

"Good job girl, this is exactly what we needed!" He told her proudly as he patted her head affectionately.

Pushing against the closed glass door he found it locked, stepping back from the door he cocked his leg back and kicked the glass with all his might. His booted foot impacted the thick glass shattering it with a loud tinkling sound as it fell to the ground. Stepping through the now open door he waved Alli off not wanting her to walk through the glass.

Clothes hung from racks all around him stretching to the back of the building. Clothes for women, clothes for little girls, if you were female then the store had it all. Towards the back near the changing rooms, he found what he was looking for. Scarves, thin sheer gauzy stylish ones and thick long scarves designed for warmth lined the wall. Grabbing two of each, he stuffed them into his inventory before wrapping a long woolen scarf around his head twice and then tying it off behind his head.

It was secure enough that it would stay on without any problem, and yet it was loose enough that he could still breathe easily with it on. Smiling to himself, he made his way back through the store, stopping when something caught his eyes next to the checkout counters. It was a flat black baseball cap, snagging it he shoved it on his head after quickly brushing the ash from his hair.

Outside the store he found Alli waiting for him in the same place she had been when he entered the store. She hadn't moved at all. Pulling a sheer blue scarf from his inventory he leaned over and removed his shirt from her face and then wrapped the scarf around her muzzle. The long edges hung well below her mouth, allowing her to have it open without worry.

Brushing the ash that had gathered on her head, he urged her on. "Come on, we need to make our way through the city, let's see if we can avoid the monsters for now. Alright?"

Alli gave a quiet yip of acknowledgement before turning and leading the way down the road. Behind her, Charles kept his eyes moving constantly, looking for any sign of life. An eerie silence had fallen over the world, everything was muffled and dim when there was sound at all. There were no screams of people in the distance or the grunts of monsters walking the land for the first time in thousands of years. There was nothing, even the constant Colorado wind had quieted.

He decided to keep his full attention on the road around him for now, choosing to not meditate while walking. Without being able to see everything around him, he needed to be alert and paying attention for any hidden dangers that might find them. He could meditate at night if he was alive.

Ahead of him, Alli would run off into the smoke from time to time before returning with pieces of different colored flesh and blood hanging from a sodden scarf. Only once did anything get close to him when it leaped from the top of a two-story building and onto the road landing in front of him. Alli had just vanished from view when the attack happened, leaving Charles scrambling backward while bringing his hand up for his attack. With a thought, he felt the energy course through his hand and into the glove as a bolt of lightning shot through the monster and into the car behind it.

A flare of pain coursed through his hand and into his thigh just like it had the last time he had used the glove sending him to his knees in pain. Moving his trembling hand to his thigh he activated his healing magic sighing in relief as he felt it take effect. Pulling himself to his feet he closed the notification without reading it and looted the monster before continuing on.

Now that he knew he could heal the pain that using the glove caused he would be able to fight more often. He didn't think that he would be able to use it on more than one monster at a time unless they were lined up. It was progress though; it was a step in the right direction.

Every time he used the glove, he became a little more confident in its power and that he would be able to remain alive. As long as he had the power of the glove, he could fight the monsters and come out on top.

Alli ran back through the smoke as the monster fell to the ashy ground behind him, neither of them paying any attention to what kind of monster it had been in the first place.

As, the day wore on the large, broken buildings of the Denver skyline filled the hazy air behind them casting deep shadows through the smoke. They hadn't seen any monsters near them for some time when Charles noticed that the air was clearing up some as they left the ashy fires behind. The air was still thick with smoke, but the ash that had obscured everything and muffled all sound had all but vanished.

As the air cleared and the distance they could see increased Alli left his side to explore and clear the area of enemies. To the sides of the highway, he could see small groups of people sporting homemade weapons alongside firearms. The groups were moving from house to house undoubtedly scavenging for food and supplies.

As he continued walking, he steered well clear of them and began to notice that all the other groups were doing the exact same thing. Each of them was avoiding the other groups, none of them were cooperating or even talking with each other. Instead, they all seemed afraid of one another, like the other group of people were rabid and diseased.

The sole exceptions to this rule were when it came to the stores. Each grocery and sporting goods store that he walked past had at least one group of people camped out in front of it, with most having two. They were laying claim to their territory, marking it as theirs, something that they would fight to protect and keep from other people.

He saw little fighting happening that day, people avoided the monsters even more than they did other humans. They didn't seem interested in fighting them, only in remaining alive. Charles could only shake his head at the way everyone was acting. Each of them already seemed to have forgotten what it meant to be human and had devolved into nearly mindless beasts themselves.

He knew that he wasn't being fair to people; it was because he had the power to fight that he thought this way. That wasn't necessarily true though either, all these people had the ability to level-up. Unlike him, they could get stronger. People needed to change, the age of technology and comfort that was always at the ready was gone. The age of the gods and of fighting had returned, and there was nothing that anyone could do about it.

Chapter 5

A head of him, Alli yipped loud enough for it to carry back to him but soft enough that it wouldn't alert everyone else in the area. He hurried to her side and followed the direction her head was pointing in to see what she had noticed. To the right of the road, four orcs were gathered in a circle eating the bloody remains of a group of people.

In shock at the unexpected sight, he sank to his knees next to the large dog and leaned against her for support. He had not been expecting to see so much blood or them eating so openly. Once again, he found himself being shocked by something that he knew intellectually was happening but emotionally he had been unprepared for. Knowing and seeing were entirely different things, a fact that had been driven home repeatedly over the course of the last couple of days.

"Come on," He whispered quietly next to her upright ears. "We can't fight that many at once yet, those people are already dead. There is nothing we can do for them now." Alli turned to look at him her wide mismatched eyes expressing her disappointment in him as she huffed and turned away from the monsters.

Charles felt bad letting her down, but for now, at least it was the truth. He had one attack he could reasonably count on and that was the glove but using it would leave him vulnerable until he could recover from the pain that using it caused. He wasn't going to risk her for something like that. He knew she was stronger and bigger than when he had first found her.

He had seen the blood and gore that had accumulated on her throughout the day. He knew she was fighting without him, trying to keep him safe. Until he saw her fighting for himself, though he had no way of gauging just how strong she had gotten.

No, leaving the group of monsters behind without attacking them was the right move for now at least. Once he learned more spells, he wouldn't have to do something like that again. It was decided. He knew what he would be focusing on that night while he meditated.

The constant pounding of his feet on the hard pavement filled his being as he walked along behind Alli, trusting in her to keep him safe. He was unused to walking this much; he had been a programmer just days before. Sitting behind a desk and moving his fingers day in and day out and then walking to his car had been the extent of his daily exercise. His precious time off was used for things he found enjoyable and not for exercising and causing his body pain.

He was regretting that lifestyle now, none of the money he had saved up from working so hard did anything for him now. The entirety of his earthly possessions he now carried with him in his inventory. Absentmindedly he chewed on some jerky as he walked tossing a piece to Alli whenever she came close enough. Soon he was going to need to find more food, hopefully, something with a little more variety and nutrition than jerky had.

Above him, the sky darkened as a late-season storm crawled over the plains and obscured the sun. The large stormy clouds were a dark roiling grey, cooling everything with their mere presence. The rain they would soon be releasing on the world would be cold and the temperature outside would drop with it. He needed to find a place for them to rest soon. It was maybe an hour or two sooner than he would have liked, but they didn't have a choice in the matter. Getting wet in Colorado even in the middle of the summer was never a good idea. The rain was ice cold here at the warmest of times, in the middle of September, it would be downright frigid.

He whistled for Alli as he hurried towards the first road exit he saw. She ran back to him, her head tilted to the side in confusion. Laughing softly to himself at the very human response, he explained what was about to happen to her as they neared the first group of townhouses.

Looking towards the rapidly darkening sky, he decided they had enough time to run quickly through a couple of the houses. With Alli beside him, he rushed into the first house they came across and to the back of the house where the kitchen was. Finding the pantry to the side of the now useless refrigerator, he swept everything into his inventory without stopping to sort through it. He could do that later before the light failed fully for the day. For now, it was more important to get as much as possible in as short of an amount of time as possible.

Running back through the house he hurried on to the next house and then the next, managing to grab food from three separate houses before the rain hit. Large drops of icy rain hit the ground around them as they ran to a new house where they would rest for the night.

Charles pushed through the door and then stopped to turn around and look at the mountain bike that was resting beside the door underneath an overhang that protected it from the weather. Grinning to himself he pulled it inside the house before turning to watch Alli stand in the rain. Her blood blackened scarf hung heavily over her snout dripping small rivers of red whenever she shook her fur ridding herself of the ash that had clung to her all day.

Shaking his head, he walked inside, leaving the door open for her. At the rear of the house just before the kitchen, he found a bathroom with large white towels on a rack beside the door. Grabbing an armful of them he returned to the entryway and waited for Alli to finish cleaning herself. If he was being honest with himself then the idea of getting clean sounded divine right, then. He was covered in blood and ash and sweat from the last couple of days.

Then again, this might be the last opportunity he had for a while to get properly cleaned. Shrugging his clothes off, he sat down on the stoop while he waited for his clothes to get wet enough to wash. Sitting there in nothing but his boxers he could already feel a chill setting in.

Running his hand through his sopping hair he washed the ash from his scalp and then from his body as the thick grey water pooled around his feet. Feeling clean enough for the moment he stepped over to his clothes and rubbed them together in an effort to get rid of the worst of the stains. If he had taken the time to look through the house, he probably would have found detergent he could use while washing them, but he hadn't thought of it beforehand. Now he was too cold to stop and run inside to look for anything. If he stopped, then he knew he would not be coming back out. The shivers he was barely holding at bay attested to that.

Deciding he had had enough he rushed back into the house, holding his dripping wet clothes under one arm. Alli was waiting for him inside the house next to the pile of towels he had left there, she had shaken herself mostly dry but was still dripping a little bit of water on the floor. Grabbing the first towel he dropped the clothes from his arms and began wiping himself down before the shivers fully took over. He was still somehow holding them at bay, but he could feel them fighting to come out.

Quickly he wiped Alli down, shifting her scarf so that it hung from her neck for now. Picking up his wet clothes from where he had dropped them, he carried them into the kitchen and lay them over the chairs where they could dry out overnight. Then going back to the front door, he made sure it was closed and locked before heading upstairs to where the bedrooms were. He ran into the first one he came to, delighted to see that it had a large king-sized bed as he dove underneath the covers. Above him, he could feel Alli laying down across the bed her large body heating the blankets quickly as he shivered uncontrollably.

The room was fully dark when he came out from underneath the covers no longer shivering. Sitting against the headboard he pulled out some food and water for them to eat and drink while he began going through everything in his inventory. What he had initially thought of as a lot of space was instead something that quickly became full when you had to carry everything with you. Anything that had stacked into a single slot he left alone for now choosing to go through everything else. Cans of food and spices he left alone, though he tossed all the boxes of pasta which for some reason hadn't stacked.

He needed to find some more backpacks to put things in soon, if he put items that didn't stack in the bags then he would be able to carry a lot more. Considering that he was now carrying all their food and supplies, he was going to need to be able to carry as much as possible.

When he had finished going through the food in his inventory, he pulled the health flask from where he had stored it during his impromptu shower and motioned for Alli to drink it. He knew she had been fighting all day, working to keep him safe. He didn't know if she had been injured at all, but he was unwilling to risk it. Letting her drink, the health potion each night would be the least he could do for her. During the day they would use it for emergencies, but at night he would give it to her to drink.

He watched as she held the mouth of the flask in her teeth and tilted her head back, letting its contents fall right into her throat. In so many ways she did not act like a normal dog, he knew she was intelligent and that she could understand him but seeing her act like that really drove it home. She was no longer just a normal dog; she was something else. She was changing alongside him and the rest of the world.

Taking the flask from her he put the top back on it, watching as the glowing numbers came into being and began their countdown. Placing the flask in his inventory, he settled back to meditate for the night, focused on learning some attack spells. He had already decided earlier in the day that he would be using fire for his attacks, at least for now. Most things burned after all, and the things that didn't he could use his glove on them and hope there wasn't more than one at a time.

It was odd not being able to sleep, in some ways he missed it, and in some, he didn't. He wasn't sure if the gods truly knew what they had done for him, by not needing to sleep he gained hours that he could spend meditating each night. Meditating was restful, but normally it would have been no substitute for a good night's sleep. If the gods hadn't cursed him like they had, then he would have only been able to meditate for a single hour or two max each night. Instead, he was making progress meditating on magic because he didn't need to sleep. Their curse was actually helping him, although he knew that without the ability to meditate the long sleepless nights would have quickly made him go insane.

Alli shifted around on the bed throughout the night, pulling him from his meditations to look around the room. Each time once he saw that she was merely trying to get comfortable and not alert him to something, he would heal the mounting pressure in his head and the go right back to his meditations. The hypnotic sight of flames danced behind his eyelids all night long as the glove guided his trance-like meditation towards the mysteries of fire magic. In the morning he had learned two fire spells.

Congratulations, you have learned the spell 'Firestarter'.
Firestarter is a fire spell used to start fires.

Congratulations, you have learned the spell 'Firebolt'.
Firebolt is a basic attack fire spell that hurls a bolt of fire in front of the caster. Max range of sixty feet.

Oddly enough, though there was not a mana cost associated with using the spell, actually now that he thought about it there hadn't been one on his healing spells either. It didn't make sense to him, there had to be a cost for using the spells. He had a mana bar it was right there on his status page. Granted, there weren't any numbers next to it, but casting spells always had a cost. During the day he would have to try casting the spell repeatedly to see what his limits were.

Alli stretched on the bed for a second before hopping off and waiting for him. She was larger again, now slightly taller than his knees. Pulling up her information, he saw that she had gained another level the day before. She was now level three. It seemed every time she gained a level she grew in size. He wondered how long that would go on for, hopefully not too much longer, or she would be too big to take inside.

Pushing Alli to the side with a nudge of his leg he walked past her and down the stairs to the kitchen and his hopefully dry clothes. The sun was just barely rising on the horizon and hadn't had a chance yet to warm the rain-chilled air. Unfortunately, his clothes were still a little damp. They would dry off pretty quickly with him wearing them, but they would be uncomfortable until they did.

Dressed in his moist uncomfortable clothes and his leather bomber jacket, Charles brought out some food and water for them to eat before they got going. Alli had a look of disgust on her face as she ate the jerky he laid out for them to eat. Unfortunately, much of the food he now had in his inventory required prep work and cooking time or was full of sugar. There was little ready to eat food to be found.

Pushing his chair back from the table he walked over to the pantry remembering they hadn't looked through it the night before. Inside the shelved space, he found it full of sugary products and dog food. Whoever had lived in this house before had obviously had kids, and possibly a dog, or maybe the kids had just like the taste of dog food. Pulling one of the bags behind him he dragged it over for Alli to see.

"I found some dog food you can eat instead if you want." He said as the open bag began to spill onto the floor in front of her.

The face she made at the dry hard food was almost as bad as the one she had made for the jerky. Apparently, she didn't like dog food either. It was really too bad that neither of them had a lot of choice in the matter anymore. Deciding to leave the other bag of dog food in the pantry, he went back upstairs to look for clothes. The shirts were too big, and the pants were too small. The coats were more like glorified tents. In fact, the only thing he found that helped him was an unopened package of socks that were buried at the bottom of the drawer.

Throwing the lone package of socks into his inventory he made his back to the kitchen where he found Alli laying next to a now empty bag of dog food. She had finished the entire twenty-pound bag of food in one sitting.

"Do you want me to grab the other bag of food for later?" He asked in amazement. He hadn't realized she was that hungry.

Picking her head up off the floor she looked at him for a few seconds before looking away climbing to unsteadily to her feet. Her stomach was swollen from all the food. Shaking her head at him, she waddled past him towards the front door.

Taking her response as a 'no' he walked past her and opened the door before grabbing the bike that he had brought in the night before. Looking at the bike and then the size of the clothes upstairs, he'd bet that it had seen very little use since it had been purchased. It was there to sit outside their house to make the owner feel better about themselves and nothing more.

It was too bad too; the bike seemed like a fairly nice model with shocks and disc brakes. Granted at this point in his life, though he knew next to nothing about mountain bikes. For all he knew this could be a cheapo bike purchased at the local superstore.

Alli walked by his side as he walked the bike to the main road and prepared to set out for the day. Straddling the cushy gel seat, he remembered that he had one last thing he needed to do before setting out. Reaching into his inventory he pulled the health flask that he had stored there the night before and attached it back to his hip. He didn't notice that the countdown timer on the lid of the flask showed nearly a full twelve hours until they could use it again.

Bending down, he rearranged the scarf so that it covered Alli's mouth and nose then did the same for his own. Putting his feet on the pedals he pushed shakily forward as he rode a bike for the first time in six years. Keeping his eyes on the road, he soon regained confidence in his ability to pedal a bike without falling over and began to speed up.

The crisp morning air streamed around him making his eyes water, the morning air was clearer than it had been in days. The rain from the night before having washed away much of the falling ash and smoke.

Looking behind him, Charles was able to clearly see for the first time the full extent of the damage that until then he had only seen small glimpses of. The city was ruined, and in spots he could see where smoke continued to drift into the sky from flames that still raged. Looking back at the husk of a city made him wonder just how he had managed to survive at all.

There were only a small handful of buildings taller than five stories that still stood in one piece. Everything else had either been destroyed by fire or some other catastrophe. It was no wonder the ash and smoke had been so thick in the city, looking at it now it seemed like almost everything had been on fire.

Charles continued to stare at the ruined skyline fighting to regain the breath that had left his body when he saw the extent of the damage. It boggled his mind to comprehend the idea that anyone could survive something like that. Let alone that someone was able to walk through the center of it and never know the devastation that was hidden within the veil of smoke.

The sound of Alli growling next to him is what finally brought him back to reality. Turning back around on the bike, he immediately saw what she was snarling at. Two large grey skinned trolls, each holding a rust-colored bone club in their large hands. Rolls of fat and flabby skin jiggled and waved with each step they took, making it seem like they were in constant motion.

His eyes fixed on the bone clubs he knew the rust color for what it truly was. Dried blood. Resting his hand on Alli's head, he swung his leg off of the bike, putting the kickstand down as he did so. Then bending over next to her ear, "Go get them!" He told her firmly, and he tried out his flame attack for the first time.

Chapter 6

The bolt of fire shot from his hand as Alli sped towards the monsters with a teeth-baring snarl. She took the one on the right as his bolt of flame impacted the troll on the left. With a scream of terror, the large flabby grey-skinned monster turned to run from the fire as it was engulfed by the blast. With a panicked scream, it fell to the ground as the flames spread over its entire body. Apparently, trolls were incredibly flammable.

Alli snarled viciously as she attacked the other troll, her strong jaws snapping shut on the wrist that held the bone club. There was a loud crack as its wrist snapped under her jaws, the club falling from its limp fingers. Alli let go of the wrist as the other troll fell to the ground behind the monster she was attacking. Jumping away from the troll, she took a few quick springing steps moving away from them. Planting her front paws firmly on the ground, she spun in place and charged back towards the monster. Slamming her shoulder into the distracted troll, she used her weight and momentum to push it backward.

It stumbled into the flaming thrashing troll; the flames leaping from one monster to the next in that single second of contact. The second troll stopped moving as its massive shiny bald head swiveled down to look at the flames speeding up its leg. Falling to the ground, it too began rolling around on the ground screaming in terror.

Alli sprung away from them and ran to Charles side, as they both watched in dumbfounded surprise. They both tuned out the screams of the monsters that echoed through the air as they looked at each other. His Firebolt didn't seem to cause a lot of actual damage, but the trolls were so flammable that in this case, it didn't even matter.

Moving away from them, they watched as the flames slowly ate away at the monsters. Minutes later, everything finally fell silent as the flames slowly petered out, leaving small wisps of smoke in their wake. The monsters were dead, and though it had been horrifying, it had also been easy. The monsters had a weakness that was incredibly easy to exploit if you had a strong enough stomach for it.

Grabbing the bike, they skirted the burnt husks of the trolls as they quickly moved past them. The stench emanating from their burnt flesh was incredible, bringing tears to their eyes with the slightest of whiffs. There was no way he was even going to try, to loot either of them.

Keeping his eyes on the horizon as he steadied the bike, he walked carefully his mind on the magic he had used. The lack of known mana cost was bugging him for some reason, whenever he cast his magic, he hadn't felt anything. There was no drain of energy or buildup and release of power. It just was. He thought of the magic he wanted to use, and it came into being just like that.

He could feel the shifting of magic inside himself, that had been the first thing he had learned. That first night before he had been able to use spells, he had learned the basics of mana usage. That had allowed him to feel the movements of mana within his own body, but whenever he was casting magic, the power for the spells wasn't coming from him. Instead, it was focused around the glove on his casting hand.

Pushing the bike along as he walked, he trusted in Alli to alert him to any danger as his mind remained focused on other things. Focusing his senses on the flow of magic he extended his hand and cast firebolt. The flame shot from his hand and eventually dissipated into the air when it didn't hit anything. His mind was focused on what he had sensed around his hand and noticed none of that.

When he had cast the spell, a stream of pure mana had extended into the air from his glove. The glove was taking the cost of the spells from everything around him. He didn't understand how it was possible, but then again, he only had a basic understanding of magic at that point. Very little of it made sense at all.

Deciding to experiment, he extended his left arm, dropping his right and concentrated on casting the magic from the raised hand. The bolt of fire formed more slowly as he felt it drain his energy before launching from his hand. His feet stumbled at the sudden loss of energy using the spell had caused.

Ahead of him, Alli looked back as he stumbled and then loped back to him as he stopped moving altogether.

Charles stared at his left hand, amazed at what he had just learned. He didn't know if the gods had intended for this effect or not, but the glove allowed him to cast magic without the usual cost. He had, in essence infinite mana, or at least as much as the area could provide. With this new knowledge, he could cast spells constantly and work at possibly leveling them up for better versions. He was sure that the key to learning more about magic was using it and meditating on it.

Laughing softly to himself, he started walking again, pushing the bike along with his left hand. With his empty right hand, he began to repeatedly cast Firestarter, leaving a trail of small flickering flames in his wake.

Ten minutes later he shook his head and stopped casting the simple spell. He needed to focus, Firestarter was a useful spell, but he doubted it would level-up into anything better. He needed to concentrate on his attack and healing spells for now, and he also needed to figure out a way to do it while riding the bike. Walking was too slow, and their journey was going to take long enough as it was.

Maybe during sections of the road when he didn't need both hands to control the bike, he could cast something then? Things were never easy, were they? No matter what the world became, there would always be something more that needed to be done.

Swinging his leg over the seat, he settled his feet onto the pedals and pushed off feeling the crisp morning air brush past his face.

Alli kept pace next to him as he pedaled nonstop, his breath coming in short gasps on the hills and then slowly evening out as he would coast down the other side. Groups of monsters began to appear on the road more frequently. Each time Alli would run from his side and engage the monsters pulling them away from him. He would then pepper their backsides with bolts of flame as the large silver husky would employ hit-and-run tactics on soft or exposed spots. Everything was fair game for her as long as she could reach it, throats, groins, tendons, if she could reach it with her teeth, she did.

Then when they were all on the ground he would move in and finish them off with his lightning attack. With every use, the pain in his hand grew worse, and he would fall to his knees as his thigh burned along with his hand. Healing his leg proved some relief, but he was unable to heal the pain in his hand no matter how hard he tried.

By the time the light had started to fail his right hand hung limply at his side, twitching in time with his heartbeat. The fingers of the hand were useless as he leaned against the seat of the bike and walked along using it as a crutch. His fire spell seemed to do more damage as the day got on, but it was still a weak spell. Without the glove, he could only cast the spell six times, which was just barely enough to finish off an Orc. They had learned that during their last fight when the monster had jumped out at them while Alli was busy scaring off a pack of feral dogs.

He had only used the lightning attack three times that day, but apparently, that was the limit. The first time the pain in his hand had gradually gone away. The second time it had stayed, and the third time had rendered his entire arm useless.

In the future, he would have to very careful how much he used the lightning attack.

The bike had proven to be a double-edged sword. They had indeed been able to cover more ground that day, but they had also been attacked more as a result.

Charles had never felt so tired in his life, he wanted nothing more than to be able to sleep but knew he wouldn't be able to. For the first time since this had started, he wanted to break down and start crying like a baby. It was too much for him. It had all finally become too much.

Next to him, he felt Alli nudge her wet nose into his injured hand, sending a bolt of electricity through it as it spasmed painfully. Dropping the bike, he fell to his knees, ignoring the gravel that dug into his skin. And just like that, the tears started to fall.

Alli licked his face repeatedly before giving up and pressing her body against his. Letting her very presence provide the comfort that he so desperately needed at that moment. He felt wrung out emotionally and exhausted physically when he finished letting out all the emotions that had piled up over the last few days.

His eyes felt dry and gritty as he gently hugged Alli and then pushed her away, so he could get to his feet. The sun had vanished behind the mountains, leaving only a few streaks of light in the sky far overhead. Charles looked at where they were as Alli trotted away and stood in front of a closed glass door. They were in the parking lot of a military surplus store.

He had been following her mindlessly for some time at the end there; he had no idea where they even were anymore. Regardless she had brought him to some place great. The kind of supplies they would be able to find in a surplus store like this would be great.

Kicking the glass of the door he watched as it spider-webbed out from the spot he had kicked but stubbornly held together. Kicking it again, he watched in satisfaction as it shattered falling to the ground noisily. Peering inside, he spotted some shirts hanging around a rack by the door. Grabbing all of them he scattered them across the ground around the door covering the glass so Alli could walk safely over it.

Nudging him softly, she moved past him and into the darkened store. Using the last little bit of light that trickled in he sped through the aisles searching for the one thing that he was sure a store like this possessed. Glow sticks! They may no longer have flashlights, but glow sticks would still work.

Perched on the top of the counter right next to the cash register, he found a box of them just waiting to be used. Cracking three of them right away he sighed in relief as they provided the light he needed to see by.

Taking the sticks of light, he walked back through the door and into the now dark parking lot. He had dropped the bike earlier and then forgotten about it; he needed to retrieve it and store it before someone stole it. The bike was still laying where he had left it the paint chipped from where it had hit the ground. Holding the glow sticks between his teeth, he picked the bike up with his left hand and tried to put it in his inventory. Nothing happened, it didn't vanish. Growling in annoyance he pushed the bike into the store and rested it against the wall.

Alli appeared in front of him holding a folded-up blanket between her teeth. Nodding at her, he let her lead him through the maze of aisles to the back of the store and the waiting backroom. He was too tired and weak to even think about doing anything but follow her.

Putting his back to the wall after they had closed the backroom door, he slid to the ground with his feet outstretched in front of him. Awkwardly reaching around himself, he took the flask his hip and unscrewed the top so Alli could drink it.

Shaking her head, she used her nose to push the hand holding the flask to his mouth. Apparently, she wanted him to use it that night. Nodding at her gratefully, he tilted his head back and waited for the pain of healing to begin.

The rush of fire from the potion sped through his body, burning away impurities and scouring nerves in its wake. The fire seemed concentrated on his right arm and shoulder, everything on that side of his body burned hotter. Then the sweet rush of ice swept the pain away, numbing everything and returning feeling to his extremities.

Charles gasped in relief as he opened his eyes after it was over, using the potion was always a rush of conflicting feelings. The pain was intense, but the sheer relief afterward was equally intense. Experimentally he flexed his gloved hand and moved his arm. The pain was gone, and he could move everything normally again.

Not being able to use his hand or the glove had been terrifying. He was counting on it to help him stay alive, if he couldn't move his arm then he was more or less helpless. He would have to be more careful in the future. Gradually he was learning his limits, now he just needed to be able to stay within them.

He slipped the flask onto his hip and watched as Alli curled up next to his side and snuggled with him. Grabbing the edge of the blanket he shook it out and wrapped it around himself and Alli, making sure that she could breathe without any problems. She huffed lightly as he wrapped the blanket around her and snuggled even tighter against his side. Her eyes were closed with her head resting on her paws. She was already settled in for the night.

Settling against the wall, he looked down at her with a slight smile pulling against his lips. He didn't know what he would do without her. She was constantly saving him and protecting him, even from himself. At the back of his mind, he knew the way he was reacting to everything was more than slightly strange. It wasn't just that he was rolling with the punches; it was like he barely even registered that anything had changed. Maybe his mind was broken. Why else would he be so accepting that the world had ended? Everything about his life had changed, and for some reason, he couldn't bring himself to properly care or even mourn.

Sighing softly to himself, he focused on his meditations for the night and closed his eyes. Pressing the meditation spot on the glove, he delved into the mysteries of water magic. He felt his mind being pulled in separate directions, as parts of his mind splintered to further explore the magic he had already learned. His normally whole mind diverged to focus on different things. Right away, he could feel the beginnings of a massive headache. He would have to stop more often that night to heal it.

It would become more painful to learn different magic types if this continued. Pushing that thought from his mind he focused on the magic he was going to try to learn that night. Water was something that was going to become harder and harder to get, the longer he stayed on the road. For now, at least he needed to focus on utility water magic, not attack magic. If he could conjure drinking and washing water, then that would be one less thing that was taking up precious space in his inventory.

Throughout the night he had to stop his meditations whenever it became too painful to continue. Healing his head worked for the physical pain, the mental pain and fatigue was something else altogether. In the morning, however, all the pain was worth it when he saw the messages he had been ignoring.

You have come somewhat closer to discovering the secrets of magic! Keep trying and soon you may find more revealed to you.

Congratulations, you have leveled up. You are now level 4; you have gained 5 status points for distribution.

Your animal Companion 'Alli' has leveled-up from level 3 to level 5. Her status points have been automatically distributed.

Congratulations, you have learned the spell 'Water Spout'. Water Spout is a water spell that produces drinking water.

Congratulations, you have learned the spell 'Clean'. Clean is a water spell that cleans all dirt and sweat from the target and their clothes.

Dismissing the rest of the notifications and messages he climbed to his feet while Alli yawned loudly next to him. The bulk of the messages were useless to him. He was unable to truly level-up, so it was useless to even pay attention to how much experience he was or wasn't getting from the various monsters. As for the information about the monsters, he didn't particularly pay any attention to that either. It wasn't like he could realistically run from most of the fights, so it was pointless to know whether it was a level 4 or a level 6.

Maybe someday that would all change, but for now, at least he just didn't care. Next to him, Alli finished her yawn and stretched out her long body. Finishing her stretch, she stood up revealing that she now stood almost as tall as his hip.

Chapter 7

S miling down at her wide, heterochromatic eyes, he cast his new cleaning spell on her. A thin layer of water encased her entire body moving rapidly in a circular fashion. There were two small openings at her muzzle for her to breathe through, but everything else was covered in the spinning water. The water spun faster and faster as it began gathering all the dirt and grime towards the rear of her body. Her fur was shiny and gently fluffed in the wake of the cleaning spell until it reached the end of her tail and then dripped onto the ground. The water vanished as soon as it hit the floor, leaving behind a small pile of dirt that it had scoured from her body.

Alli shook herself lightly before letting her tongue dangle from her open mouth in a smile. It seemed she was pleased with the results of the cleaning spell. Stepping away from her, he cast the spell on himself. The movement of the water as it glided over his clothes and skin reminded him of a light full body massage. Almost as soon as he began to enjoy it, however, it began to shift downwards. The water had taken on a brownish-grey coloring as it crept down his body towards his boots. He felt it tickling his toes and then the water ran back up his boots and down the sides to the flooring where it evaporated. The pile of dirt and filth it left behind was significantly larger for him than it had been for Alli.

Alli looked down at the pile of grime and stepped away from him with a sniff of her upturned nose.

"Oh, don't start with that. You were smelling pretty ripe there too princess." Charles said snarkily as she continued to back away from him with her mouth hanging open.

It was true; the spell had even taken care of the smell. For the first time in days, his clothes actually felt clean, not to mention his body. His skin felt smooth and thoroughly cleaned after that, his pores exfoliated and clear. There were still a couple of stains on his clothes where the cloth had already changed color permanently, but other than that they were clean!

A smile on his face, he picked up the blanket from where it had fallen and began folding it as he walked towards the front of the store. Golden streams of sunlight lit up the interior of the store for them. It looked like the store hadn't been looted at all. On one wall there was a long glass case full of guns and ammunition, green metal cans designed to carry ammunition were stacked next to them. On the other wall, tents and large hiking backpacks lined the wall. In between the walls, the aisles were loaded with all kinds of camping gear. On the back wall closest to them were boxes labeled MRE's and other kinds of ready-made food.

This store was paradise! It had practically everything they needed to survive, and with his inventory, it would be interesting to see just how much of it they could bring with them.

Stepping back into the backroom, Charles began emptying his inventory. All the food and bottles of water he had found up till that point he stacked in a corner away from the dirt. With the contents of this store and his new spells, he no longer needed any of it.

Leaving everything in the back, he walked over to the wall with the tents and bags and began pulling it all to the ground. He grabbed several tents and stuffed them into one of the bags before dropping it into his inventory. You never knew when you might need an extra after all, and just maybe he would find someone along the way that needed one. Another bag he filled with sleeping bags and another with heavy-duty coats. Clothes of all kind went into another.

Dragging several bags through the aisles, he began filling them with everything that caught his eye. Knives, sharpening stones, matches, a couple of large machetes, more glow sticks, cooking supplies, it all went into a couple of bags. Carefully he set aside a machete and knife pair in his inventory, so he could wear them later. He might not need it himself, but surely someone would. Besides, it would be valuable in the future as items for bartering he was sure.

Pulling more of the empty bags from his inventory he made his way over to the guns and ammo. Again, he set aside a Glock 9mm handgun, a thigh-holster, and some ammunition into his inventory. Everything else he loaded into the bags and ammo cans. He left nothing behind; he knew how valuable ammo and guns would now be. If only this store had bows and arrows as well!

Moving to the back wall, he threw boxes of food into his inventory and filled the rest of the bags. When he was done most of the store had ended up inside his inventory, with some room left over. If he hadn't been able to put bags full of items in there, and if certain items hadn't stacked, then he wouldn't have been able to carry even a portion of what he was a way.

"What else do we need, girl?" Charles asked as he absentmindedly scratched her ears.

Alli cocked her head at his question before running to the far corner of the store, returning with a large circular metal bowl held in her jaws. Dropping it at his feet, she sat on her haunches and waited. He had forgotten to get her a water bowl; she was probably beyond thirsty at this point. Each time they had stopped for a break she had downed bottle after bottle of water.

Wincing at his own thoughtlessness he cast his water spout spell to begin filling it as he apologized to his companion. "Sorry, Alli, I forgot about your needs. Am I forgetting anything else? Anything you might need?"

Turning her head away from him, she huffed loudly before dipping her head and beginning to drink thirstily. It seemed she was more than a little annoyed with him forgetting about her. It wasn't entirely his fault though, or at least that's how he reasoned it out in his mind. She acted so much like a human in her mannerisms sometimes that he had forgotten that she wasn't. He could see that she was a dog, but in his mind, she had become a quiet human girl.

Pulling out a box of beef jerky, he opened a couple of packages before returning the box to his inventory. He had been eating nothing but jerky the last few days. Why was it that none of the houses he had stopped at had any kind of fruit? He didn't care if it was fresh or canned; he hadn't seen any at all!

He watched as Alli drank her water, his eyes drawn to her silky-smooth coat. There was something different about it today, or maybe it was because it was clean that he was noticing it. Her hair was longer than it had been before. Reaching his hand out, he felt her silky hair petting her softly, feeling the hard muscles that now lay just underneath her fine coat. Leveling-up was definitely changing her, she wasn't only growing larger and more intelligent each time but also stronger and probably faster as well!

Abruptly Alli raised her head from the bowl of water and growled, her head focused on the door of the store. Quickly Charles tipped the rest of the water from the bowl and threw it into his inventory. With Alli still growling beside him, he hurried to the door and out into the open.

Walking towards the front of the store was a group, five armed men. Each of them was covered in dirt and filth and carrying guns that had clearly seen better days. Wary looks of uncertainty crossed their faces as he stepped into view walking through the door he had broken the night before. Alli hung back letting the inside of the store hide her for the time being.

The looks of wariness and uncertainty vanished from their faces as they got a good look at him. Standing there in front of the store was a clean unarmed person, someone who had clearly not been doing any kind of fighting and leveling up. Someone they could take everything from without worry.

"What are you doing there, boy?" One of the filthy men asked. Charles focused on the speaker, his enhanced vision showing the lice that clung to his matted colorless hair.

Boy? Really, he was twenty-four for Pete's sake! He hadn't been a boy in years. Moving just the tips of his fingers, he motioned for Alli to join him outside the store.

He answered as she walked silently to his side. "I was resting for the night with my companion here. What do the five of you want?" He was getting a bad feeling from them, not exactly blood thirst but it was close. Whatever it was they wanted, it most certainly was not going to be good for him and Alli. Speaking of bloodthirst didn't he have a skill related to that? Why hadn't it been working? He would have to look into it later when he had a chance.

"We want what's inside that there store! And we want the nine items you undoubtedly took and put in your inventory!" Charles fought to keep the muscles of his face under control as the man spoke. He had been right they were up to no good, more than that though he had just learned something important. His inventory was different from everyone else's. His was much larger! Was it because of the glove or because he used magic? His mind sped through the different possibilities as Alli began to growl again next to him.

"Keep your freak of a dog under control, or we'll put it down!" One of the men said nastily as he raised his gun and aimed it at her.

"Her!" Charles said firmly.

"What was that? Speak up, boy!" The first speaker said before spitting nastily to the side, the stream of brown liquid splattering on his companions' boot.

"I said, her! She's not an it, and she is not a freak!" He said firmly his voice loud enough for them all to hear clearly. Next, to him, Alli nudged his leg warmly, appreciating his words.

The five men looked dumbstruck for a second before they began cackling at him. "Boy, she's a freak if we call her one! Besides who cares what its gender it is after we take everything from you, we're going to kill you and then we're going to use your giant freak of a dog for target practice!"

Charles felt his skin prickle and his hair stood on end as the man explained what he was going to do to them. Next, to him Alli's growl deepened and her legs separated into a crouch. She was ready for a fight. His hand flexed lightly as he made sure it still worked without issue, the problems from the night before had made him understandably cautious in that regard.

No matter what he was not going to let them hurt Alli. They may have been human, but they were acting like monsters! If they wanted to fight, then he wouldn't hesitate, to him, they meant nothing while Alli meant everything. Over the course of the last few days, she had come to mean more to him than anyone but his family. They were dead though, only his sister now remained, and she was thousands of miles away on the other side of the country. He only had Alli, and he would protect her above all else!

Each of the men pulled their guns to the ready as they aimed at Alli, flickers of fear flashing across their faces at her growl.

"Get your animal under control, or we'll kill it first before we do you! You're unarmed, and we are going to get inside that store! Whether we do that with the items from your inventory or without them is up to you, but we are going inside and there is nothing you can do to stop us!" His voice echoed loudly across the parking lot as he raised the sight of his rifle to his eye and fired.

The ground in front of Alli's paws exploded, pieces of asphalt pelting her muzzle and drawing a line of blood across Charles's cheek. He stilled as he felt the bloody streak begin to drip down his cheek, when that man had fired at Alli something had changed within him! The hot feelings of anger and uncertainty had fled, up till that point he hadn't been sure that he would be able to fight them.

Then they had fired, and all emotion had fled from his body, only cold hard rage remained. No longer was he uncertain about hurting them, killing them, now the only problem was how much was he going to make them suffer before they finally died?

Raising his gloved hand, he extended it towards the men and spread his fingers. "You handle the one on the far right!" He said quietly, his voice bone-chillingly cold and devoid of emotion.

Alli leaped forward her muzzle pulled back in a snarl as she launched herself at her target.

His eyes fixed on the first of the five men, the dirtiest and most vocal of them. It was the man who had dared to shoot at Alli; he launched a firebolt lighting the man on fire. The quick change in circumstances left the other men stunned and unable to move as they watched their leader fall screaming to the ground. Their diverted attention proved fatal as Alli reached her designated target and began to ravage him with her sharp teeth. Dual screams echoed through the parking lot as another man fell to the ground, his rifle falling to the ground forgotten and useless.

As one all three of the remaining men stumbled backward in shock, one of them falling down. Charles watched dispassionately as one drew ahead of the others as they ran away, launching another firebolt at the man in the lead. More screams rent the air, making the listeners cringe at the pain that was being expressed.

Alli finished off her target and growled at the man who had fallen down and was trying to scramble away without being noticed. He froze though his eyes watched as the last of their group ran away passing a writhing flaming body.

Desperately, Charles clung to his emotionless state for just a little longer as he stood over the frozen man. "Just because the world has changed doesn't mean you have to act like the very monsters that are now attacking us!" He said venomously as he pulled up the information on the man.

John Boardman Lv. 2 Age 32

"Go John and warn everyone you meet that they should not forget themselves! It is us against the monsters! Most of humanity has already perished. Would you aid them in killing the rest of us off?" The man stiffened completely when his name was spoken, his shock obvious at Charles somehow knowing it.

"Who are you? What did you just do?" His voice was shaking as the last of the screams faded as they succumbed to the sweet embrace of death. The sickly sweet smell of burned flesh and hair filled the air underneath an endless clear blue sky. In the distance, smoke could be seen hugging to the ruined building of the once bustling city.

"It doesn't matter who I am, leave, and make sure you tell everyone you meet what I said!" Charles reiterated as he felt his emotions starting to come back. "Now LEAVE!" He roared.

The man jumped to his feet and ran leaving his weapon and the bodies of his companions behind. Charles managed to hold on long enough for the man to disappear from view before he sank to the ground and was sick. Everything he had eaten or drank since he had woken was violently expelled across the asphalt. His stomach continued to convulse until it was empty, and he was left feeling wrung out. This was the first time he had killed an actual person, and while he didn't necessarily regret his actions, knowing that he was capable of doing it in such a casual manner left him feeling conflicted.

They had threatened him and they had shot at Alli. They were bad men, and they deserved what had happened to them, at least that is what he told himself. For the most part, he even believed it to be true. Emotionally though, it would take some time for him to come to terms with what he had done.

Charles looked up as Alli stepped closer to him, avoiding the vomit that was splattered across the ground around him. Blood covered her muzzle and front paws from her attack on the thug. Looking away, he cast the cleaning spell on her, letting it take away the evidence of their actions.

Getting to his feet he forced himself to face the bodies, then reaching down he looted each of them in turn. Looking at what he got from them, he had to sigh in annoyance. They each carried a small amount of ammunition and water, but that was all. He didn't know if it was because they needed the space to carry whatever they looted from the store or if they just didn't have more than that.

Alli licked his hand as he turned away from the bodies and headed back into the store. It was time to get the bike and then get back on the road before anything else happened. He doubted that this would the last time he would be forced to defend himself from humans, but it would be the last time he spilled tears over what he was forced to do. They had been the attackers not him; he needed to survive, and he would do what he needed to make sure he did.

Chapter 8

Charles pedaled along, the quickly heating road passing silently beneath the tires of the bike. He still felt a certain amount of turmoil over his actions in that parking lot but seeing Alli's silver body running ahead of him settled any lingering emotions he felt over the matter. He would do anything he needed to keep her safe, and that was it. He wasn't the only one that needed to survive, Alli did as well.

As he continued pedaling, he noticed that Alli would disappear more and more often, each time returning bloody and with gore covering her muzzle. She would come over to his side whenever she needed healing. During the course of the day, he noticed something odd about her. She had very few bleeding wounds of her own, her silver coat was now like a coat of armor. She had deep bruises but nothing more, which he was glad for. He did not particularly want to test how much damage his healing spell could fix and be found wanting.

It was when they stopped for lunch that he remembered he had yet to equip any of the stuff he had set aside that morning. Having it all on display might help to discourage more people from thinking them helpless and attacking them.

The holster and gun were affixed to his right thigh, the knife and machete were hanging from his belt on the left. He made sure both were visible, although he had no intention of using them. He had his own built-in weapons, after all, these weapons were for show, meant to discourage would-be attackers. He had no experience using any of those weapons and knew it would be foolish to act like he did.

He filled up Alli's water bowl multiple times during their break as she drank her fill and then began running her paws through the water cooling herself down. The pavement was starting to heat up underneath the hot Colorado sun, he could only imagine how much her paws must be hurting her.

"Come here, Alli," He called her as he sat down next to the metal tub of water. "Show me your paws!" He told her firmly, lifting his hand for her to put it in. Looking to the side he could see faint tinges of red mixed in with dirt clouding the water.

Holding her paw in his hand he gently turned it to the side, so he could look at the soft pad's underneath. The water had soaked them and cleaned the bulk of the blood away from the torn and tender skin. Already he could see fresh blood welling to the surface and staining the dark pads red with fresh blood.

"Oh Alli, why didn't you let me know your paws were hurting you?" He asked softly as he imagined how much walking must have been hurting her.

Alli hung her head low as he began to heal the pads of her paws in turn. "Next time just tell me, and I'll heal them. There is no reason you should be in pain while walking, alright?" She licked his face as he finished speaking, accepting what he was telling her. He knew she was intelligent, she had proven it many times over! So, he couldn't understand why she would prefer to walk in pain than having him heal her?

Shaking his head, he cleared it of things he couldn't understand and stood brushing the dirt from her paws off his clothes. Tipping over the metal tub he spilled the remaining water across the ground before putting it into his inventory.

Getting on the bike he pushed off and began pedaling as Alli ran out ahead of him. They continued moving throughout the rest of the day. He only had to get involved in two separate fights, once when Alli got overwhelmed and once when an orc holding a large wooden club began to sneak up on her. He had peppered the orc with firebolt after firebolt until it finally succumbed to the concentrated fire.

As the sun began to dip beyond the horizon, they started to notice more people crowding around the various stores they passed. They never stopped to talk to any of them, after that morning, they had no desire to interact with more people. There was no point in pushing their luck, and nothing drove that sentiment home like what they came across a few minutes later.

In front of a large grocery store, one group of people were attacking another group. People were fighting over supplies, killing each other instead of talking. They remained motionless on the road watching the two warring groups as they fought until blood coated their blades and flowed over the heated ground.

Alli cocked her head and looked to the left of the building where a darkened alleyway ran alongside the store. Following her gaze, Charles saw a group of giant orcs approaching, drawn by the sound of fighting and the smell of blood.

Charles focused on them his enhanced vision, bringing them into sharp focus. They were larger than any of the other orcs he had seen and there were eight of them! Looking at each, in turn, he saw that they were also higher levels than the others he had seen. They were all level sevens and equipped with makeshift metal clubs fashioned from old signposts they had ripped from the ground.

He and Alli hung back for a second to see if the people would notice the incoming monsters. They were too absorbed in fighting though, and the noise they were making would prevent them from hearing if he tried yelling to them. Dropping the bike on the road he set off at a run, Alli outpacing him almost immediately.

Alli's warning howl finally drew the attention of the people fighting, making everyone focus on them. Pointing behind them, Charles launched a firebolt making the two groups scatter as the flaming bolt flew past them and hitting the chest of the orc in the front. They were all silent as they saw him use his magic, their eyes following it as it flew past them and into the group of giant green monsters.

First one and then another of the gathered people began to scream as they saw the monsters. Alli flew past them in a silver streak as Charles continued to throw firebolt after firebolt into the group of monsters. Seeing them attack the on-coming Orcs, the two previously warring groups began to work together and attacked the monsters. Behind them Charles moved to the side, getting into a position where he could continue to attack without hitting anyone.

The first orc fell to Alli's sharp teeth, its arm hanging limply at its side and a gaping hole where its throat had once been. The second fell to damage from the bolts of fire that Charles was flinging at them, its green hide charred a deep black. From the corner of his eye, he saw someone get flung from the group and into the side of the building. The body crumpled to the ground and didn't move again.

Two more of the orcs fell to the ground beneath the constant onslaught of the attacking people. Alli leaped from one monster to the next, keeping their attention on her as she ripped large chunks of flesh from wherever her teeth landed. One more fell to Charles and someone else, a knife had been plunged through its eye as it fell dead to the ground. Alli used its carcass as a springboard, launching her large body high into the air above their heads. Using her size to her advantage, she forced an orc to the ground and crushed its face with her massive jaws.

The two remaining orcs seeing the rest of their group fall turned and ran back the way they had come. Deciding to make a point, Charles extended his hand and used his lighting attack aiming for the one in the lead. The bolt of lightning shot through the air with a muffled crack boring a smoking hole through the chest of his target.

Charles let his arm fall to his side as he used a healing spell on his burning leg, fighting to remain standing and to keep the pain of using that attack off his face. He couldn't show weakness to these people, he had to make sure that they understood just how weak they were and that they needed to be working together instead of fighting.

Thankfully Alli seemed to be able to read his mind and pulled everyone's attention back to her as she growled loudly. All the muscles in her body coiled tightly as she crouched. Her growl became an ear-piercing howl as she launched herself at the last remaining orc. Her feet struck the ground, and then she leaped into the air her mouth opened at an angle. Her feet planted firmly into the monsters back, forcing it to the ground as her jaws closed around the back of its neck.

The front of the orc slammed against the ground as Alli used her powerful legs to rip out the back of its neck. Blood pooled around the monster as its arms flopped uselessly to the ground beside it. She had ripped out part of its spinal column. Alli sat next to the head of the gasping orc and looked at all the gathered people. Her large mismatched eyes held no pity for the being that was bleeding out at her feet.

Everyone was silent with their attention fixed on the gruesome scene in front of them. Behind them, Charles breathed out in relief as the strength came back to his limbs. Walking through the standing people he walked up to Alli and the now motionless orc. Putting his hand on her head, he scratched her ears lightly as everyone watched them. Reaching over to the monster he quickly looted it and a moment later the body disappeared leaving only its blood behind.

With Alli at his side, they walked through the crowd of people and looted each of the monsters they had killed in turn. No one said anything as the bodies disappeared in turn, with one last baleful glare and a snarl from Alli, they walked away. The people still had yet to move when they rode away and vanished around a bend in the road.

The light had nearly vanished from the sky by the time the fight had finished, and they rode away. Alli moved into the lead as they hurried down the road. He wanted to get some distance between them and that group of idiots. There was no way they were going to spend the night anywhere near people like that.

People that acted like that did not deserve his respect or help. He had only helped them this time because the monsters had appeared right in front of them. He had nothing against helping people, but people that were actively attacking others was something else entirely. People like that did not deserve his or Alli's help. Now if only he could convince Alli of that, she seemed to have a desire to help everyone they came across. He would, of course, keep Alli safe, there was no question of that at all.

Empty houses stretched out into the darkness on one side of the road. Open space and scrub brush were on the other side of the road. The moon hung full in the sky as stars began to appear in the cloudless sky.

"Which house should we sleep in for the night?" He asked Alli softly as he looked behind them. They hadn't seen anyone since the fight about an hour earlier. Still, he couldn't shake the feeling that something was out there following them. Waiting for them to let down their guard.

Beside him, Alli looked behind them as well and then focused on the houses to the side of the road. The only light around them was from the moon and stars, making the world seem far emptier than it truly was.

Leaving the road behind them, Charles followed Alli, letting her pick where they would be staying for the night. Houses loomed darkly on either side of them as they walked between several of the unlit buildings. Instead of choosing one of the houses closest to the highway, she led them into the depths of the subdivision. The houses were built close together, blocking the light of the moon from providing any illumination.

Slivers of light were all that kept him from tripping over his feet as he followed along behind her. Her silver coat was easy to see in the blackness of night keeping him from getting lost. In the future no matter how much, he wanted to go on they needed to stop sooner. It wouldn't do to be stumbling along without being able to see.

Ahead of him, he saw Alli waiting for him in front of an open door, the darkness inside the house was absolute. Resting the bike against the side of the house he put a hand on her head, letting her guide him inside the house. She led him through darkened hallways and to a set of steps that led upstairs. A window above the steps let moonlight in as they climbed to the second floor.

Leading him into a room with a bed, she waited for him to climb onto it before joining him and curling up next to him. Scratching her lightly behind the ears, he apologized. "Sorry, Alli, it's too dark for me to see anything. I can't put out any water for you to drink. Drink this though!" He told her as he pulled the health flask from his hip and opened it for her.

He felt the flask pulled from his grip, followed by the sound of swallowing as she tipped the contents of the flask into her throat. Taking it back from her when she was finished, he wiped off the mouth of the flask and affixed it to his hip once more.

Alli shifted against his side as she got comfortable. He ignored the grumbling noises of his stomach as he closed his eyes and pressed his finger against the meditation point affixed to the back of the glove. Walking in the dark had revealed a significant weakness he now had, he needed to be able to see at night and in dark places. It was time to focus on learning light magic.

With his focus in mind, he felt his mind splinter and separate as he began his meditation. His world expanded as he felt something tug at the center of his being. It resisted the pull of his mind like nothing else had until then. It was slippery and hard to control only bending to his will after repeated attempts.

Chapter 9

Something about this magic was different from the others. Neither fire nor water or even healing had made him struggle like this. Neither of them had caused a pulling sensation at the core of his body. The longer he concentrated, the more he began to ache, and unlike the headaches his meditations caused it could not be healed away.

Half-way through the night, he had to give up and let his meditation have free rein, no longer guiding its direction.

When the light of the morning sun began to shine into the room causing Alli to stir from her slumber, the ache had finally disappeared into the ether. Opening his eyes, he pulled his finger away from the meditation point on the glove and looked at the messages from the day before. Immediately closing any message related to the fights and the monsters. When he was done skimming through them, only four messages were of any importance.

Congratulations, you have leveled up. You are now level 5; you have gained 5 status points for distribution.

Congratulations, your animal companion Alli has leveled up. She is now level 6; her status points have been automatically distributed.

Congratulations, you have learned the spell 'Divine Wisp'. Divine Wisp is a holy spell that provides a bright light whose movements can be controlled. The light it produces also protects all who are in its glow from the effects of fear.

Congratulations, you have learned to use the gfas;khgf$lkghfdl*gfapthwkidg.

It was nice to see that he and Alli had leveled up again, even if it meant nothing for him personally. It did affect her and how smart and strong she was. It was interesting to see that the spell he had learned during the night was a holy spell, however. He had been concentrating on learning a light spell, so why had it ended up as something else? Then there was the last message! He had never seen a scrambled message before. What did it mean?

Closing the last of the messages he looked over to where Alli was doing her morning stretch and wondered how much larger she had gotten this time? Standing from the bed, he cracked his back and pulled out her water tub as she hopped from the bed and stood next to him. She was now even with his hip. Shaking his head in amazement at how big she had gotten over the last few days, he began to fill it with water.

Pulling out a bunch of food he sat next to her on the floor and began to eat. It still wasn't exactly a balanced diet, but thanks to everything he had gotten from the store the day before it was closer to resembling something healthy.

Standing up, he walked downstairs and began to rifle through the cupboards, finding them all empty. Someone had already looted them all, leaving nothing behind. "Come on, Alli!" He called as he closed the pantry in annoyance. It wasn't that he needed the supplies now, but every little bit helped. Opening the front door of the house, he waited for Alli to run past him before closing the door behind them. Hopping onto his bike, he pedaled behind her as they headed for the highway.

"Don't forget Alli, you need to let me know when your paws are hurting you! I don't want you hurting for no reason." He told her with feeling as he pulled up alongside her. She gave a yip of agreement before pulling ahead of him as the highway appeared in front of them.

I-70 stretched in front of them, the hard-black road cutting a dark swath through the landscape. Fewer cars occupied the road the farther they got from the city, letting them see the groups of monsters that roved in front of them. Some of the groups stuck to the road, searching the cars for remains. Others wandered across the short crabby grass that grew everywhere in Colorado. They looked to be heading to the various houses that were scattered around the area.

The air was clear underneath the blue sky. They had gotten far enough from the bulk of the fires that smoke no longer hung heavy around them. Behind them, however, they could see a dark cloud of it sitting above the far-off city.

For the first time since Alli had joined him, he could actively watch as she ran off and began attacking the monsters. She used hit-and-run tactics to keep them focused on her while drawing them away from the road. Whenever one of them would get ahead of the others, she would be there a second later attacking them. Ankles, the backs of knees, their throats, everything was bitten or clawed. Lines of blood trailed behind the monsters as she whittled their health away. Then he noticed something interesting, after each monster fell dead Alli would run back to them. She would stand above them for only a second before continuing on, but the monsters would disappear after she did so. She was looting them! She had an inventory as well!

Alli ran back to him when she was done, showing him her side where she had been struck. In amazement, he shook his head as he healed her. She had finished off a group of four monsters and only been slightly injured. She had come a long way since he had found her about to die at the hands of a single orc. Now she was able to handle them on her own like they weren't even a problem.

"I didn't know you had an inventory and could loot monsters!" He told her as he lifted a paw to look at the soft pad beneath.

The look she gave him made him wish she could actually talk, reading the expressions on a dog's face was hard at the best of times. She may be intelligent and had adopted a lot of human mannerisms, but they were still on a dog's face.

Flicking his eyes from the dirty but otherwise healthy paw he saw her do what he could only describe as roll her eyes. He hadn't even known dogs could do that! Then again, it was a very human gesture, so he shouldn't be that surprised to never have seen an animal do it before.

Rolling his eyes back at her, he patted her head and let her paw fall to the ground. "Be careful, if any of the monsters are too much for you, just bring them to me, and we'll take them down together! You understand?" The concern he felt for her was plain in his voice as he spoke. Her head bobbing up and down as she rubbed against his leg and then ran off to attack the next group of monsters.

He had to admit it was nice being able to see the monsters before they attacked him. It allowed him to concentrate on his pedaling. Riding a bike for hours on end was exhausting, but he knew he was covering more ground than he would if he was walking. Looking at how far he had to go, though, was daunting. It was over two thousand miles to Massachusetts, which meant he was going to be stuck on this bike for the foreseeable future. If only he could find an old truck or something conveniently sitting at the top of a hill, he could use for a compression start. Something like that would never happen though.

The longer he pedaled the farther apart everything grew. He no longer saw humans in the distance or around the houses. What few houses he saw still standing, that is, many of them were nothing more than rubble. Monsters crowded around the remains of those buildings, letting him know exactly what had happened to them.

Looking away from that disturbing sight he found Alli was walking next to him having finished clearing out the monsters that were closest to them. She was looking at him like she was trying to figure out a puzzle of some kind. It was more than a little odd and slightly disconcerting to see that look on a dog's face.

"You know Alli, I don't know how smart you are at this point, but I think it is obvious that you are at least as smart as my neighbors were. That being said, I once caught the older one eating paint chips." He didn't even know what he was saying anymore, the world was just so quiet! He needed to hear someone talk, even if it was just himself.

"What am I even doing, Alli?" Charlie asked as he shifted on the bike seat that had started to become more uncomfortable the longer he sat on it. "Up until a few days ago I was just another programmer, I was no one special! I was just a guy that liked watching his favorite TV show, nothing more, nothing less." He was rambling, and he knew it, that didn't stop him from continuing, however.

Next, to him, Alli seemed focused on his words, her wide mismatched eyes seemed to glow as the light hit them just right.

Looking down at her he stopped speaking for a second as her eyes drew him in. Shaking his head to dispel the effect, he focused on the road and continued speaking. "My favorite show is the one that caused this entire issue. I mean for me, not the world! I had nothing to do with that! No, I was up late the night before all this started watching episode after episode." He sighed in melancholy as he thought about never being able to watch that show again. "I think you would have liked it. It's called 'Chuck', it's a show about a nerd who accidentally becomes a spy. There's a beautiful lady named Sarah who is his love interest, and a scary tough guy named Casey. It's a great show!" He was silent for a while as he thought about all the times, he had watched the show.

"Can I tell you a secret, Alli?" He asked quietly looking down at her.

She gave a soft yip and a nod of her silver head in response.

"That's all I really wanted, a girl like that. Someone strong, who can push me to be better. Someone who I can see myself spending the rest of my life with. I never wanted to be a fighter or someone with power. I was happy to live in the shadows and just do my own thing. That's the thing about life though, if you want a girl like that, then you can't stick to the shadows. If you do, then you'll never get noticed by them either." He had tears in his eyes as he spilled the secrets of his life to her. For the first time, he was realizing just how much time he had wasted doing nothing! It was only now, looking back on his life that he saw what he had been doing. He had been hiding, scared to pursue the things that really mattered. He had been content to maintain the status quo instead of pushing forward and striving to become a better person. A person that someone like Sarah would actually look at.

Before everything had changed, he had never put himself out there. He had never pushed himself. In a way, it was ironic that it had taken the end of the world to make him realize something so simple. Now he was doing nothing but putting himself out there.

Beside him, Alli growled and then shot off as she spotted another monster that needed to be taken care of. Shaking his head, he pushed the introspective thoughts from his mind and focused on pedaling. Far in the distance, he could see that while the roads were indeed less crowded than before, there were also a greater number of semi's occupying the road.

Apparently, the various groups of monsters had figured out that the trailers sometimes held interesting things. Monsters crowded around the trailers, pounding on them and tearing at the metal wherever they could. They had managed to actually push at least one trailer onto its side and were jumping on top of its crumpled side. The thin metal flexed beneath their massive feet and then with a scream of tearing metal one of them fell through, vanishing inside the trailer.

Charles avoided them as best as he could as he kept one eye on Alli making sure she stayed safe. Which is exactly what she was not doing. Ahead of them, Alli was running from trailer to trailer biting and clawing at each of the monsters.

Cries of pain mixed with roars of annoyance echoed softly through the air as she harassed them. They ran after her, leaving the road devoid of monsters as he pedaled faster trying to keep her in sight. Alli's sleek silver form flashed in the sunlight as she ran beside the road, a line of monsters trailing her.

The sun hung low in the sky when he saw it. Far to the side of the road, the remains of an old abandoned gas station. The pumps had been removed, and the signs leaned heavily against the side of the building. Weeds grew haphazardly from the pitted concrete surrounding the building and the overhang was broken where it had been pulled to the ground by heavy snows sometime in the past.

Pulling the bike alongside the building, he swung his legs stiffly from it and sank to the ground as his legs gave out. Biking all day long was not something he was used to, and everything hurt. He had gotten more exercise in the last few days than he had gotten in the last couple of years combined. His body was protesting at the sudden change as well. He could heal the worst of the aches and pains away, but there was nothing he could do about his lack of muscle or stamina. Simply healing everything away didn't miraculously give him more energy, it just made his exhausted state more comfortable. More than that, it seemed that he had found the limit for his current level of healing ability. Abusing his muscles all day like he had been, was too much built up damage for it to fully fix.

Lying down on the hard and dirty concrete, he gave a groan of pure pleasure as he relaxed against the hot ground his back relaxing. Alli ran up to him and flopped beside him with a huff. She had been running all day and was surely equally exhausted. He'd had to heal her paws numerous times alongside her other varied injuries. He knew he was pushing them both hard, but the thought of his brainiac sister struggling to stay alive kept him pushing forward.

Rolling onto his front he pushed himself to his knees and then to his feet as he hobbled stiffly over to the door of the gas station. Leaning against it he swung his hip near the handle and the door popped open with a groan of rusty hinges.

Dust lay thick over the floor as he shuffled inside with Alli at his heels. He closed the door behind them and then pulled a blanket from his inventory shaking it out over the floor, so they didn't have to sit in the dust for the rest of the night. Putting his back against the wall he waited for Alli to curl up beside him before pulling out another blanket and wrapping them both in its warmth.

He was too tired to eat, making himself drink some water and having Alli drink the health potion was almost more than he could manage. Leaning his head against the wall, his hand crept over to the meditation point as he focused on speed. They needed to be faster, they would never reach his sister before winter set in at their current speed.

Chapter 10

Charles stopped as he looked at the notification for his newest magic. It was exactly what he had been hoping for. That was not the problem, half-way through the night, the pressure on his mind had eased. He could tell it was still split in different directions, but the pressure the splits had caused was suddenly gone. It had left him feeling, disjointed and afraid to look at the messages he was constantly minimizing. One of them undoubtedly held the reason for the sudden change.

What if he had damaged himself? What if his constant meditations and the pursuit of magic had damaged his mind in some way? He knew it was silly not looking right away, but as long as he didn't look then he didn't have to acknowledge that something was wrong. So, he had put off on reading the messages until morning and just continued with his meditations.

Now the time had come to face whatever they said.

Congratulations, you have learned the spell 'Haste'. Haste is a time spell that increases movement speed on foot by 15%, or on a vehicle by 40%. The effect's duration lasts for one hour.

Casting that spell while he was on a bike would be great and casting it on Alli would allow her to keep up with him. The next message was the last one, it would tell him what had changed during the night.

Due to the constant splitting of your mind, the skill 'Mental Partition' has been learned. This skill allows your mind to split into separate partitions that can each focus on a designated task. Certain conditions must be met for this skill to successfully activate.

Closing that last message with a sigh of relief he looked down to his side where Alli had been curled up at his side all night long. Her body heat combined with the blanket had kept him nice and warm, she had barely stirred the entire night though. All the fighting she was doing must be tiring her out like nothing else. At least there hadn't been a message saying she had leveled up, that had surprised him actually. With how many monsters there were on the road, he was sure it would happen tonight.

The morning light let him see a number of things that he had missed the night before. Namely, the dusty and somewhat outdated roadmap. Getting stiffly to his feet he shook out the dusty blanket and stuffed it into his inventory before more dust could latch onto it. A cloud of the obnoxious filth filled the air as the movements of the blanket disturbed the air in the room.

Next, to him Alli got to her feet with a sneeze and hurried over to the door with a glare. Bending over he scooped up the book of maps and brushed it off as he opened the door to outside.

He studied the roads on the map as he chewed mechanically on some jerky and Alli noisily drank from her water tub. He had a basic idea on how to get to his sister, but that was it. According to the map, he would first go into Kansas by following the interstate he was on now. More than that now that he knew the actual distance, he was able to work out how long it would approximately take it to go that far. It was worse than he thought, if he could cover a minimum of thirty miles a day, he was looking at over two-and-a-half months of being on the road.

That was more than a little daunting! He would do it, there was no question of that. The number represented something else to him besides distance, how many monsters they were going to need to fight. Even with his new spell, he wasn't sure how much farther they would be able to go each day. The farther they went in a day, the more monsters they would come across. The faster they went, the faster they would come across those monsters. With the new spell he would be effectively doubling the fighting they would be doing each day.

Putting everything away he called out to Alli and cast the haste spell on her. She appeared to blur out of focus for a second as her entire body suddenly sped up looking like it was slightly out of sync with the rest of the world. Shaking away the momentary disorientation seeing her blur had caused, he swung his leg over the bike and prepared to cast it on himself.

His eyes closed, he cast the spell. Nothing changed, he didn't feel any different, certainly not any faster! Opening his eyes, he saw something that was more than slightly disorienting. The world had slowed down! Everything felt slower, the motes of dust that hung in the air fell slower. The sounds in the air were elongated and stretched on for longer than they should have.

Closing his eyes, he focused on the beat of his heart, letting its steady, somewhat rapid beat calm him. Focusing his senses on the internal metronome beat of his heart, he began to peddle. Alli kept pace with him initially before running ahead to do her usual thing. For his part, he kept his eyes firmly on the road and not too far ahead. Seeing the world under the effects of his spell was just to stomach churning. As long as he focused on things near him and nothing that was living, he could fool his mind into believing everything was normal.

It worked too, for a little while. Until he came upon the first monster of the day, seeing how slowly it moved and breathed undid all the progress he had made. Stretching his hand forward, he paused as he looked at the monster. It was something new; it wasn't an orc or a troll. He had seen more than enough of those by this point. No, this was something else.

It was short, maybe three feet tall and green. Its ears were short and pointy with ragged tears on both sides. It had a long pointy nose with beady yellow eyes and a wide mouth with sharp serrated teeth. Long arms that hung to its knees with knobby hands and extra-long fingers that appeared to have two extra joints. It was an ugly little monster.

Above its head, the words 'Goblin Lv. 5' appeared.

It was the first new kind of monster he had seen in a while, but it did confirm something for him with its presence. Whatever the gods had done to the world was nowhere near finished. The changes were still ongoing, and the world was only going to get more dangerous.

The goblin's eyes widened as it stepped away from the car it had been rummaging through and drew its small rusty knife. There was a flash of silver behind the car as Alli stepped out from the behind it and growled. She was larger than the small monster who began to screech at the sight of the big dog.

It was hit by the first firebolt as it took a step away from them, the force of the blast throwing the small monster into Alli's waiting jaws. Her mouth snapped shut around its green head with a crunch as her teeth pierced the skin and punctured the skull.

The screech turned into a howling scream as its head was slowly crushed under Alli's powerful jaws. With a final crunch, she shook her head the small body swinging in the air as its spine snapped with a loud crack.

Charles could only watch on as the green-skinned monster shimmered and then vanished from her mouth. Seeing her take care of the monster like that drove home just how much she was doing for him. He knew she had been protecting him this entire time; he had even seen her taking out the monsters in the distance. Attacking it first with his magic and then seeing her attack, he realized just how weak he truly was. It was pitiful, the only reason he was still alive was because of her. He needed to do more. He needed to be more. He needed to get stronger, he couldn't keep depending on her or anyone else's strength.

Focusing his mind, he cast haste on them both and tried to concentrate as he pedaled down the road. He couldn't hold the meditation spot on his glove while riding the bike, but he was determined to find another way.

He had been meditating at night for days at this point, he was familiar with how it felt. If he could just get it to work without using his hands, then he could continue to meditate all day long. When he was walking, he hadn't been able to do that because of a number of different circumstances, least of which was not being able to see through the smoke. Now though he could see his surroundings, and with his partitioned mind, he was hopeful that he would remain aware of his surroundings as he meditated.

It was a struggle to force his mind to operate in a way it was never meant to. It didn't matter that he had meditated before, using the glove created a connection where none had been before. Trying to create that same connection through the power of his mind alone was giving him a headache.

Remembering how he felt every time he meditated, he struggled to clear his mind. Taking a deep breath, he felt the magic settle around his head. His eyes were open, but his focus was somewhere else. Mindlessly he pedaled on, his eyes barely perceiving the road in front of him. He trusted Alli to keep him safe and that if she couldn't, she would alert him in time. It wasn't something he wanted to do all the time, but he knew he could trust her.

The sun was in a different place in the sky each time Alli warned him of monsters. Her growls and howls pulling him from his ever-growing headache. He had let his haste spell lapse multiple times throughout the day, though he made sure to recast it every time Alli needed healing.

It was late in the afternoon when he felt something shift in the back of his mind and a new notification popped into being in front of his eyes.

Congratulations, you have managed to unlock the skill 'Magical Meditation'. This skill allows your mind to meditate on the properties of magic without the use of items or equipment.

Finally, it had worked. He had gotten the skill to meditate without needing to use the glove! Closing the message, he focused on the road in front of him, really seeing it for the first time in hours. In front of him, Alli ran through the abandoned cars and trucks. She was huffing and out of breath with her tongue hanging limply from her mouth.

He could tell that she was thirsty as she drew near. "I'm sorry, Alli! I didn't realize how thirsty you had gotten." He apologized as he hopped off the bike and put his back to a car. Sinking to the ground in the shade of the car he pulled out her tub and began to fill it with water.

Next to him, Alli flopped onto the ground, her silver body kicking up dirt and dust as she settled into place with her head stuck in the tub of water. She noisily lapped at the water, drinking her fill while he set out healing his aching muscles. He wasn't used to exerting himself physically like this every day. He couldn't even remember the last time he had gone to the gym. If he was being honest with himself, he was actually rather impressed with how well he had been doing. First, he had been walking all day and now with the biking, his body was changing at a rapid and surprising pace.

He could feel muscles on his body, where days before there hadn't been any, even his pants were slightly looser. Granted, he had never been fat, and he wasn't eating enough currently. He couldn't help but think that his body was changing too fast though.

The sound of water being noisily consumed ceased as Alli stood and then put all four paws into the tub of water. Reaching up, Charles began scratching behind her ear as she stood there. "You were getting hot, huh, you know I wish you could talk. I've never had a dog before. I don't know if I'm taking good care of you or if I'm doing a terrible job." A wave of depression coated his voice as he spoke softly to her. Shaking her head, she stepped out of the water and licked his face reassuringly. "Thanks, I'll try to do better regardless!" He said with a laugh as his brief flare of depression vanished.

Looking at her this closely he could see just how tired she was, they had managed to cover a lot of ground that day. It was more than that though and he knew it. While he had been concentrating on getting his meditation to work, she had been fighting, keeping him safe.

Wrapping his arms around her, he hugged her as she huffed into his ear. "Just a little longer, we'll stop as soon as we find a good place to rest for the night!" He felt his eyes prick hotly as the tenuous control over his emotions slipped. Burying his face into her dusty coat, he wiped the tears from his eyes. Breathing out, he pushed away from her and breathed in deeply feeling his chest expand to the limit. Closing his eyes, he repeated the deep breaths until he was sure that he was once more in control.

Focusing his mind, he released her and pushed off of the ground getting to his feet. "Let's go, just a little more today." He assured her once more as he cast the haste spell on them both and started peddling.

Starting his meditations, he immediately noticed a difference from before. The split and shift in his mind were more pronounced, but there was no pain or disorientation accompanying it. Instead, it felt completely natural to be able to concentrate on several different things at once. For each different type of magic, he had learned there was a partition in his mind that separated the thoughts from one another. There was even a partition in place that let him concentrate on the world around him.

He didn't know what would pull him from his meditations. It was clear to him though, that for now at least he could meditate day in and day out. The sheer amount of time he could now spend on learning new magic was staggering. He couldn't help but be somewhat suspicious of the way he was learning magic. Something, he couldn't quite place his finger on, seemed off about it. He was sure that he was missing something that should have been obvious.

Ahead of him, he saw a goblin crawl out from under a car and into the path of his bike. His reactions were slowed from the meditating as he failed to respond in time to the threat. He had found the weakness of meditating on the road it seemed. The partitions in his mind allowed his thoughts to be clear, but forcing his mind in so many different directions slowed his ability to react.

A loud screech filled the air as he collided with the green monster and was thrown from the bike and into the air. Time seemed to slow as the partitions in his mind disintegrated and created a backlash effect that left his body stunned and unable to move. With a crash, he hit the windshield of a car unable to brace himself for the impact.

The air was forced from his lungs as something shifted in his stomach. A flare of pain seized him as he tumbled from the car and onto the warm asphalt of the road. Gritting his teeth, he pushed himself to his knees and forced himself to look around. Behind him, he saw the goblin separating itself from the warped wreckage of the bicycle still screeching as loud as it could.

In the distance he saw Alli running back to him, a veritable tide of monsters was behind her as more began appearing from beneath the cars. His legs shook as he leaned against the car struggling to his feet. Pointing at the lone goblin behind him he launched three rapid firebolts one after another. The loud screeching morphed into a terrified scream of pain and then petered out. For the first time, he was able to hear the approach of the oncoming swarm.

Grunts, hisses, growls and more occupied the air as the ground began to rumble beneath the rapid pounding of innumerable feet. Focusing his eyes on the coming horde he felt his bowels loosen slightly at what he saw. There must have been over forty of them, a mix of rabid animals, orcs, trolls, goblins and more. What made him lose his courage though were their levels, none of them were below level 10. Even the animals were a higher level than he and Alli. The monsters themselves ranged between levels 12 and 15.

It was too much; he was only level 5, and he was unable to even distribute his points. Alli was doing better than him, but there was no way she would be able to stand up to those levels.

Each breath was filled with pain and a feeling of something grinding in his stomach. Moving to the side of the road where there were no obstacles, he faced the monsters and raised his hand. Desperately he tried something new, something that he had not even considered possible before that very moment. Casting the lightning spell, he tried to hold on to it and force more power through the glove.

A shifting blue and white glow suffused his arm as he held onto the spell for several beats of his racing heart. Releasing the control he had on the spell, he watched in stunned awe as a thick bolt of lightning leaped from his smoking hand. There was a deafening crack of thunder in the wake of the super-heated bolt of plasma. Great arcs of electricity wormed through the air hitting everything near them. The paint on cars blackened and glass melted as five of the monsters and several nearby animals appeared to freeze and then drip onto the ground. Their flesh and bones turned into boiling liquid in the wake of the lightning strike.

Flicking his wide eyes from the destruction he had wrought to his still smoking hand he noticed that he could no longer feel his hand at all. His leg collapsed beneath him as his entire thigh filled with fire. His gloved hand fell uselessly to his side as his other hand clasped his thigh. Relentlessly he healed his leg waiting for it to take effect. His teeth were clenched painfully, and dots filled his vision as he only dimly saw the aftermath of the initial spell.

Alli was desperately flinging herself from one monster to another, blood coated her liberally, but still, the monsters ran on.

Pushing through the pain in his leg and the exhaustion healing himself had caused he crawled desperately away from the road. Brambles and sharp rocks cut into his knees and tore apart his pants. Distantly he could hear the cries of the monsters being attacked by Alli. Terror filled his mind, robbing him of all rational thought and pushing away the pain he was feeling, and the difficulty he had breathing to the farthest reaches of his mind.

His body was on autopilot as his leaden legs curled up beneath him. With a powerful heave, he found himself on his feet and running away from everything that threatened his life. His conscious mind fought against the terror that controlled his body, desperate to not leave Alli behind. He couldn't leave her, he couldn't abandon her!

With a herculean effort that left his mind reeling, he retook control of his body and fell to his face gasping for air. With every breath he took, the grinding in his chest got worse. His left leg felt like the skin had been flayed from it and then the muscle carved from his bone.

In front of him, he could see the remains of an old barn obscured through the spots of light that kept appearing in his eyes. His unfeeling right arm dragged on the ground as he pushed himself forward. His left leg refused to cooperate, forcing him to worm his way across the rough ground. Tears dripped from his wide eyes as his left arm and right leg worked in tandem to drag him closer to the barn.

The grinding in his chest got worse, before slowly fading into the background as his focus shifted. His world narrowed to the movements of his one good arm and leg, everything else buried beneath a fog of pain.

The thin grey weather-worn planks of wood that made up the side of the barn filled his vision. If he could just reach that wall, he would be able to rest. If he could just reach that wall, everything would be better.

If he could just... the tip of his nose bumped into the rough wood as his glazed eyes refocused. His scattered thoughts sluggishly fell into line as with a groan he flipped around so that his back was against the wall.

The wall against his back was the most comfortable thing he had ever felt. Who needed a soft bed to lay on? He had a hard wall to lean against! His eyes drooped as the world grew fuzzy and dim, even the sounds he had been ignoring seemed to grow distant.

It would be nice to sleep again. He was so tired, and breathing was so hard. Everything would be better after a nap.

The sound of something growling near him made him open his eyes. Something large and grey or was it silver crouched over his legs growling. There was a slight tickle in the back of his mind as his eyes refused to focus and his thoughts remained scattered.

What had he been doing? Oh, that was right! He had been trying to sleep, he could feel the surface of something supremely comfortable pressing against his back. The lids of his eyes fell closed, protecting him from the confusing world around him. It would still be there when he woke, he was sure of it.

Something soft and hairy hit his face. With a groan, he opened his eyes once more determined to make whatever it was go away. It was sleepy time. Why would someone bother him during that holy time? If his eyes weren't so hot, he was sure that tears would have been falling from them. He wasn't sure why he felt like crying, but there was a feeling in his chest that seemed to think it was the right move.

There was a thump against his back as the wall buckled and splintered. Whoever was there had deprived him of his sleeping wall, it was the most comfortable wall he had ever felt!

NO ONE DEPRIVED HIM OF HIS WALL!!!

The world slammed into focus as a silver tail batted at his face again. In front of the giant silver animal were the monsters that wouldn't let him sleep, no they were supposed to be behind him. Thoughts began slipping from his grasp as he pulled himself to his feet struggling when only one leg and one arm responded properly.

Without understanding why he used his left arm to raise his right with his hand outstretched. The tips of his fingers looked blackened, matching the color of the curious glove that covered his hand. Something sparked in his mind at the sight of the glove, something about fire and lightning.

As he thought about lightning, he noticed flickers of light dancing across the tips of his fingers like little arcs of electricity. The mesmerizing sight morphed into something else as all the little arcs of flashing light combined into one at the tips of his fingers.

He wished he could focus; he was just so tired though.

The bolt of crackling light leaped from his fingers faster than the eyes could follow. A charred, blackened hole appeared in the chest of a monster as the bolt ripped through him and into the monster behind it and the one behind it.

With a laugh that seemed somewhat hysterical to his addled mind, he used his left arm to shift the aim from his right and repeated the action.

Distantly in the far reaches of his mind, there was something screaming at him to stop. That he was hurting himself, that thought made him pause as he registered that his leg was no longer hurting. Indeed, he couldn't feel it at all, it was as numb as his entire right arm.

Another laugh bubbled up from within his chest with a wet sounding gurgle. Everything was so funny. He wondered what had happened to that giant silver dog? He was sure that it would be laughing right alongside him.

The wall he had been leaning against crumbled under an impact from something within the building. The force of the impact spun Charles around as he fell to his knees and then to his back.

Had he ever seen a sky so orange before? And why was the world suddenly so silent?

Next to him, a lump of bloody silvery fur fell to the ground stirring up the dust around them. His eyes tracked back to the endless sky above as everything grew blurry, and he knew no more.

Intermission

B rigit stared at the shadow clad person sitting at the head of the table and thought about what he had just asked her.

Did she want to make Charles her chosen hero for the coming game? It was something that she had been giving a lot of thought too, not least because all of the other gods had originally decided that he should remain an unknown factor. Then again, if she chose him, then she might actually be able to finish the game with everyone without needing to create additional characters like she always had in the past. The flip-side to that, of course, was having all of the other gods get mad at her, and that could affect the game as a whole. They had proven to be fairly petty in the past, and she wouldn't put it past any of them to put a target on his back as a result.

"No," She said, making up her mind. "I don't think I will choose him. I find him interesting and surprising for a human, but I will follow what we all agreed upon and leave him free."

"Very well, do you have someone else in mind then, or do you need more time?"

She thought for a moment as someone she had been keeping an eye on came to mind. "Actually, I believe I do know which person I am going to choose as my hero. My hero's name is Kira Lourne!"

"Very well, as the first player to choose a hero, you are allowed to give her a single personalized quest." The DM stopped speaking as he started shuffling through the papers in front of him. "Has anyone else decided on their hero or do we require more time? The world is still stabilizing from the massive upheaval we unleashed, so we can't begin the game just yet in any case. The sooner you make your selections, however, the sooner you can start moving them into position."

There were scattered mutterings around the table at Brigit's selection. No matter what they had said, some of them had wanted her to choose Charles as her hero. With the gifts they had given him, there was a possibility that he would become a strong player. Which is exactly what she needed, her characters had the rather unfortunate habit of dying quickly. Keeping her players in the game longer would only benefit them all, then again if he was her hero then he might die quickly rather than living longer to entertain them.

With a shake of their respective heads they thrust the matter from their minds, they would just have to live with more of her tantrums if that was the case. They were doing this to have fun after all, and the game which had not even begun yet was already proving far more entertaining than anything else in the last few hundred years.

Chapter 11

Kira

Kira Lourne was not having a very good day. It wasn't that she was having a bad day, she just wasn't having a good one. She was almost done fixing the truck, she just needed to get back to the garage with the cans of gas she now had in her inventory. That right there was the problem, since the apocalypse, or whatever you wanted to call it, she had been stranded in the middle of nowhere near the border of Kansas and Colorado.

Now the way back home was in sight, and she was faced with two separate problems. One was the monsters in between her and the garage, the second and far more annoying item was the message that kept blinking into being in the middle of her vision. No matter how many times she closed it, it came right back to annoy her.

You have been offered a quest by the gods! Rescue Charles Byrne before his life expires!

Following the message were a series of directions on where to find the hapless idiot. She had no intention of going to rescue someone. She needed to get back home to Kansas City and check on her family! Her family was important, not some idiot who couldn't even take care of himself!

With an annoyed growl, she denied the quest and closed the message for the fifteenth time. She was a mechanic, a pretty good one too. She was not, however, someone who went out and helped other people from the goodness of her heart.

She hated people! They were deceitful, lying sacks of crap that she couldn't care less for if she tried!

It was why she was a mechanic, cars, specifically older ones made sense to her. They didn't lie or cheat, they either worked or they didn't. It was as simple as that. New cars, on the other hand lied, all those sensors that were always malfunctioning.

Okay, so maybe she had an issue with people, but hey, she had long ago acknowledged that and taken steps to avoid people.

That was one of the good things about the end of the world as far she was concerned, sure electronics no longer worked, and batteries had all seemed to have lost their charge. But there were fewer people in the world, fewer people meant she had to interact with them less. That was a major plus in her book, regardless of how it came to pass, and hey it wasn't like she had known or cared for the people that had died. That was why she wanted to get home so that she could make sure that her family was alive and taken care of.

Plus, beating up on monsters was really doing something for all those pent-up anger issues therapists had been telling her she had for years. She had never believed them until now, and she still didn't quite believe it.

The message popped into being again, causing her to scream in annoyance. All the monsters in the area swiveled and focused on her. Okay, so maybe she had some anger issues, but at least now she had an outlet for them.

Pushing the message to the side she ignored it as she ran out of her hiding spot and attacked the first green monster she came to. The massive wrench she had been more than a little surprised to find at the garage had saved her life more times than she could count in the last week. It had to weigh at least ten to twenty pounds easy and was over three feet long. It was a wrench she would expect to see on an oil rig, not at a small-town garage.

Her hand was clenched tightly through part of the 12 point closed end as she swung it over her head and smashed it into the face of the monster with all her might. There was an explosion of blood and a short gurgling cry, but she was already focused on her next target. She had to be quick, getting tied down for too long meant they would surround her. If they surrounded her then, there was a chance she would get injured, and she did not want to get cut by the rusty knives they all seemed to carry.

She did not want to get infected with some monster disease that there was no way of curing. She didn't want to get infected at all!

Over the last week, she had gotten adept at choosing her battles and attacking them one at a time. She didn't have that luxury right now, though, and needed to focus. Luckily, this was easier than it would have been in the beginning. She had been leveling up quite a bit thanks to all her fights. She was now level 6 and had the stats to back it up.

She wasn't concentrating on any one stat in particular at this point. She saw the value each might have, at the same time though, she wasn't sure what effect each might actually have on her. Certain ones were easy like strength and dexterity, she could tell that she was physically stronger and more coordinated and faster. Others like intelligence and wisdom had a less obvious effect. So, until she could figure out how everything worked, she had been trying to keep everything mostly even. Her strength and dexterity stats were still higher than any of the other stats though.

She knew that no matter what, those were the ones that would be keeping her alive for the foreseeable future.

Kira bounced from one target to the next, remaining on the outside of the gathering monsters. Her arms were shaking from exhaustion when the final monster hit the ground dead. She didn't worry about looting them; she didn't have the room to carry anything but the gas.

The vultures could have them she didn't care. Stumbling forward, she opened the door to the darkened garage with a shaking hand and slipped inside. Right on cue, the message appeared in front of her again as she leaned against the closed door with a groan. She read through the message again, noticing that this one was slightly different.

The gods have given you a quest! Rescue Charles Byrne before he expires. This quest has been accepted automatically as it has been assigned to you personally. The rewards for personal quests given by the gods are generous upon their completion. Failure to complete such quests often has dire consequences!

Her hands curled into fists and shook as she tried to hold in the scream of rage that was threatening to burst forth. Now she was being forced into doing something, and if that wasn't enough, she was being blackmailed as well! She had noticed that it didn't specify just who those dire consequences would affect, it could be her, or her parents or even her little sister!

Everything seemed tinged in red as her entire body shook with impotent rage at what she was being forced to do. It didn't even matter what the gods wanted because she didn't even know if she could get the truck running to rescue him in the first place! She had been working on it all week, and she had fixed everything that she could think of, putting gas in it was just the second to last step. The actual last step was getting the stupid thing started, and she couldn't do that alone, a fact that she had been ignoring the entire week.

It was an old enough truck from the fifties that she could theoretically compression start it without a problem as long as she had fixed everything. The problem lay in that she needed an additional person or a hill to start the truck like that. Neither of which she had available. Kansas was a flat wasteland of wind and scrub-brush where she was.

Kira stopped next to the truck and put the cans of gas in the open bed. Later she would put some into the carburetor and then the rest would go into the tank, for now, she needed to think. She couldn't risk whatever dire consequences the gods might think up, which meant she had to rescue this Charles idiot before he kicked the bucket.

If she was going to rescue him, then she needed the truck running to get there in time! Which brought her back to her current issue of how to get the blasted thing started by herself. There was only one thing she could try, and she hoped it would work since it was her only chance.

Popping the hood of the truck, Kira unwound the air filter that sat over the carburetor and poured in some gas. Next, she emptied the can and all the others into the gas tank, filling it as much as she could. Storing the now empty cans in her inventory, she hurried back to the main door of the garage and opened it after a quick peek to make sure there weren't any monsters hanging around.

The doors open, Kira went back to the truck and released the brake while putting the transmission into neutral. Then she pushed, it was easier than it would have been the week before. Her increased stats in strength showing their usefulness.

Carefully, she pushed the truck back onto the road and made sure it was pointed in the right direction. Kira cracked her neck and stretched her arms across her shoulders. It was go time!

With the driver's side door open and one hand on the frame of the truck and the other on the steering wheel, she began to push. The flat road actually helped her somewhat, making it easier for the truck to coast. Gradually, Kira began to pick up speed until she was running with the truck.

Kira hopped into the driver's seat and jammed in the clutch while she shifted the transmission into second gear. Releasing the clutch caused the truck to buck slightly and the engine to cough as it began to turn over. This was where the gas she had poured into the carburetor came into play. The gas lines running to the engine were likely empty, which normally would have meant spending time cranking the engine while the lines filled. The gas she had poured into it though would allow the truck to start for hopefully long enough for the lines to fill normally.

The engine gave another cough as the truck began to slow, then with a roar, the engine caught, and the old truck shot forward. Kira shifted gears as quickly as the old truck could accelerate. The engine sounded strong, and she wasn't feeling any odd vibrations through her booted feet.

The speedometer climbed past fifty as the engine sputtered and died for a second before coming back strong. The gas lines were now full, and she was on her way.

Thankfully, she shouldn't have to do this again. Older vehicles like this truck used a regulator to charge the battery instead of an alternator. Whatever the gods had done had turned nearly all electronics into scrap metal, anything with a coil had arcing damage melting the metal together. She had yet to see an intact alternator at this point, even the ones that had been sitting on the shelf in the garage had been damaged.

It made no sense, but then again, they were dealing with gods. Mythical beings that no one even believed existed before this week, or was it last week? Without her phone to tell her the date, Kira was finding it hard to keep track of the days. Since this had started the days had started to just melt together, she didn't have time to wonder if it was a Tuesday or a Friday. It no longer mattered!

The breeze through the open window next to her held a pleasant chill as she drove down the highway. Her hands were fixed firmly on the wheel as she dodged all the dead and dormant cars that littered the roadway. Reddish brown smears were everywhere, all leading into the scrub and brush before vanishing from sight.

Countless people had died over the last few days, but Kira could not quite bring herself to care. She hadn't known them; they weren't special to her in any way. They were nothing, their existence was nothing more than a passing blip on her radar.

The sights around her held no sway over her, however, as her mind was fixated on getting to Charles in time. He was another nothing, a person who normally would have never mattered to her. Thanks to the god's involvement, however, that had changed. She was being forced to care about the safety of someone that she had never even met or knew existed before that morning.

The back molars in her mouth ground together as her teeth clenched tightly together. This was not the direction she wanted to be going. It was, in fact, the complete opposite direction! No matter how many times she reminded herself that she didn't really have a choice in the matter, she remained angry.

The pedal to the floor helped the time pass quickly as she sped across the state line and into Colorado. According to the directions provided by the quest, she should be getting fairly close, not more than another thirty minutes at the speed she was going. This far from the cities, the roads had been fairly empty when everything stopped working. There were occasional clumps of trucks and cars, but for the most part, the roads were barren.

Even with the quirks and shakes that came with such an old truck, she was making excellent time. Not to mention that she had not had to deal with any monsters the entire time that she had been driving. She had, of course seen some in the distance, but they were never near enough to the road to bother her. The few that had turned towards her had quickly found themselves outdistanced by the racing vehicle.

Glancing at the quest information that she had settled in the corner of her version she saw that she was almost on top of where he was. Slowing the truck, she topped a rise and saw destruction laced bodies covering the road and making a line towards an old crumbling barn in the distance.

Kira stopped the truck at the top of the hill and looked around the area. She couldn't see anything moving in the distance, it looked like all the monsters in the area had been killed earlier. Though, for the life of her she couldn't figure out what had happened. She saw bodies with charred holes in them and melted glass that had run down the sides of blackened and warped cars. She hadn't met a monster that could do something like that yet, and she didn't want to. It was rare to even see monsters fighting each other, not unheard of, but it wasn't exactly a common occurrence.

Shifting into first she steered the truck off the road and began following the trail of bodies. Some of the bodies were burned in some fashion, but the vast majority of them were covered in bite marks. The closer she got to the crumbling barn, the clearer the picture became. Bodies ringed the side of the building, and she could see that part of the wall had been bashed through.

She pulled the truck alongside the bodies and hopped out, her desire to find Charles momentarily overwritten by curiosity. She wanted to see what these monsters had wanted so badly, more than that she wanted to find whatever had killed them all! If all of these things led her to Charles, then maybe he wasn't as worthless as she had been thinking. He might even prove useful.

A large silvery head perked up as she climbed out of the truck but left it running. The largest dog she had ever seen was lying next to a thoroughly mangled man, even if he wasn't dead yet she didn't think he would survive much longer. And she didn't have the medical expertise to help someone with that level of damage.

Blood had pooled around his body and into the ground soaking his clothes. The fingers, on one hand, were blackened and charred to the edges of a dark glove, and his left leg was twitching spastically. The constant shifting of his leg revealed a swirling silver tattoo on his thigh through a rip in his pants. There were multiple knives sticking out of his legs from where he had been stabbed and the blades left in.

He was a mess, and she had never seen someone in worse shape and still be alive. At least she thought he was alive, the twitching of his leg seemed to hint that he was in any case.

The dog that was lying next to him weakly pulled itself to its feet and walked towards Kira. One of its rear legs wasn't working and was dragged through the dirt with every limping step. Kira stepped towards the tall partially crouched dog when it didn't seem hostile and placed her hand on its head, careful to avoid the eye that was swollen shut.

"Help him, please!" Echoed through Kira's head as soon as her hand touched the dog's head.

Kira stepped back in shock, dislodging her hand from its head. With a pained grunt, the dog stepped to her and touched her with its nose.

"Please help Charles. He won't survive much longer." The voice was feminine and full of pain as it entered her mind.

She looked down at the dog in surprise and shock. "You can talk?"

The silvery head bobbed weakly before touching her again. "I can, but only when touching you. Will you help him?"

"I wish I could, but I don't know how. There is far too much damage for me to do anything that might save him!" She said with only a trace of emotion.

"I will tell you what to do. First accept the invitation to our party." While the dog was speaking, a new message appeared before Kira's eyes.

You have been invited by 'Alli' to join an existing party. Do you wish to accept?

"So, your name is Alli huh, pretty name," Kira said as she accepted the invitation.

"Thank you, I rather like it myself." Alli's voice held a touch of amusement. "Now on Charles's hip, you will find a flask, pull the top off, and pour the contents down his throat. After you do that, pull the blades from his legs and then step away from him."

"Uh, alright?" Kira agreed somewhat confused and stepped away from Alli. Walking past the massive dog, she saw just how big she truly was, even crouched like she had been her head had come up to her breast. If she had been able to stand, Alli would probably have been almost as tall or taller than herself. She was huge!

Hurrying to Charles side she found the flask Alli had told her about and pulled off the top, then tilting his head back she dumped the contents into his mouth. As soon as the liquid hit his mouth, his back arched and all his muscles seemed to tighten. Kira dropped the flask and pulled the various knives from his legs before stepping away.

Her eyes were wide as she watched his back bend at an almost impossible angle. Beside her, Alli slumped to the ground her breath coming in fast short gasps.

A scream erupted from Charles pulling her eyes away from the injured dog. The muscles beneath his skin were shifting and the injuries all over his body were closing and then vanishing. The charred fingers on his right hand became pink as the burnt skin sloughed off and fell to the ground. The scream petered out as his back slowly relaxed until he was flat on the ground and a soft whimper fell from his lips. The muscles all throughout his body continued shifting for a few more seconds before setting down. He looked much stronger than before and with the injuries gone he no longer resembled a scrawny corpse.

"Alli, where is Alli?" He asked in a dry raspy voice as his eyes flickered open.

Kira stepped closer until she was standing right next to him, her eyes wide in amazement.

Chapter 12

H is entire body hurt, and frankly, he had no idea how he was even alive. The last thing Charles remembered was passing out with Alli next to him. He knew there had been a fight of some kind, he could remember the beginning of it, but then everything went fuzzy until Alli dropped to the ground next to him.

"Alli, where is Alli?" Charles asked as his eyes flickered open. The question was meant to be rhetorical but to his surprise, there was a woman standing above him in the fading light pointing behind her.

Charles lifted his body with a groan until he could see where she was pointing. There was an old truck idling there with Alli laying beside it her stomach pumping in and out as she breathed rapidly. Terror gripped his insides as he saw that her eyes were closed, and her side was misshapen where something had hit her.

Scrambling to his feet, he weaved unsteadily as his vision swam in and out of focus. The ache of his muscles was forgotten as he took one unsteady step after another until he reached Alli's side. Dimly he noticed that while the fingers on his right hand were no longer burned, he was having difficulty controlling that hand.

Using his left hand to guide his right he lay both hands gently on her side and began to heal her. The strange girl that had been standing over him was forgotten as he pushed all the energy he had and more into healing Alli.

Constantly casting healing spell after healing spell, he could feel the slow progress he was making. Gradually, bones shifted back into place, smashed veins expanded to allow fresh blood to flow through them. Tears in her muscles began to knit, shattered and chipped teeth regrew, and the deep bruising and barely functioning organs began to heal.

He was aware that tears were falling freely from his eyes and wetting her silver coat as he pushed the last of his energy through his left hand and began to rely solely on his gloved right hand.

The woman had tried to get his attention when he first began healing her, and a greenish glow had covered Alli's entire body. She had since fallen silent, however.

The sun had long since fallen below the horizon and the moon was high overhead when Charles felt that he had done all he could. Everything that he hadn't been able to fix, hopefully, the potion would when he was able to use it again.

Charles stared almost unseeing as his hands fell from her side. His knees had cramped from kneeling next to her for so long as he fell to his side next to her and tried to straighten them.

Messages that had filled his vision since he had first awoken fought for his attention as they crowded together, blocking everything behind them. He had been wholly focused on healing Alli and nothing else had mattered until he was sure that she would be alright.

He skimmed through the messages about the monsters that they had slain and focused on the level up information.

Congratulations, you have leveled up. You are now level 6;
you have gained 5 status points for distribution.

...

Congratulations, you have leveled up. You are now level 12; you have gained 5 status points for distribution.

Congratulations, your base stats have been decided as such your status point are now able to be assigned. No changes will be made until after you fall asleep.

Congratulations, your animal companion Alli has leveled up. She is now level 7; her status points have been automatically distributed.

...

Congratulations, your animal companion Alli has leveled up. She is now level 14; her status points have been automatically distributed.

Congratulations, your animal companion 'Alli' has learned the advanced trait 'Telepathy'.

Alli has invited Kira Lourne to join your party.

Kira Lourne has joined your party.

Congratulations, your spell 'Basic Heal' has been upgraded to 'Heal'.

Congratulations, you have learned the spell 'Heal'. Heal is an intermediate level healing spell capable of healing even severe injuries.

Charles was shocked as he went through the various messages. Both he and Alli had leveled up a ton, he knew that they had only barely survived the fight, but this was ridiculous. Thankfully, his healing spell had been upgraded he was sure that had helped with Alli.

Then there was the message about his stats having been decided and the points finally being available for use. Did being unconscious count as sleeping? Was that the reason for the sudden change? Charles closed the remaining messages and pulled up his status page, shocked at how different it looked now than before.

Charles Byrne || Level: 12 || Exp to next Level: 1326

Strength: 22 || Intelligence: 29

Dexterity: 28 || Magic: 27

Constitution: 30 || Agility: 28

Cursed by the gods with 'Sleepless' || Available Status Points: 60

His base stats seemed rather high to him, but if they had only just been decided then maybe everything that he had gone through the last few days counted towards them. It might also explain while he suddenly felt stronger as well, part of the reason he had had such trouble walking to Alli when he first woke up was because of that. He was going to have to get used to his entire body again, and probably every time he leveled up from here on out.

If he could only level up when he was knocked out, then the changes were going to all come at once. Then there was the sheer amount of status points he had available, it was just too many. Or maybe it wasn't, it wasn't like he knew what the stats were for the average human. It was entirely possible that he was below average!

Charles thought back to one of the messages he had closed before turning to look at the woman sitting on the ground behind him watching.

"Kira Lourne, what are your stats?" His voice was raspy and his mouth dry as he spoke.

"How do you know my name?" Kira asked him, sitting up straight and ignoring his question.

"There was a message that had your name when you joined our party." He informed her, keeping his gaze steady.

"Just call me Kira," She finally responded after grinding her teeth for a minute.

"And your stats?" He asked again.

"None of your business!" She said vehemently. "It's my turn to ask a few questions. What are you? How did you heal her, what was in that flask I gave you? How is she able to talk and is she going to be alright?"

Charles found himself focusing on her questions at the end. "She can talk? Hmm, that's new. I wonder if it's an effect from her leveling up?" His voice was quiet and barely carried across the ground between them.

"What did you do to her? Is she going to be alright?" Kira seemed more interested in Alli than she did in him.

Charles dropped his hand to his thigh and angled the flask, so he could look at the countdown timer on the top. There were just under ten hours on it before they could use it on Alli. Kira looked down at her lap in shock, surprised not to find the flask where she had set it hours before.

"When I can use this flask again, it will heal her the rest of the way. For now, though, I was able to heal her enough that she isn't in any life-threatening danger." He explained tiredly as his eyes flickered shut. He had used all his energy to heal Alli, and while he may not be able to sleep, exhaustion still forced his eyes shut.

"How did you heal her? Do you have magic of some kind?" She asked with a disbelieving laugh.

"Yes, I am able to use magic," Charles said as he pulled a water bottle from his inventory. He was too tired right now to use his water spell. Cool water splashed down his throat as he drank thirstily, bringing sweet relief to the desert that had been his mouth.

"Magic doesn't exist!" Kira said belligerently as she clambered to her feet.

"Neither do gods!" He replied in turn.

"Yeah, well, I'm still not convinced this isn't all some terrible dream!"

"Then it shouldn't matter either way," Charles said obviously done with the conversation. "Why are you even here, anyway?"

"I'm here because of the gods," Kira said with a sigh as she sat down on the ground next to him.

"What does that mean?" Charles asked, not bothering to open his eyes.

"It means they forced a quest on me to save your stupid hide and that instead of going to Kansas City where my family is, I had to go in the opposite direction to help someone that I didn't even know!" Her face was red and the veins on her forehead taut with pressure as she yelled at him.

Charles kept his eyes closed as he lay on the ground and listened to her holler at him. He wondered who had given her the quest, for that matter he wondered who all the gods were, so far, he had only met Brigit, but he knew there were more.

"Well, since you have a truck that appears to work, and I have magic and am heading somewhat in that direction why don't I join you?" Charles opened his eyes slightly, so he could see the shocked look on her face at his offer.

"Just because the gods blackmailed me into saving you, doesn't mean I want to spend any more time than I need to with you!" Kira replied hotly, standing with fisted hands trembling at her side.

"It was just an offer. I need to get to Massachusetts and riding with you to Kansas City would shorten that trip." Charles was finding it hard to not start begging her to take them with her. They had never been outside during the night, and with Alli out of commission, they were stuck. If Kira agreed, then they could put Alli in the back of the truck and with any luck get away from the area before any more monsters showed up.

Kira stomped away from him for a few steps and then stomped back to stand above him. "Fine, you can come with me, but I'm only doing it because of Alli! I want to make sure she is okay."

Charles tried to keep the relieved grin from his face as he clambered to his feet next to her. Cracking sounds filled the air as his joints popped in quick succession and Charles groaned in pleasure. "She will be, let's get her into the back of the truck and then get out of here before any more monsters show up. I have a feeling that we're pushing it as it is." Even passed out and needing to be healed Alli was still helping him out. How had he ever managed to get such a good friend?

Kira unlatched the tailgate of the truck and let it drop as she hurried over to grab Alli's legs. She had to agree with Charles, nights were dangerous, and they had pushed their luck enough staying in one place as long as they had.

Together they carefully lifted Alli's massive body and set her into the truck bed. "She's grown again!" Charles remarked aloud as they carried her.

"How big was she before?" Kira asked with a grunt as they lowered her onto the rusty metal truck bed.

"This morning or rather yesterday morning," Charles began as he looked at star-strewn night sky. "She was around my hip area, now she'd probably just below my shoulder. I hope she doesn't get any bigger, or she is going to start having issues."

"Was she your dog from before all this?" Kira asked as she hopped out of the back of the truck and opened the driver-side door.

"Uh, no I found her trying to take on a monster by herself that first day. She was injured, but I was able to use the potion to heal her right up. I gave her a name with her help, and the rest is history." Charles slid onto the long bench in the truck and closed his door as Kira started the truck with a twist of the key.

Washed out yellow light illuminated the area in front of the truck as Kira slipped it into first gear and twisted the wheel. She kept the speed low as she drove over the rocky terrain and onto the road. "How did you get that potion?" Kira finally asked once the truck was back on paved roads.

Charles stared at her for several seconds, his eyes struggling to make out details in the darkened interior of the truck. "A goddess gave it to me." He eventually replied keeping it simple for the moment.

A short bark of laughter came from Kira as she focused on the road in front of them. She looked at him and then back to the road. "Uh, you're not serious." She paused her eyes, flickering back to him for a beat. "Oh... is that how you came to have magic as well?"

Charles kept his eyes on the darkened landscape as he thought about how he should respond. So far Kira had been helpful, but she also seemed to be somewhat in denial. What he didn't know was whether she was in denial to herself or just acting like it? It wouldn't do to tell her everything until he was sure of what kind of person she was.

"I can drive if you need to get some sleep?" He offered, deciding to just ignore her question for now.

"Actually, we're going to need to stop soon for gas." She glanced down at the instrument gauge and the needle that was hovering just above the empty icon.

"How did you get gas before?" Charles asked curiously, turning to face her.

"I siphoned it from a bunch of different cars. I have some tubing and gas cans in the back of the truck with Alli that I used. We need to find some slightly older cars though; most newer models can't be siphoned from. There are other ways to get the gas from them, of course, but they are more time-consuming. And since it is night, it's not something I think we want to spend a lot of extra time doing."

Charles tilted his head as he looked at her. "What is it you did before all this went down?"

The hands around the steering wheel flexed and whitened as she gripped it tighter. "I was a mechanic and restorer! Do you have a problem with that?" She asked clearly defensive.

This was clearly a sore topic for her. "No, why would I? I mean look at us right now, you're the one with the working truck, and I was the one riding a bicycle that got mobbed by monsters! I think you might have a bit more of an advantage than I do in this new world." He was serious in what he was saying to her, even if the circumstances could have been better. In this new world, a mechanic who could get vehicles running again would be treated like royalty. She needed to know that before someone tried to take advantage of her.

A dusty green sign appeared on the side of the road telling them that there was gas and food at the next exit. "If you want to stop at this exit, I'll see if I can find some more gas cans we can use." Charles offered breaking the stifling silence.

Kira's grip loosened slightly as he spoke breaking her from her inner reverie. "Food and water too, I haven't eaten all day and all my inventory slots earlier were taken up with the gas cans." Her voice was hoarse and had taken on a distinct dry raspy edge since she had last spoken.

"Oh, why didn't you say something?" Charles asked as he pulled a package of jerky and several bottles of water from his inventory.

Kira started slightly as he offered them to her. "I didn't say anything because I didn't think you had any more in your inventory. I thought it would be full of useful items, like a weapon and a sleeping bag."

Charles only grunted and looked back out the window. That was another thing that was different for him, how much inventory space he had. According to the men he had encountered outside the store, they only had nine slots. He had far more than that! He just couldn't decide what to share with her and what not too! For now, he would just concentrate on the present and ignore the other thoughts. She may have helped him and Alli, but that didn't mean she was trustworthy.

The truck slowed as she took the exit with one hand on the wheel and the other gripping an open bottle of water. She thirstily drank the entire bottle and opened the second one before letting the truck glide to a stop at the bottom of the exit.

"I've never been here before, which way should I turn for the gas station?"

"How should I know! I've never been here either, go right. There's probably one on both sides of the highway." Charles said squinting into the darkness.

Kira turned the trucked to the right and gave the old truck some gas to get it moving faster.

"Wait, turn into this parking lot!" Charles said suddenly as he spotted a large dark blob. "I think it might be a hotel or something."

"So?" Kira asked as she pulled into the parking lot of what was indeed a hotel.

"So, a hotel will have cars in the parking lot. You said you got your gas by siphoning it from other cars, so we don't actually need to go to the gas station we just need a place with a bunch of cars." Charles explained as the headlights revealed over a dozen cars and trucks just waiting for them.

Kira grunted in annoyance that she hadn't thought of it as she pulled the truck alongside them and shut it off. "This is going to be difficult in the dark!" Her door creaked loudly as she opened it.

"That won't be a problem!" Charles said as he cast his light spell and attached it to her.

Charles gently shook Alli's body as Kira reached into the back and stuffed the empty gas cans into her inventory. The only thing she had in her hands as she walked away was a length of thin tubing.

"Poor girl, she must have been exhausted from everything that happened today." A tear rolled down Charles' cheek as he softly talked to himself. Alli's eyes didn't so much as flutter from his attempt to wake her. Just thinking of everything that she had done for him was hard and remembering how close he had come to losing her was even worse. So, he would let her sleep as long as she needed, she had earned it!

Charles cast a light spell for himself as he hurried to Kira's side. She had a gas can on the ground already and a thin stream of gas flowing into it from her tube. "I'm going to try to find more gas cans. Alli is still asleep in the back of the truck. Please keep an eye on her. She means everything to me."

"I know she does, so hurry up and find some more cans. See if you can find some more tubing like this as well." She ordered him without looking away from what she was doing.

Charles walked away, hoping it was the right thing to do. He thought she had a soft spot for Alli, but this would be the first time he had ever entrusted her safety to another person.

Chapter 13

Charles heard Kira give a sigh of relief as he walked away. Undoubtedly, she was glad to be rid of him for a while. He wasn't sure if it was him. She didn't like or if it was just people in general, and since there were no other people around, he figured he wouldn't know for some time.

His right hand still felt clumsy whenever he tried to use it like he was wearing a thick ill-fitting glove over it. It was better than earlier, but he couldn't help but be worried about what it meant. The potion was supposed to heal everything, but it hadn't fixed his hand. The goddess Brigit had warned him not to over-use the glove, and then he had gone and done it, anyway. Twice.

The potion had fixed the damage the first time, but he had also stopped using the glove then. The fight from earlier was still hazy and murky at the best of times, but he was sure he hadn't stopped using the glove. Which meant that if he continued using the glove in that fashion then he might damage himself in a way that even the potion couldn't fix. A chill ran through his body as he considered that.

The street was dark beyond the light of his wisp and the night quiet. A wind blew through the area kicking up dust and trash that swirled in an eddy before moving on. Charles was certain that it was too quiet. Monsters were everywhere during the day, it had to be worse at night. Everyone knew that the truly nasty monsters came out to play at night.

So, why was it that they hadn't seen or heard anything?

Charles felt his heart begin to beat faster as he began running. Somewhere behind him, there was a soft rhythmic thumping, a short screech filled the air. He dove to the side of the road and rolled feeling something clip the edge of his boot.

Scrambling to his feet, Charles ran down the road to where he hoped he would find a gas station. He needed to get inside and away from whatever had just tried to attack him!

With a wave of his hand, Charles cast another light spell and sent the bright wisp of light rocketing forward. He needed the extra light to know where to go, he couldn't take the time to go slow. Bits of rock and dirt crunched under his booted feet as he ran. Just beyond the edge of his lights, he could see a smaller building with a large covered area in front of it.

Praying that it was a gas station he put everything he had into his legs and ran towards the darkened area.

The soft rhythmic thumping filled the air again as he neared the large overhang. Charles twisted his body as he dove and caught a glimpse of something large and dark diving from the sky with a screech. He scrambled backward as he watched the darkness, his back against a no longer working gas-pump.

Charles waited for his heart to stop racing and his lungs to stop screaming at him before pushing off the pump and onto his feet. The world swam in his vision for a second as the blood rushed from various parts of his body, making him feel simultaneously light and heavy at the same time.

The world settled, and Charles hurried into the dark and abandoned building. Glass covered the concrete in front of the windows and door crunching noisily under his boots. To his left, Charles heard a few crickets begin to make noise and then the world came alive with a cadence all its own.

Feeling more at ease, Charles stepped through the shattered door and inspected the interior. Someone had already gone through it and ransacked the place. All the drinks and snacks in the place had been looted leaving rows of empty shelves.

In the far back corner, was a large pile that contained all the bottles of oil and windshield cleaner in the place. Underneath the blue and red bottles of oil, a gas can peeked through. Charles kicked through the pile and stored the six large gas cans he found buried at the bottom.

Eager to get back to Alli and the truck, Charles left everything else where it was and ran from the store. He didn't think that Kira would leave him behind, but he wasn't willing to bet Alli on it.

In the distance, he could see Kira's form bent over beside a car with a red can at her feet. The wisp he had left with her illuminating the area. Slowing to a jog he jumped over the small ditch to the side of the road and into a corner of the parking lot.

"Kira," He called out, not wanting to startle her.

For the first time, Charles got a good look at her, He had barely seen her when he first awoke, and then it had been too dark to truly see anything. She had short auburn hair with purple highlights in a stylish pixie cut. Her arms were bare and lined with lean muscle in her oil and grease stained tank top. Her long legs were covered by a pair of black cargo pants and boots.

"Back all ready?" She asked calmly turning to face him and letting the end of the tubing drop into the gas can at her feet.

The light from his wisp highlighted her face as she stared at him. She had chocolate brown eyes with flecks of gold in them that glittered softly in the light. Long eyelashes highlighted her eyes drawing attention away from her slightly crooked nose.

"Ye, yes," Charles stammered somewhat stunned from actually seeing her for the first time.

"What do I have something on my face?" She asked impatiently which actually he now saw that she did.

"You have some grease above your eyebrows and on your cheek." He told her grateful that she didn't actually know why he had been staring.

"I'll clean it up later. Were you able to find any more cans?" She asked brushing aside how she looked.

Charles blinked, still trying to pull himself together. "Uh, yes I was able to find six large cans." He said as he pulled them all from his inventory where they had stacked to occupy a single slot.

Kira's eyes glittered back at him as they narrowed suspiciously. "Just what do you have in your inventory?"

His mind raced for a decent answer. "What does it matter?" He asked as he lifted two of the gas cans she had filled. "I'm going to start filling the truck."

Kira growled as he avoided her question and hurried over to the truck.

"Also, before I forget, there was a flying monster chasing me earlier. I have no idea if it still around, but it dived at me twice and then disappeared." Charles avoided looking at her as he threaded the nozzle on the can into the truck and began to pour.

"I figured there had to be something in the area. It was far too quiet when we got here." She replied thoughtfully.

"Well, thanks for warning me, it's not like I went running off on my own or anything. No, I was just taking a leisurely stroll down the road without a care in sight!" Charles didn't bother to conceal the edge of anger in his voice.

"Hey if you're too stupid to figure things like that out on your own, then you are too stupid to live!" She yelled back.

"Shhh, what are you crazy?" Charles whispered harshly.

They both quieted and looked around the area waiting. When nothing happened, they went back to their separate activities in silence.

"Are you going to tell me anything about yourself?" Kira asked in an even voice as she moved onto the next car in line.

"Are you?" Charles returned. "I've asked you several questions, and you have avoided answering all but one."

Kira let the hose hang down into the can as she moved two more of the full cans to Charles' side. "What are we four years old? Is this a tit for tat situation? I answer one of your questions. You answer one of mine." She grabbed the can he had emptied into the truck and moved back to the car.

"Sounds good to me. I'll start." Charles tipped the can up as high as he could, emptying the last of the gas into the truck. "How old are you?"

"Haven't you ever heard you're not supposed to ask a lady her age?" Kira chuckled.

"That's not an answer," Charles said in a sing-song voice.

Kira snorted. "I'm twenty-eight, my turn, how old are you?"

"I'm twenty-four. What family do you have in Kansas City?"

"Both my parents live there along with my younger sister. Why do you need to get to Massachusetts?"

"My older sister is at MIT. Last I heard she was alive with a group of other people there." She didn't need to know about the quest or how he had learned she was still alive. If she wanted to waste a question asking, then that was another matter. "Are you close with your sister?"

Kira paused, obviously thinking about just that thing. "I think I am, she means a lot to me. My parents had her late in life, so she is only fourteen this year. I try to visit her as often as I can, but it's difficult. When she was younger, I was practically her idol! In the last couple of years though, we've had to pull away from each other." She sniffled lightly and wiped away the glittering traces of tears on her cheeks. "I just want to make sure that they're alive." She swallowed thickly and cleared her throat. "Who are you, and can you help me keep my family safe?"

A dribble of gas ran down the side of the truck as Charles pulled the half-full can away from the now full truck. "That's two questions."

"I don't care, answer me!"

Charles brought the can over to her and leaned against the car she was currently siphoning gas from. "I was just your normal desk jockey before the gods decided they wanted to mess with the world. I had been up working for several days straight and then stayed up really late the night before the apocalypse and slept through the god's announcement. Apparently, they took offense to that, when I woke that morning a goddess was in my room and I had been cursed by the gods." His voice wry and devoid of any other emotion. "I was given the potion and the ability to learn magic by her."

"What's the curse?" Kira asked, interrupting him.

"I can't sleep, and because I can't sleep, I am unable to level-up properly."

"Can it be removed?"

"Yes, but I have to complete a bunch of different challenges for that to happen. You realize you now owe me a bunch of answers, right?" Charles asked, changing tact.

"I do, and you still have part of my original question that you need to answer. Can you help me keep my family safe?"

Charles hesitated unsure of how to respond. "I don't know. I need to continue on to my sister."

"What if I gave you the truck? Would you be willing to stay and help for a little while?" Kira exchanged the cans she was filling at her feet before looking at him.

"Depending on how long you wanted me to stay, I could probably do that." Charles continued to think as another option came to mind. "Or you could all come with me? I plan to stay near my sister when I find her, it might be a better and safer option in the long run."

"What about everyone else?" Kira asked, clearly intrigued by the idea.

"What about them? My loyalty is to my sister and Alli. I've seen how people are acting already and I want no part of it. If you want to worry about a bunch of people that you don't even know and may want to hurt you, that is your problem, but I won't be a part of it!" Charles pushed off the side of the car and walked to the back of the truck where Alli lay sleeping. He ran his fingers through her soft dense hair and wished that she was awake.

Charles pulled up the last of the messages that he had been ignoring since he woke, leaving his hand on her warm body.

The ability 'Pain Resistance' can now be upgraded. The upgrade you choose will affect further growth options. Which would you like to select:

'External Pain Resistance', you will be able to ignore a greater amount of external damage.

'Internal Pain Resistance', you have suffered numerous internal injuries, and now you can ignore some of them.

Charles thought about what each option might mean, the first was fairly clear, the second one though was a different matter. He wasn't aware that he had suffered that many internal injuries, and if he selected that choice then would he still have his normal 'Pain Resistance' ability?

His right hand tingled where it rested on the truck. Was that it? Was the damage from the glove internal? He guessed it made sense, and if that was the case, then would he be able to use the glove more times before his hand stopped working?

Before he could change his mind, he selected the second option.

Congratulations, you have selected the upgrade path
'Internal Pain Resistance', this does not remove the effects of
the initial ability but instead augments it.

Charles smirked as the tingles faded from his gloved hand and feeling returned. Now for the last message.

The ability 'Detect Bloodthirst' has not yet been activated
for the first time, would you like to activate this ability, or
would you like to roll for a different ability?

Well, that explained a lot, Charles had wondered why he had never known when a monster was near. Outside of that first time in his apartment building, he had never felt anything, and now he knew why. The ability was an active instead of passive ability; it needed to be activated. He hated active abilities, needing to remember to activate them every time they wore off was not something he wanted to worry about constantly.

Charles selected the option to roll for a different ability and held his breath as a glowing twenty-sided dice appeared in front of him. Using his now fully working right-hand Charles picked up the dice and tossed it up.

"What are you doing?" Kira asked curiously, having seen him toss something glowing into the air.

Charles spun around losing sight of the dice as it fell to the ground and rolled under the truck. "I was rerolling an ability."

"Can you do that? What did you get?" Kira asked in quick succession, not waiting for an answer.

"Um, apparently you can. I didn't know until just now either, but I was given the option to roll for a new ability and I chose it." Charles said distractedly while getting on his knees to look for the glowing icosahedron. "I can't find it."

"Does it even matter?" Kira asked, coming to stand next to him. "You're not the one who decides what ability you get, so do you even need to know what you rolled?"

Charles stopped and closed his eyes as his forehead sank to the ground in annoyance. "No, you're right I don't need to know."

"The gas cans are all full, help me put them in the back or in inventory, and then we can leave," Kira told him, changing the subject as he stood and brushed off his knees.

A new message flashed into view before he could move.

Congratulations, you have been chosen by one of the gods to act as their hero of choice in the days to come. At this time the god who has chosen you wishes to remain anonymous, as such you may choose a name for your god. What would you like to call your god?

Charles tilted his head in confusion at what he was reading. "Bob, I will call you Bob." He muttered with a snicker.

"What's going on?" Kira asked, coming up behind him.

"Uh, nothing just reading some new messages."

"About the ability?" Kira asked, dropping two gas cans in the back of the truck.

"I think so, hold on let me finish reading them," Charles said distractedly.

As the chosen hero of the god 'Bob' your growth will be faster and more pronounced, this also affects your animal companion 'Alli'.

Well, that would at least be useful, especially since it would help Alli. There was one last message.

The god who has claimed you has affected the roll of the dice, you have been given the unique ability 'Second Chance'. The unique ability 'Second Chance' has properties known only to 'Bob' at this time, you will learn them in time.

"It doesn't tell me what the ability does, only its name?" Charles said dismissing the last message. "Are you ready to go?" He asked, not wanting to talk about what the message might mean.

"Sure, I need to get some sleep though, are you up for driving?" Kira asked, stepping back from him.

"I can't sleep. I might as well be the one driving. Hop in, I'll secure the gas cans." He told her as he transferred the cans into his inventory.

Jogging to the driver's door of the truck he pulled it open and slid in next to Kira. "Here use these to get comfortable," Charlie said as he pulled a blanket and camping pillow out of his inventory for her.

Kira accepted them and settled into position against the door. "We need to talk about your inventory when I wake up. There is something different about it!"

Charles pumped the gas twice, priming the carburetor before starting the truck on the first try. "No, we don't, it's my business, not yours. Now go to sleep."

He slipped the transmission into first gear and slowly let off the clutch while giving it some gas. It had been quite a few years since he had last driven a manual transmission. The truck shuddered as it rolled forward needing more gas. With another jerk and a shudder, they started picking up speed.

Steering back onto the highway, he rolled down the window to blow fresh air on his face. Kira curled her legs under herself and draped the blanket over her legs.

Chapter 14

The constant vibrations of the truck running over the paved highway lulled Kira to sleep quickly. The soft sounds of her breathing filled the cab of the truck and drifted out through the open window. With one last look at her, Charles started meditating, splitting his mind for the first time since he had woken with Kira standing above him.

Charles decided that it was time to learn earth magic and let his mind focus on that branch of magic as another partition slid into place in his mind. A portion of his mind remained clear and focused on the road ahead of them.

He kept the speed of the truck at fifty miles an hour, the beams of the headlights not allowing him to drive any faster. With dead vehicles popping up suddenly no matter the lane he was in, he had to be extra careful not to hit them. When the sun came up illuminating the world around them, then he would be able to drive faster.

There was a shift in the back of the truck as Alli turned over, causing the truck to shimmy from side to side.

"Charles, are you there?" A warm panicky voice rolled through his mind.

Charles pressed on the brake slowing the truck before the shimmy could get any worse as Alli shifted again.

"I'm right here!" He said as he stopped the truck completely and hopped out.

Alli's wide, mismatched eyes looked back at him from where she was crouched. Her body slowly relaxed as she saw him until her head was resting on the metal of the truck bed.

"What is going on? I do not feel well." Her eyes tracked his movements as he climbed into the back with her.

"You were really injured after our last fight. Kira gave me the potion, and I then healed you as much as I could. We're waiting for the potion to be usable again and then you'll take it and be healed the rest of the way." His hand ruffled the hair on her large head as he stretched out next to her.

"I understand, I'm glad she was able to save you!" The voice in his head was thick with emotion as a tear rolled down her hairy cheek and onto her muzzle.

"We need to get moving again. Can you hear me if I'm driving and talking in the cab?" He asked as he gave her a hug and pressed his lips to her muzzle.

"It shouldn't be a problem; my senses have grown stronger since I met you." She nuzzled against his neck for a second. "Go, before the monsters come. I can hear them moving in the darkness!"

Charles held her for a second longer and then sprang out of the back of the truck. "Good, because it seems that we have a lot to talk about."

"Yes, we do! Now that I can finally talk to you, there is much that I need to tell you. I will warn you though, it seems that you are the only one I can talk to without needing to directly touch them. When I spoke with Kira earlier, she wasn't able to hear me until I touched her."

Kira stirred and opened her eyes as he slid back into the cab and closed the door. "Alli is awake." He told her as the truck began accelerating.

"Good!" Her eyes flickered shut and relaxed against the door once more.

"We need to go faster Charles!" Alli's words spurring him to jam the gas pedal to the floor.

The engine screamed, and the truck vibrated as he shifted into second gear and then a few seconds later into third.

"Alli, are we good now, or do I need to speed up more?" Charles angled his head, so he was speaking towards the open window.

Kira stirred slightly but didn't open her eyes.

"The distance is increasing, I believe that we are fine now. I hear something flying above us, but they are ignoring us for now. They seem to be hunting smaller prey at this time."

Charles shifted the transmission into fourth gear and eased off the accelerator, holding the speed steady. "Okay, Alli, let's talk. What's going on with you? Are you still growing or has that stopped?"

"It seems to have stopped. It is my belief that me developing the ability to telepathically communicate was the next step. It is likely that the ability will get stronger as I continue to level-up. I must confess I find myself curious as to how I will continue to grow and evolve in the coming days." She sounded happy as the prospect of becoming stronger.

Charles felt a shiver run down his back as a terrible thought came to mind. "Alli, do you want to stay with me?" His voice was soft and barely carried to the window.

There was a thump against the rear window of the cab as Alli hit it with her muzzle. "Of course, I want to stay! Where is this coming from? Charles, do you not want me to stay with you any longer?" The thoughts carried a heavy wave of emotion as he felt her heart was on the verge of breaking.

"Don't even think those thoughts!" Charles said harshly. "Of course, I want you to stay with me! What I'm trying to say is that the choice is up to you. I don't want you to think I'm forcing you to stay with me. You're my friend and I care about you, but I don't own you."

There was another lighter thump against the window. "I know that. I've always known that. You have never treated me like I was your pet, but as a person who couldn't talk. Now that I can nothing is different. I am going to stay with you, I am going to fight by your side, and we will survive together. If you are inclined to let Kira accompany us, then I might even be willing to fight by her side. She did save your life after all. She might be useful to keep around."

"Yeah, I don't think that's going to happen. I get the impression that she doesn't really like me, or anyone but her family for that matter." He said quietly his eyes flickering to the form sleeping on the other side of the cab.

"I think that she has problems trusting others. She will see eventually that you are trustworthy."

"And if she doesn't?" Charles asked, keeping his eyes on the road.

"Then she will leave us, and we will continue on by ourselves. It would be nice to have another person in our group, but it is not needed. If it was the wrong person, then they could cause more harm than good. Do not forget you have many secrets, secrets that would put you in danger if others knew of them." Alli's voice was soft and gentle in his head.

"Who are you talking to?" Kira asked, her eyes opening and glinting softly.

"I'm talking to Alli. She is awake in the back."

"Oh. Why can't I hear her then?" Kira asked sitting up, so she could see through the back window.

Charles steered the speeding truck around a group of stopped cars before responding. "She told me earlier that for everyone outside of me that she needs to be touching them before they can hear her voice."

"Oh, that's too bad. She seemed nice," Kira said, looking forlornly at Alli through the glass window.

Charles drummed his fingers on the steering wheel as he thought of something to say. "Kira, can I ask you something?" He finally asked, thinking of something that had been bothering him for a while now.

"I guess," She said with a shrug looking at him carefully.

"How many people have you encountered since this began?"

Kira tilted her head as she thought. "I saw a few people in the distance that first day, but after that, I hadn't seen anyone until you. Why?"

"Doesn't that seem odd to you?" Charles asked, his grip tightening. "I lived in Denver, home to nearly a million people, and I have only seen a few scattered groups. I know a lot of people died when it first happened, but it just seems like there are too few people!"

Kira was silent as she thought over what he had said. "So?" She finally said with a shrug. "It doesn't really affect us either way, personally I think the fewer people the better!"

Charles winced at the harsh tone in her voice. "You really don't like people, do you?"

"Is there any reason I should? People are disgusting creatures that lie, cheat, and hurt others for their own pleasure and momentary benefit!" Kira's hands were gripped in white-knuckled fists as she spoke.

"See, I told she had trust issues!" Alli told him smugly.

"Still," Charles began.

"Still nothing!" Kira said, interrupting him. "The fewer people there are, the easier time we will have. In case you have forgotten the world has ended, that means as a race that we have to start over! Food weapons, clothes, everything is about to become an extremely precious commodity. The fewer people we have to share with the better!"

"That... that is really cold-blooded." Charles finally said.

"Oh, get over yourself, it's every person for themselves! We don't have the luxury of worrying about others in this new world, or are you really going to tell me that you stopped and helped every person that you saw?"

"No, I'm not, because I can't. Alli and I were attacked by some of them, and we did help a group of people that were fighting each other as they were about to be attacked by monsters. That's it though, after seeing how stupid people are, I decided to just keep moving and not stop again. That doesn't mean I wish they were all dead though!"

"Then you're deluding yourself! The only good person is a dead person!" Kira shouted at him, her eyes wide and her back straight.

Charles stared at her in shock for a second before he was able to drag his eyes back to the empty road. "What happened to you?" He asked softly.

"I am no longer sure that she would be a good traveling companion," Alli told him from the back. "She seems to be slightly unhinged. I wonder if she was this way before everything changed or if this is new?"

Kira shook for a second before relaxing and turning to look out the window, no longer facing him. "That is none of your concern. Keep your eyes on the road. I want to make it to Kansas City sometime today. I need to check on my family."

Charles held back from saying anything and focused on his meditations and driving. He felt the truck shift slightly as Kira settled back into position and promptly fell asleep once more.

"What are we going to do, Alli?" Charles asked out loud speaking as softly as he could.

The truck shifted again as Alli moved into a more comfortable position. "I do not know, I do not think she is dangerous to us but if that is truly the way she feels then she may bring trouble upon us. We should take care in how we proceed with her."

Charles pulled the flask from his hip and looked at the top. "Agreed, now get some sleep. We have a few more hours before we can use the healing potion again."

Settling back in the truck bench, he settled into a more comfortable position, resigned to drive through the night. A gradual lightening in the distance was the only hint that night was coming to an end. The increase in light allowed Charles to see farther ahead. He increased the speed of the truck until the speedometer was pegged at eighty-five and the truck had started to shake.

He kept an eye on the gas gauge as they sped past exit after exit. Older model trucks were not known for their gas mileage and driving fast only made it guzzle the gas that much faster. The world was still and silent outside the roaring truck, with no monsters showing themselves despite the truck being the sole spot of noise in the area.

Charles lifted his foot off the gas pedal as a sign for the next exit appeared promising gas and a hotel. Reaching his hand across the bench he lightly shook Kira's shoulder. "Kira, wake up. We need to stop for more gas. I thought we would take the time to fill the containers at the same time."

Kira stiffened at his touch and pushed herself against the door. "How much farther to Kansas City?"

"Another couple of hours at least, the last sign that mentioned Kansas City had it listed as over three-hundred miles away. That was a while ago though, so I can't actually say for certain." He told her as he withdrew his hand in shock at her reaction to the simple touch.

Her arms wrapped firmly around herself with the blanket bunching up in her hands and her eyes hidden from view. "Don't touch me!" Her voice was like steel that cut through the otherwise quiet cab of the truck.

Charles kept his hand in the air and away from her. "Uh, sorry about that! I didn't mean anything by it, I just wanted to wake you."

"Do not ever touch me again!" Kira's eyes flashed dangerously in the early morning light.

Lowering his hand to the steering wheel, Charles focused on driving down the off-ramp and finding some place with a lot of cars.

"What do you think happened to her? Her reaction to a simple touch is not normal!" Kira's steely gaze kept him from replying to Alli.

Charles didn't bother to stop at the stop sign instead blowing past it without a care in the world. A four-story hotel sat right next to the left side of the road. A large parking lot in front of it contained a measly four vehicles.

"Four cars should be enough to fill the truck again, when we stop Alli will carefully hop out of the back and check the area. I'll start filling the truck from the containers we filled before, then I'll give the empties to you to fill again. Just like last time, is that all right?" Charles asked as he pulled into the parking lot.

"That's fine," Kira said, her voice utterly devoid of all emotion.

Alli moved slowly from the back as the truck stopped, landing on the hard pavement heavily, her movements slightly off and jerky from the incomplete healing. Charles leaped from the truck and ran over to her when he saw how she was walking.

"Alli, are you alright?" He glanced at the flask quickly. "We have another thirty minutes, and then we can use the flask on you."

"I'm alright for now, the bones in my hips feel off though. I don't think I will be able to walk very far until I'm healed properly." Alli's voice was suddenly drowned out by the sound of the truck revving followed the screeching of its wheels. Spinning around Charles was able to make out the tail-lights of the rapidly vanishing truck.

Kira had just left them behind!

Chapter 15

The reflected sunlight from the hotel windows shined down on Alli's eyes, making them glow brightly as she growled in the direction Kira had driven. "Forget everything I said about her, it's not worth putting up with her crap to keep her around. That girl has too many issues and too much baggage, for her to be a viable candidate as a companion of any sorts."

"Calm down, Alli," Charles said, reaching up to pet her head. She was nearly as tall as his shoulder now, standing at least 5ft8. "She won't get very far. The truck has very little gas in it and I have all the gas cans. Even if she stops next to more cars, she doesn't have a container to put the gas in."

"How far can she go on what is left in the tank?" Alli asked calming slightly.

Charles scratched behind her ear and then dropped his hand. "I don't know for sure, it's fairly close to empty though. If I had to guess I would say no more than twenty miles max."

"We'll have to wait until I'm healed then. I can't walk that far just yet. On the plus side, once I am healed, I should be able to carry you on my back." Alli told him as she began limping towards the hotel lobby.

"What are you, a dire wolf?" Charles asked with a soft laugh.

Alli gave a laughing yip. "No, I'm just really big and strong now. Let's eat breakfast and drink some water inside while we wait for the potion to be usable."

Alli took a step and then stopped, tilting her nose into the wind. "I don't smell any monsters in the area." She said in a puzzled manner.

"What do you smell then?" Charles asked equally confused.

"I smell plenty of blood and death in the area, and I can hear a rabbit moving through the grass behind the hotel, but that is all. I don't smell or hear other humans or monsters in the area. This place is completely empty!" Alli told him as she tilted her head to the side.

Charles spun in a slow circle as he scanned the horizon and thought. "Now that you mention it, I saw one flying monster last night, but that was it. I haven't seen or heard any others since we were attacked yesterday!"

Alli took a slow limping step towards the building, nudging the glass doors open with her nose. Charles followed along behind her, his thoughts filled with what the lack of monsters might mean. Walking across the empty lobby he pulled out her tub for water and began filling it as he pulled out some food for the both of them.

Charles finished eating the food he had taken out of his inventory and cracked his neck. "Since there aren't any monsters around to worry about, I'm going to grab as much canned goods as I can find from the kitchen and supply rooms."

Alli pulled her head from the water tub, her muzzle wet and dripping. Her nose in the air she sniffed deeply and put her head back into the tub. "I don't smell anything, so it should be safe. Stay on guard just in case though, if you get in trouble, I can't get to you quickly right now." Her hip made a clicking noise as she lifted her leg and gingerly set it down again, illustrating her point.

"I'll be back in a few minutes, as soon as the countdown is finished," Charles said as he brushed her tail in passing.

Charles had managed to keep his meditations going this entire time, it seemed that as long as he wasn't being too active, he could maintain it now. Large glass windows lit the halls in early morning sunlight as he wandered from one area to the next looking for the kitchen.

Charles wasn't sure what he had expected to find when he did find it, but it wasn't the small nook of a room that allowed for reheating and nothing more. The gleaming stainless-steel kitchens that he had seen on TV were nowhere to be found. Instead, there was a large supply room full of canned and dehydrated goods that would be reconstituted for breakfast.

The cans went into his inventory without a second thought, followed by a small can opener. With plenty of food now secured, Charles hurried back to Alli's side, ready to use the potion on her. As he walked, he noticed that the faster he moved the more strenuous the hold on his meditations became. Charles was smiling widely when he walked back into the lobby of the small hotel.

"What, has you so happy?" Alli asked him as soon as she saw him. "Did you find some good food?"

"No, well maybe. I don't know everything is in cans right now, no I just figured out what one of the limits for my meditation is all. I was hurrying back here when I noticed that the partitions in my mind were becoming strained and unsteady. As soon as I slowed down, they all snapped back into place." Charles told her as he settled onto the ground next to her.

"Are you going to try to keep your meditations going all the time?" She asked as he pulled the flask off of his hip.

Charles' hands paused as he struggled to answer in a way that made sense. "The way I figure it, the reason that I am able to learn magic as fast as I have been, is because of two things. One, the goddess Brigit blessed me with an ability to learn things quickly. Two, and possibly more important, is that I don't sleep. I spend my nights in meditation, which means that I am able to spend far more time doing so than anyone else. What would normally take a week I can do in a night, and so on." Charles glanced at the now blank lid of the flask before pulling the cap off. "If I can keep my meditations going all day, then the progress I can make will be enormous. Magic and you are the only things keeping me alive for now, and I have to be able to do my part to keep you safe as well. Now open your mouth!"

Alli opened her mouth as requested and drank down the potion in two gulps before collapsing onto the ground in pain.

Charles could only hold her head as he watched the muscle around her hips squirm underneath her skin. With loud audible pops, the joints in her legs settled into their proper positions. Alli's eyes were clenched shut even as she whimpered against the wave of pain that was undoubtedly running through her massive frame.

The short bristles of the worn cream-colored carpet dug into the skin of Charles' knees as he knelt there holding Alli. His heavy-duty cargo pants had been ripped and torn in their last fight and were now barely more than scraps that were stained with gore and blood. It was as Charles was putting the flask back on his belt that he noticed a silver line running down his thigh. A tear in his pants stretched tight across his muscled leg prevented him from seeing any more.

Alli was still whimpering slightly as the last of the potion's effects rocketed through her body. He had to wait for her to be alright before he looked at what was on his leg. She came first, and he was not going to ignore her just to satisfy his own curiosity.

His fingers softly stroked her pointy silky soft ears as he waited for the pain to leave her body. Her breath stuttered and evened out as she breathed in deeply and opened her eyes.

"That was painful, feeling the bones in my body shift like that is not something I want to experience again!" Alli told him as she gingerly pulled away from him.

Charles grimaced before replying. "Sorry about that, it won't happen again. My healing spell is stronger now and doesn't require as much input from me. The spell I was using to heal you originally needed me to guide it.

Unfortunately, I'm not a doctor, so I wasn't able to properly heal certain injuries."

Alli nudged his hand with her nose and opened her mouth wide in a yawn. "I'm not blaming you, Charles. I know you did the best you could. Nobody can ask for more than that, if you hadn't healed me, I wouldn't be here now. I think that a little bit of pain is worth it, don't you?"

Charles pulled himself to his feet and stepped away from Alli. "Of course, I do!" His shoulders slumped. "Regardless, now that you're all healed why don't you scout the area. I need to check a few more things, and then we can go after Kira."

Alli bobbed her head once and stretched her body before heading toward the doors and pushing one of the glass doors open.

Looking at the large glass windows and doors that lined the front of the lobby, Charles backed-away. Even though he knew there was no one else around, changing his clothes in plain view like that was not something he could do. The carpet felt stiff under his boots as he stepped into the office that was hidden behind the front desk.

Stepping behind the thin wooden door, Charles pulled his bomber jacket off first and stored it in his inventory. His shirt was next and was tossed it in a corner of the room. Next, he unlaced his boots and toed them off before dropping his pants and looking down at his bare thigh. Swirling lines of silver glinted softly in the dim lighting of the room.

Charles dropped his hand to his thigh, feeling the lines running underneath his skin. The lines flexed as he nudged them with the tips of his fingers. The skin where the lines were was smooth and devoid of imperfections.

He felt the muscles in his face slowly relax as he continued to study his leg. It was odd yes, but no more so than anything else that had been happening recently. It didn't hurt at least, nor did it seem to affect how he moved. Actually, thinking about the pain he should be feeling in his leg made him remember the pain that would engulf his thigh every time he used the glove.

Charles brought his gloved right hand alongside his leg and compared the two. The loops and swirls on his leg were more complex, but they were definitely similar. He found it hard to believe now that he was thinking about it that the two items were unrelated. They were too similar, and the odd pain he would feel in his thigh when he used the glove would indicate that they were related as well.

Brushing his fingers against his leg he straightened and leaned against the wall at his back. What was one more unexplained thing, he thought? A short hysterical laugh bubbled up his throat before he was able to shove it back down. He had been shoving most of his emotions and reactions into the back of his mind where he didn't have to deal with them.

In the beginning, it had been easy, with each new event though he was finding it harder and harder to ignore them. Worse, each new emotion threatened to bring everything he had buried and tried to forget back to the surface.

The sound of a door in the lobby opening brought Charles back to reality, forcing him from his mind. Quickly he cast the spell to clean himself and started pulling clothes from his inventory. A pair of thick black cargo pants replaced the rags his prior pair of pants had become. A long sleeve forest green shirt went on next, he left the bomber jacket off for the moment but put another flat black ball cap on his head to replace the one he had lost earlier.

The weapons he had hung on his belt had all gone missing during the fight the day before. Since they had been there for decorative purposes only Charles decided against replacing them as he threaded the belt through his pants.

Picking up his boots, Charles stepped into the lobby and spotted Alli waiting for him. "Did you find anything in the area?" He asked as he stepped into his boots and laced them.

"No, the area is completely empty. The smell of old blood is plentiful, but there are no bodies. Also, all the monsters seemed to be heading in the same direction when they left."

"What direction was that?" He asked finishing with his boots.

Alli looked out the large windows at the front of the lobby before responding. "It is the same direction as that large city Kira wanted us to go to."

Charles pushed open a door and stepped out into the fresh breeze and sunlight. "How old was the smell?"

Alli walked out behind him, her silvery hair shining. "Judging by how little it had faded, I would say they left sometime yesterday morning!"

Charles stepped to the side of the four-story building and looked at the distant horizon. He felt the shift in his eyes as the far-off hills came into clear focus. They were all empty with nothing stirring in sight.

"We should hurry and catch up to Kira, if all the monsters are making for the city then they are going to need all the help they can get!" Charles said as he spun to look Alli in the eye.

She crouched in front of him. "Hop on then, I believe that I am now big enough to carry you. If you cast your haste spell on me as well, then I shouldn't be that much slower than the truck."

"All right, just don't hurt yourself!" Charles told her as he straddled her back. This was not going to be a comfortable ride, no matter how big and strong she was now, she wasn't a horse.

She stood carefully, bringing her legs up underneath her as she steadied getting used to the feeling of having someone on her back. "I'll be careful, now hold on tight!"

Charles leaned forward and gripped her neck before casting the haste spell on her. "Let's go, we need to catch up to Kira as quickly as possible. I don't think she will be in danger, but we shouldn't risk it, regardless."

Alli bunched her long-muscled legs and launched them across the ground. She ran alongside the highway, keeping to the slightly softer dirt as her paws pounded rapidly into the ground. The air rushed past Charles's face as he clung to her neck.

Stretching out to her full length, Alli wrung every ounce of speed from her body. "Can you heal the pads on my paws from up there?" She asked after a couple of minutes of running at full speed.

"I don't know. Do you need me to try?" Charles asked, speaking directly into her ear.

"Yes, the extra weight from having you on my back combined with the tough ground is tearing the skin from them."

Charles focused on the spell, concentrating on how it moved through her body. A dull green glow encased each of her paws as he sent the healing magic through her body. Directing the magic like this was actually easier than he would have thought, he was getting more used to using the healing spell. When he had healed her earlier, he had been doing something similar to this without realizing it.

"How is that?" He asked while trying to control the spell even more. If he could keep the spell going at a low enough level, then it would heal her wounds as they came or at least over time. He had never tried to learn a new spell through anything but meditation. What he was trying to force the spell to do was act like a Regeneration spell.

"Better, they are no longer hurting. Something feels different though, are you keeping the spell going?" Her steps never faltered as she spoke with him.

"That's good, yeah I was trying to get the spell to heal the damage automatically. It doesn't seem like I will be able to get the spell to work that way just yet, for the time being, though I'll keep circulating the healing spell through you." Charles readjusted his grip on her neck and closed his eyes against the wind that battered at his sensitive eyes.

The sun hung low over the eastern horizon as Alli streaked over the barren dirt. Kansas was a windy, flat expanse, full of scrub brush, telephone poles and little else. The dark lines of the highway stretched across the ground as Alli ran alongside it.

Charles felt his mind drift along as he clung to her heaving sides. Where had the monsters gone? What was causing them all to leave? Was Kira's family in danger? What was happening with his own sister? He wanted to be there for her, but things kept getting in the way! Did he really want to spend the time helping these people when he needed to be making his way towards her!

"Kira's smell is growing stronger, I believe that we are getting closer to her!" Alli told him, pulling him from his thoughts.

Sure, enough as soon as they topped a small rise, they could see the truck stopped in the middle of the road. Apparently, Kira hadn't seen the point in pulling off to the side of the road when the truck ran out of gas. What was the point, after all, it wasn't like anyone was going to hit it!

Stopping at the top of the hill, they were able to look down at the truck and the small form of Kira ranting and raving at the heavens.

Chapter 16

"What is she saying?" Charles asked Alli as they watched Kira wave her arms at the cloudless sky.

"Err, you probably don't want to know." Alli began hesitantly her ears twitching spastically. "Her words are rather vulgar, and some of them are aimed at you and your apparently dubious parentage."

Charles coughed before chuckling softly. "Well, it's nice to know she hasn't forgotten us completely after leaving like that."

Alli slowly walked down the small hill and towards the stomping Kira. "Be nice to her, Charles."

"Why, I thought you said she wasn't worth keeping around as a companion?" He asked, interrupting her.

Alli hung her head low as she responded. "I did, and I still mean it. Another part of me, though, just sees someone who has been treated wrong by the world. It was easy to be dismissive about her earlier when she wasn't in front of us, now I am finding it harder to think of her that way."

Charles ran his hands along Alli's neck comfortingly. He knew that she was a caring person, err animal. There had been more than a few times that she had wanted to stop and help the people they saw from the road. "So, what do we do then?"

"Same plan as before, just without her in it at the end. We go to her parents, make sure they are safe, and then we move on towards your sister. If we are lucky, she'll let us have the truck. More than likely though you'll be stuck on my back for the journey."

Charles winced and dropped a hand to his tender groin. Riding on Alli was certainly faster than walking or riding a bicycle, but it was by no means comfortable. He'd just have to find some pillows. He was not going to suggest getting a saddle to her! "Alright, sounds good, let's do this already. I'm surprised she hasn't seen us already."

Alli snorted softly. "I'm not. She is very focused on her cursing. It takes some serious concentration to come up with what she is spouting!"

"I almost wish I could hear some of them," Charles said.

Alli's ears twitched once and then lay flat on her head. "Uh no, you really don't."

Charles swore he could feel her blushing in his mind. "What did she say this time?"

Alli shook her head as she increased her pace. "Nothing I am comfortable repeating!"

"Sierra, this all your fault!" The sound of Kira's voice finally reached his ears.

"Who's Sierra?" Charles whispered softly.

"I don't know, but Kira seems to really hate her! Her name has been coming up quite frequently." Alli answered what had been meant to be a rhetorical question.

In front of them, Kira dropped her arms to her sides and let loose a blood-curdling scream at the sky before sinking to the ground.

"Let me off, it'll be better if we are both walking when she sees us," Charles told Alli softly.

Alli crouched low enough for Charles to slide off her back and then shook herself violently when the weight vanished from her back. Charles fell into step beside her as they walked past the truck and closer to where Kira sat slumped over with her eyes closed.

The sound of Charles boots crunching over loose gravel caused her to stir as she raised her head and looked at them with dead hollow eyes. "What are you doing here? The truck is out of gas." She asked and then brushed the question aside just as quickly.

Charles stopped mid-step a shiver running through him from her eyes and watched her carefully. "It's alright, I have the full gas cans in my inventory still." He said slowly.

Beside him, Alli stopped as well and sank to her haunches. "Are you feeling alright Kira?"

Kira's face was devoid of all emotion as she looked away from them and stared at the ground. "The truck is out of gas." She repeated again, before closing her eyes.

"I think something is wrong with her mentally." Alli said watching her. "Can you heal her mind or something?"

"No, I don't think I can. The potion might be able to, but I don't have a spell that will do that yet." Charles replied to her in a low voice. "I'm not entirely sure what is going on, but I think we should just give her some time and space, for now. I'm going to go fill the truck's gas tank. You keep an eye on her while I'm doing that."

Charles walked back to the truck and pulled the gas cans from his inventory, trying to keep his eyes from drifting back to the slumped over form of Kira. He had a feeling that everything Alli had said about the woman was true. She most definitely carried a remarkable amount of baggage, it was equally obvious however that there was a deeper issue at play with her. The way she was acting was not the way someone that was well adjusted and had lived a comfortable life did.

Charles threw the now empty gas cans into his inventory and stored the couple he hadn't needed to use the same way. Opening the driver side door, he slid onto the bench and cranked the starter for a few seconds. He waited a few seconds to let the gas circulate back into the system before twisting the key again.

The sound of the truck engine turning over filled the air. Alli's ears twitched, but neither she nor Kira moved from their position. With a roar, the old truck started and settled into a rumbling purr.

Charles climbed from the truck and hurried over to Kira's side. Pulling her to her feet he wrapped an arm around her shoulder in support as she leaned against him. Her eyes were slightly glazed, and it seemed to take all her focus just to put one foot in front of the other.

Guiding her to the passenger door, he opened it and helped her inside the cab. She sank onto the old worn bench and closed her eyes, letting the purr of the engine lull her to sleep instantly. The truck rocked as Alli jumped into the back as Charles closed the passenger door and hurried to the driver's side.

"Are you comfortable?" Charles asked Alli as he passed her.

Alli snorted. "As comfortable as I can be on this hard-metal bed."

"Haha good." Charles slid behind the steering wheel and pushed in the clutch pedal. There was a slight shudder as he slipped the transmission into first gear and gave it some gas. "Well, get as comfortable as you can. We have a few hours of driving ahead of us!"

"Don't worry about me, just concentrate on your driving. The road is only going to get more crowded the closer we get to the city." Alli reminded him as the truck rocked gently as she rearranged herself in the back.

Charles shifted into second gear as the truck picked up speed. "Do you think you will be able to push them out of the way if they get in our way?"

"It shouldn't be a problem if it is just a car, anything bigger than that though, and I'll need Kira's help."

Charles looked at the sleeping woman. "Let's let her sleep for now then, hopefully, she'll be feeling better when she wakes up. Her eyes were freaking me out."

"Do you mean the emotionally vacant and dead quality they had earlier?"

Charles shivered at the thought of how hollow they had been. "I mean exactly that. I'm not sure I want to know what she must have gone through to have eyes like that!"

The feeling of Alli wincing at the thought came through the connection. "It does make me wonder though. She seems to be too focused on her family for them to be the cause."

"You're right, her family life doesn't seem to be the cause of this. Should we even bother asking her if we're not going to keep her with us then why bother?" His voice was soft as he asked Alli.

Alli sighed and was silent for several minutes before replying. "I don't know what to think anymore. I want to help her, but I know that we need to be moving on. I do not like the thought of her suffering though!" Charles didn't respond, feeling that Alli had more to say. "She was the first person I ever actually talked to. I must confess to feeling somewhat connected to her."

"What do you want to do then?"

Before Alli could reply, Kira whimpered softly in her sleep. "No Sierra don't leave me alone, not with them! They're going to hurt me!" Kira's voice rose piteously at the end.

Charles flipped the visor down as the sun reflected harshly in his eyes, tears could be seen in his squinting eyes.

"Charles, what happened to her?" Alli whispered softly into his mind.

Kira's body trembled as she continued whimpering.

"I don't know, but it must have been bad," Charles said as he reached across the cab to wake Kira.

Kira's body suddenly stilled as she spoke with a cold, emotionless voice. "Sierra, why did you let them take me? They only wanted you!"

Charles stilled his hand before it could touch her. Did he really want to wake her? She was no longer trembling, and the last time he had touched her she had exploded at him.

"Let her sleep," Alli told him. "Whatever she was dreaming about seems to have passed for now."

Refocusing on the road in front of them, Charles increased their speed. The window was open, but the air inside the cab felt stifling and no matter how fast he drove he couldn't get rid of what he had heard.

Flecks of green were interspersed throughout the constant brown of dirt, where small patches of grass or trees had managed to survive. The near constant wind buffeting the truck harshly.

"Do you smell anything, Alli?" Charles asked after they had been driving for some time.

"Yes, and it is somewhat concerning," She answered after hesitating. "The smell of monsters is indeed growing stronger, enough so that I think we have even passed some slower groups."

"Well, that doesn't sound so concerning, annoying maybe, but that is all," Charles said, trying to lighten the mood.

"I know what you are doing, but this is serious," Alli said as her mental voice took on an introspective tone. "The smell of blood has been changing over the last few minutes."

Charles spoke up when she didn't further explain. "What do you mean the smell is changing? Is it growing stronger, weaker, or something else?"

"Weaker, and something else. I will be the first to admit that my various senses have become more acute along with the other changes in my body, but this is the first time I have smelled something like this." Alli seemed reluctant to tell him what she was smelling.

"Alli, quit with the games. What are you smelling?"

"I'm smelling the same thing I was smelling from Kira earlier." She began softly. "I'm smelling terror. The smell of blood has been fading because fewer people have been killed in their cars. It seems that they were taken and forced into a group. I can smell their sweat and terror from where they were forced together."

For the first time, Charles noticed the state of the vehicles as he drove past them. He had stopped fully acknowledging them days ago. Now though he looked and saw how many of them had the doors torn off and the windows smashed.

"Was it humans or monsters?" Charles asked finally, dreading the answer. He didn't know which he was hoping for, humans could be more monstrous than the actual monsters at times.

"Monsters, they were all taken by monsters."

"Who was taken by humans or monsters?" The sound of Kira's voice startled Charles, and the truck swerved as he jerked the wheel.

"You're awake." He said simply as he eyed her suspiciously.

Kira wrapped her arms around her body protectively. "Do you have a jacket I can wear?"

Charles pulled a fleece jacket he had taken from the surplus store out of his inventory and handed it to her. She didn't let her hands touch his as she took it from him and quickly put it on.

"You didn't answer my question." She said as she settled against the door and watched him carefully.

Charles chuckled dryly as he continued driving. "Are we just going to ignore what you did then? Because frankly, I'm more interested in that than explaining anything to you!" He said hotly, somewhat surprised at the sudden burst of anger he felt.

Kira's hands clenched as she glared at him. "I don't know what the problem is! The truck is mine. I was letting you ride along with me and then I decided I no longer wanted your companionship."

"Well, you certainly did a great job by yourself!" Charles began caustically.

"Charles calm down!" Alli ordered him.

"I don't need anyone else!" Kira yelled, her face red.

"That much was obvious when we found you. You were doing just fine by yourself, out of gas, and seconds away from collapsing." Charles continued ignoring Alli for the moment.

"Get out of my truck!" Kira screamed at him.

"Charles, stop the truck!" Alli screamed at him.

The brake pedal hit the floor as the wheels locked up and the truck skidded to a sudden stop. Kira's eyes were wide as she stared at him, having braced herself with her arms when he braked suddenly.

"What was that for?" Charles yelled as he twisted to look at Alli.

"Look," She said simply her head facing forward.

Turning to face the front, Charles felt his jaw loosen at the sight in front of them. In the midst of them arguing they had arrived at the edge of the city. Smoke drifted in clouds away from them as the wind blew them away.

The sight that captured the eyes though was what Alli had spotted. Outside of the city, lines of humans had been chained together. Pens had been constructed in places and the old and young along with those too injured to escape had been placed inside.

The people that had been chained together sat in the dirt, each of them was filthy and covered in blood.

"It's a farm!" Kira whispered, horrified as she followed the direction of their eyes. "They're treating those people like farm animals!"

A sudden notification appeared in front of Charles and Kira in plain view for them both.

The gods have issued you a quest, rescue the people of Kansas City from the clutches of the monsters. This is a timed quest, as the Kansas City location will be converted into a free-spawning dungeon in 36 hours. Rewards will be given on successful completion of the quest. Do you accept this quest?

"Accept the quest Charles," Alli ordered him. "We need to help these people. We are the only chance any of them have!"

Charles didn't respond as he spotted a monster in the distance. His eyes zoomed in on the hulking monster as he analyzed it, 'Ogre Lv. 10'.

The Ogre stepped up to one of the pens and picked up someone that had been laying down. The Ogre's massive hand wrapped around the human's waist as it held it in the air and sniffed it. With a look of disgust, it released its grip allowing the filthy body to fall to the ground.

The Ogre turned on its heel and stalked away, allowing Charles to fully see the monster. It looked to be a little smaller than the many Orcs they had encountered but was covered in thick muscle. It was completely hairless and had large drooping ears that hung nearly to its shoulders. Most of its skin was a sickly yellow that gradually morphed into a blueish color the closer you got to its head. Small beady eyes peaked out underneath heavily ridged brows and a large squat nose.

"Charles!" Alli's voice rang through his head, shaking him from his thoughts. "Accept the quest, we need to help them!"

Charles wet his lips, his mouth suddenly dry and looked at Kira. "Your parents might be in there somewhere. What are you going to do?"

Her face was set into an emotionless mask that was only slightly betrayed by her thin bloodless lips. "I'm going to find them, no matter how many monsters stand in my way!"

The notification flashed once and centered in front of Charles, who accepted the quest for them. "Alright then, how do we want to do this? I saw a large monster called an Ogre that was level 10, so we should assume that is the minimum level for these monsters."

Kira looked at him with wide eyes as he spoke. "You can see their levels before killing them? How?"

"I have an ability that lets me analyze monsters and people," Charles said distractedly, his thoughts focused on what they were about to do. "How many of these 'farms' do you think there are around the city?"

"Too many," Kira said as she stepped from the truck, still eyeing him. "Leave the truck here. I don't want it damaged in the fighting."

Alli leaped from the back and nudged Kira with her side as she brushed past her. Charles pulled the key from the ignition and stored it in his inventory as he climbed out and joined them.

Suddenly Kira's eyes widened, and a large pillar of light shot down from the sky and engulfed her.

Chapter 17

The constant wind of the Kansas plains vanished as the blindingly white pillar of light engulfed Kira's form. Everything seemed to stop and even the world paused like it was holding its breath. Something was happening that everyone should be paying attention to something important.

The pillar of light tightened around her and a deep thrum that could be felt in your bones filled the air. Sound returned with shocking suddenness, pushing the void that its absence had created back.

Alli backed away from Kira and the ever-shrinking pillar of light as noise broke out from the human farm in front of them. The monsters and people around the farm had begun to notice them. Charles rested a reassuring hand on Alli's neck as he focused on Kira.

Kira's eyes could be seen widening as she read a message that only she could see. "Apparently I have been chosen by the goddess Brigit to act as her champion in the coming game of the gods!" The pillar of light condensed around her wrist and then rose into the sky. A silver bracelet covered in dark runes encircled the tan muscular flesh of her wrist.

Charles stepped towards her as she touched the runes with her other hand. With a flash of white light, the bracelet disappeared and transformed into an enormous metal Warhammer. Her hand wrapped around the grooved metal shaft and hefted the hammer that was nearly as tall as her.

With a maniacal grin stretching across her face, Kira swung the hammer experimentally. The muscles in her arm standing out and bulging beneath the weight of the hammer. "This is my reward for rescuing you. I guess completing that quest was worth it after all!" Her eyes drifted from the hammer to the trapped people in the distance.

"What are you going to do?" Charles asked following the direction of her eyes.

Kira kept her eyes on the penned and chained people as she replied. "I'm going to work through some anger issues!" She levered the hammer onto her shoulder and took off running without another word.

"Uh," Alli began as they watched Kira run. "Do you think she is going to attack the humans as well as the monsters?"

Charles flexed his gloved hand and stopped his meditations, feeling the partitions in his mind drop he began running after her as he responded. "I don't know, but there is going to be a lot of monsters, and we are going to need her help!"

"You keep her safe then. I'll concentrate on freeing everyone in chains!" Alli told him as she ran past him at full speed.

"How are you going to do that?" He whispered to himself as he focused on Kira. She was faster and stronger than him, that much was obvious. For every step he took, she took at least two and the distance between them continued to increase.

Casting haste on himself, Charles felt the world slow, but still he couldn't catch up to Kira's leveled-up speed.

From the corner of his eye, Charles saw Alli leap into the air and snatch a small winged monster from the sky. Her jaws clamped shut on a purple wing pulling the purple monster to the ground and crushing it under her feet.

For the first time, Charles noticed the monsters that were flying towards them from the city. Ahead of him Kira was entirely focused on the monsters on the ground and hadn't yet noticed the monsters nearing in the sky.

Already he could feel that something was off, there should have been more monsters appearing. The pillar of light that had engulfed Kira would have been plain to see for miles in every direction. Yet, the only monsters that he could see were the few Ogres that had already been out and about and the flying monsters.

Pulling his eyes away from the monsters in the sky, Charles looked instead at the people in chains. They were a defeated-looking bunch that kept their eyes on the ground. A couple of them were looking at Kira with interest in their otherwise dead eyes, but that was it. There was no cheering, no trying to escape. There was nothing, it was like they had seen all of this before and already knew that there was no point in even hoping.

With a chill running down his back, Charles opened his mouth to yell, but it was already too late. The ground around the people erupted and monsters leaped into view. It was a trap, one they had walked into with barely a second thought. None of them had thought that the monsters were intelligent enough to do something like this.

Another chill ran down Charles' spine as that thought ran through his mind. If the monsters were smart enough to lay traps, then what else were they capable of? Or was there something else going on here?

When the dirt had settled, and the dust blown away Kira had been surrounded. Near the people in chains, Alli was crouching with her hackles raised and a growl rumbling from her chest.

"Charles something is not right here!" Alli told him as she eyed the unmoving people in front of her.

"I know that! Help Kira!" He screamed at her as he continued running. He wasn't sure what Alli could do to help her. She was even farther from Kira than he was, but they had to do something!

Alli spun and leaped away from the unresponsive people that she had been wanting to rescue. Charles extended his hand towards the monsters surrounding Kira and felt the power surge through his hand. A long bright burst of lightning sped from him as he braced himself for the coming pain in his leg. The lightning punched through two of the monsters and arced through the air, attacking four more of the monsters surrounding Kira.

A notification flickered into being, blocking his view for a precious second before he could minimize it. The pain in his leg didn't come as he braced himself and watched as Kira swung her massive hammer over her head. Her hammer crushed the head of a monster that had been hit by his lightning, the other three jerking spastically.

Her hammer swung back into the air, flinging brain matter and gore all around her. Alli sped closer to her and leaped into the air as she prepared to attack the remaining monsters.

With a sharp yelp, Alli was flung towards Charles as the smell of burning hair and fur filled the air. Several of the flying monsters that Alli had turned away from were hovering above everyone casting spells!

Each of the purple monsters in the sky that were casting spells held staffs in their clawed hands.

"Are you alright?" Charles called out to Alli as he refocused on the magic users.

Alli stood tall as she replied to him. "That attack was nothing, the impact was greater than the actual damage."

Kira screamed as she flew limply through the air her hammer falling uselessly from her hands. In the seconds during which he had looked away from her, she had been overwhelmed. There was a brief flash of light and the hammer disappeared and reappeared as a bracelet on her arm.

A flash of lightning flew through the air followed by a ball of fire as Charles fired magic from both hands. "Grab Kira, we're leaving!" He told Alli as he began backing away from everything. Focusing on his gloved hand he felt the magic gather for the spell he was going to cast. Keeping his focus, he continued to gather magic as he delayed the spell.

Feeling his hand grow hot beneath the force of the spell, he relaxed his control and let the overcharged firebolt spell go. Charles could only watch as what should have been a simple firebolt spell grew to a ridiculous size.

A ball of fire larger than Alli in size flew from his hand and towards the suddenly scrambling monsters in the air.

Charles turned and ran, his hand tingling from the power he had forced through it. Alli ran next to him with Kira hanging limply around her neck, her eyes closed and blood seeping from her blackened and burned chest.

The monsters behind them screamed in terror and pain as they were engulfed by flames. Alli's ears flipped flat on her head as they ran from the screams and the people that they had stopped to save.

"What are we going to do now?" Alli asked him as they ran side by side. "Those people didn't even try to help, they just sat there unmoving while we risked our lives to help them!"

"Some people don't want to be saved," Charles told her as he watched Kira bury her face in Alli's neck. "In the case of those people, I think they have just given up and didn't actually believe that we had a chance of saving them."

"If they had told us, there was a trap there, we might have been able to do something for them!" Alli yelled in anger, her mouth open in a roar.

"I know that, but when people have given up on life, their thinking tends to get slightly skewed." He tried to explain to her as they neared the waiting truck.

Kira slid weakly from her back as Alli stopped next to the passenger door and Charles hurried to drivers' side. The entire truck rocked as Alli leaped into the back and the engine roared to life. Kira's hands were white and pale from blood loss as she gripped the door handle.

The rear wheels spun on the pavement as Charles floored it and spun the wheel, pointing the truck back in the direction they had come from minutes before.

"Is that how people usually act?" Alli asked, her eyes fixed on the monsters burning behind them. Their flailing bodies causing the wooden pens to flare up in flames as well.

"You'll have to figure that out for yourself!" Charles told her somewhat bitterly.

"I'm sorry. I shouldn't have attacked them without thinking!" Kira apologized to them, all color having fled from her face.

Charles grunted but didn't reply. He wasn't in the mood to hear that from her right now! She had been nothing but trouble since she had rescued him and Alli! He had been grateful to her for that; he was even willing to put up with some of her quirks. That stopped now though, she had officially endangered Alli and his life with her thoughtless actions. That was something that he was not willing to look past.

Kira rolled down the window next to her, keeping the smell of her burned flesh from overwhelming them. "I thought I could handle them!" She said weakly.

"What is wrong with you?" Charles yelled at her. "Did you actually think it over before attacking them, or did you just not care that we were there with you? We are in a group, what you do affects us as well!" He took a deep breath and squeezed the steering wheel tightly, his knuckles popping from the pressure. "Correction we were in a party!" Without another thought, he ejected her from their party.

"Charles, maybe you should heal her before she gets any worse?" Alli asked him softly.

Charles' foot punched down on the brake as he turned his head to look at her. "And you, you need to learn what is important! Faceless people that we don't know mean less than nothing to me! There is no reason we should be helping these people, trying to help them just puts us in more danger! I need to get to my sister, and you always wanting to help everyone is doing more harm than good. The world has changed, and if they don't have the strength to survive on their own, then they are better off dead!"

"I agree," Kira started, her breath coming in short gasps.

"Don't you even say anything!" Charles screamed at Kira. "You have absolutely no room to talk, your thoughtless actions are even more dangerous than her good intentions!" No matter how mad he was at Alli at that moment he wasn't about to let someone else bad mouth her.

"Sorry!" Kira coughed out, blood covering her lips.

Charles gritted his teeth and flexed his jaw as he tried to regain control of his emotions. His breath came in short rapid bursts as his cheeks flushed a deep red.

Kira and Alli were silent as they watched him regain control. The fingers on the steering wheel filled with blood as his grip loosened until finally, he released the wheel entirely.

"Come here, Kira," Charles said softly as he reached for her.

A pained expression on her face she slid weakly on the bench closer to his hand. His hand touched the crisped flesh of her stomach, causing her to flinch away from his hand. Stretching farther he touched her again and a soft green light suffused her body healing her injuries. Torn muscles and broken bones set themselves as fresh skin grew on her stomach. Kira's mouth slammed shut with an audible click as she gritted her teeth. The itch of her body healing was almost painful since she couldn't scratch it.

"What about you, Alli, do you need me to heal you as well?" Charles asked, withdrawing his hand from the new pink skin that now covered Kira's stomach.

"Oh, do you actually care about how I'm doing now?" Alli said, her head turned away and her voice pouty.

"Don't go there!" Charles growled, his anger flaring for a second. "Now answer the question! How are you feeling?"

Alli hung her head low as she slumped in the back. "I'm fine. I was mostly just shocked from the attack. It burned some hair and fur but didn't actually damage me."

Relaxing into the bench seat, Charles closed his eyes and pulled up the message he had ignored earlier.

Congratulations, due to the inscribed runes on your body reaching an acceptable level, greater magic can now be used.

The attack spell Lightning Storm has been unlocked. Lightning Storm is a wide range attack spell.

So, the silver runes he had found on his thigh allowed him to use greater forms of magic? Charles couldn't but grin regardless of how it came to pass. He now had a spell that could be used on large groups of monsters.

Closing the message, he opened his eyes and turned to look at Alli. "We have a quest to help those people, so we need to come up with a plan on how we are going to save them. This is the last time we can do this though Alli. I'm not a hero or a person that enjoys helping people because I can. If I don't personally know someone then they mean nothing to me, and a lot of the time even if I do know them, they still don't mean anything."

"I understand Charles," Alli said hesitantly.

Charles sighed as he looked at her. He knew how soft-hearted she was. She was always wanting to help people, that was just who she was. With a pang he felt deep in his bones he suddenly found himself wondering how long she would put up with him? He didn't want to think of losing her, but at the same time, he didn't know how to change or even if he wanted too. He had always been this way, for the most part, he gave absolutely no thought to the people he didn't care about. And the circle of people that he cared about had always been small.

"Let's just focus, for now, after we have completed this quest, we can talk things over." He said to her gently. It was her choice in the end, and no matter how he felt he wasn't going to take that away from her.

Kira looked over at Charles with an odd look on her face. "I think the two of us should talk later. It seems that we have certain things in common, in the way we feel about people."

Charles grunted at her, not wanting to have anything in common with an annoyance like her! "How do we want to do this? The people we saw have already been beaten into submission and I doubt that is the only group we need to find and rescue!" He told them as he climbed out of the cab and into the truck bed next to Alli.

Kira opened her door and slowly climbed into the back and laid her hand on Alli's head, so she could hear her talk as well. "Very well, let us discuss how we are going to find my family!" She announced her mind focused on what she considered to be most important.

Chapter 18

"**S**hould we split up in order to find all the groups?" Alli asked beginning the conversation.

"I do not think that would be the correct course of action in these circumstances," Kira said slowly, her left-hand fingering the new bracelet on her arm.

Charles fixed his eyes on her. "Why do you think that?"

Kira sighed. "We don't know how many monsters there are in the area for one! Mostly though, it's because splitting up is never a good idea in the stories I've read. It doesn't matter what kind of story it is, fantasy, suspense, it never turns out well."

Charles eyed her suspiciously. "You seem like you're under control again."

Kira's face flushed red in embarrassment as Alli nodded in agreement. "Yeah sorry about that, I have anger issues."

Alli snorted at that, "I think that is the understatement of the century."

"Sorry I got distracted for a moment there," Charles said before continuing. "You made some good points; the question still remains though. What are we going to do?"

"We can't fight them," Alli said with confidence. "If we try to rescue people by taking out the monsters, we will run out of time. All the monsters that I have been smelling converged on the city. That means there are going to be hundreds of monsters there minimum, likely far more."

The three were silent as they let that information fully sink in.

"So, we use hit-and-run tactics or pull them away from the people?" Kira asked hesitantly.

"It might work," Charles began, tilting his head towards the sky. "What about the traps though? What are we going to do about those?"

They fell silent as their minds explored various possibilities before mentioning any of them aloud.

"Should we just abandon them all?" Kira asked finally. "Outside of my family I don't care about anyone else, after finding them we can just leave the rest of the people. Besides the quest, we were given to rescue the people didn't have a reward of any kind listed. If I'm not getting anything from it, I don't know that I really feel like putting myself in danger for them."

Alli shifted her head to look at her and then to Charles. "I don't think I can leave everyone behind one, please, at least let's try to come up with a plan. If we can't come up with something that will save them then that is a different matter, but just abandoning them like this, is not something that I am comfortable doing."

Charles leaned against her and sighed. "Do you have a plan in mind then, because I have to be honest here. I'm not seeing a way for us to rescue everyone!"

"No, not one that will allow us to save everyone, but maybe one that will allow us to save those that haven't given up yet," Alli said somewhat sadly in return. "We'll be giving up on that first group since all of the people have already given up."

Charles could tell how hard it had been for her to say that by the muscles in her chest tightening. "Alright, what is your plan for after we get past them then?"

"Uh, that was pretty much it actually," Alli said sheepishly her head sinking in shame. "My plan is just us finding the people that want to be rescued, from there on I don't have any idea."

Kira stood, keeping her hand on Alli. "Can we even make a plan before we find those people? It's not like we know what kind of monsters we'll see there, or if more traps might be involved."

Alli stood and shook her body. "I'll act as a scout. Charles will cast his haste spell on me. Kira will drive since she knows the area and Charles will relay my findings to you from the passenger seat." She ordered before leaping from the back of the truck and waiting for them to acknowledge the plan.

"Understood!" Kira agreed readily as she hopped down to the ground next to Alli.

Charles looked carefully at Alli as she stood next to the truck waiting for him. Her head was hanging low, regardless of her words he knew that she didn't want to abandon those people. For whatever reason, she believed that everyone was worth saving, and she wanted to do so. The lesson he thought she was only just beginning to learn was that the exact opposite was true. People as a whole were worthless wastes of space, in that he agreed with Kira. The only important people were those he chose. He didn't owe these people anything. He was sure they were important to someone, and if that was the case, then that person could rescue them!

He would do everything he could for her regardless, he was sure she would learn the truth sooner or later. He could only hope she learned it before she got to hurt. With that in mind, he climbed out of the truck next to her and whispered into her ear.

"Do what you need to, just be careful and stay safe!" Pulling his face back he cast the haste spell on her and stepped back. "Let us know when you find something." He told her as he patted her flank and hurried to the passenger side of the truck as Kira started it with an engine rumbling roar.

Alli ran off towards the city as the engine settled into a fast idle. Kira eyed Charles as he sat on the bench in the cab. "I've been wondering about this since I found the two of you, but why are you so attached to Alli? It seems like you couldn't care less for people. How did she manage to become so important to you?"

Charles kept his eyes forward as he answered her thoughtfully. "Alli was simply a smart dog when I found her, and like any dog, she was loyal and caring. She has saved my life more times than I can count in the week that I've known her. People have never truly made sense to me, I find it hard to understand and believe them for the most part. With Alli, I didn't have that problem, of course, if I met her like she is now it would probably be a different story."

"You didn't have many friends growing up, did you?" Kira asked as she tapped out a rhythm on the steering wheel.

Charles kept his eyes focused on a distant shrub as he answered her. "What about you, who is Sierra? You were mumbling in your sleep about her. Was she an old friend, maybe someone who hurt you?"

Kira's hand stilled and her face grew pale as her shoulders inched inwards. "She, she was someone I thought was a friend a long time ago. Please, don't ask me about her again." Kira's voice was soft as she implored him.

The sudden change in her was enough to make Charles stop and think twice before he continued with that line of questioning. He didn't see a reason to hurt her needlessly by forcing her to relive unpleasant memories. "Alright, we'll leave it at that then. We should probably start moving, we're going to fall behind Alli at this rate."

Rolling her shoulders, Kira let out the breath she had been holding. "Tell me where to go then. I assume we'll be going off-road for some of this, so we can avoid that first farm?"

"I have to wait for Alli to tell us something so just start driving in the same direction as where she went, I'll tell you when she makes contact," Charles told her confidently, it was only now that he realized he didn't have a way to communicate with Alli when she was away from them. She was the one with the telepathy ability, not him.

With that in mind, Kira steered the old truck off-road and drove slowly after Alli, her fingers still tapping away on the steering wheel.

Charles watched her from the corner of his eye but waited for her to say something. He had known her for less than 24 hours and in that time he had seen a few different sides of her. The one thing that held true in all of them though was the simple truth that she had issues! Strangely enough, though, it was that very thing that seemed to allow them to understand each other somewhat.

He knew what it was like, wanting to lash out at the world and those around you. Something that she had done multiple times to them already. He didn't approve of her methods or losing her head in the heat of the moment, but he understood the desire behind it. And because he understood the desire, he felt like he could understand a small part of her.

The truck bounced along jostling them with every dip and bump they drove over, and still, Kira tapped her fingers with her face set in an emotionless mask. Her mouth opened and then closed without her saying anything as her eyes remained focused on the terrain in front of them.

"Are you really alright with letting everyone die like this?" Kira finally managed to ask after several minutes.

"What do you mean, I thought you didn't care one way or another?" Charles replied finally looking at her.

Her fingers stopped tapping as she thought. "I don't know how I feel in regard to this matter anymore. All I know is that it feels wrong to let them all die without at least trying to help them."

Charles sighed and closed his eyes. "If I'm being honest, then I feel the same way, but I don't see any way that we can help those that have already given up." He told her quietly. "If I hadn't let Alli think there was no other choice, then she would have gotten herself killed trying to help them. As it is, I know that she is still going to try to help them, the difference is that now she is going to give it more thought and will do it in a smarter manner. So, no we are not going to just leave them there to die, instead, we are just going to pick our battles in a way that will ensure the most people will live."

"You're different from what I thought. Every time I think I have you figured out in some way you surprise me." She ran a hand through her hair tousling it as it danced in the wind of the open window. "In the end, you're leaving their survival up to Alli then and her ability to come up with a decent plan?"

Charles caught a piece of hair that had clung to her fingers and been pulled free to drift on the wind. "She is the one who cares the most about rescuing them, there are certain things that she needs to learn and while it may be slightly cruel. I believe this is the best way for her to learn."

"Does this go back to what you were telling her earlier?"

"Yes, she needs to learn that not everyone can be saved. More than that she needs to learn that at times there is nothing you can do for people!"

Kira jerked the wheel suddenly as a wooden fence post that had fallen over appeared in front of them. Charles grabbed the door bracing himself as the truck bounced violently over yet another hole. With a snarl of annoyance, Kira yanked on the steering wheel causing the wheels to slide as they lost their traction in the dirt.

"Have you heard anything from her yet?" She asked impatiently.

"No, now quit asking and focus on your driving!" Charles ordered as they neared a grouping of houses on the outskirts of the city.

Kira slowed as she steered the truck onto the pavement and down the street picking up speed. The houses on either side of the road were abandoned with doors ripped off and laying in the yards. More than half of the houses showed signs of damage either from fires or some other destructive force.

Kira let the truck coast to a stop in the middle of an intersection. "Where to now? There aren't any tracks to follow anymore, and there is no sign of Alli in the area."

"I know I told her to do what she needed to, but I at least thought she would keep us involved," Charles muttered angrily to himself. "Whatever, keep driving. We'll search for people on our own while we wait to hear from her."

The suburbs of Kansas City stretched out around them in a confusing mass of pavement and silent empty houses. Lazy wisps of smoke curled into the air and drifted away on the winds that blew through. In the distance, a hint of gradually darkening clouds could be seen moving towards the city. A chill could be felt in the fall air even now no matter how distant the clouds were.

Neither of them paid the weather any attention as the truck rolled down the streets. Sounds carried on the wind would occasionally reach their ears through the open windows. Unfortunately, it was impossible to pinpoint where the noise was coming from as it bounced around the area.

"Stop in front of that building over there," Charles told Kira, pointing towards a building with metal stairs that ran up to the roof. "I'll get on the roof and see if I can see anything from up there."

Charles leaped from the truck as soon as it stopped, the passenger side door hanging open in his wake. A dull clanging echoed under his feet as he ran up the rusted metal steps that led to the roof. A short wall of brick edged the roof, preventing people from falling off accidentally.

Stepping carefully to the edge of the roof, Charles placed his hands on the short wall and looked over the edge to where Kira was waiting in the idling truck. Giving her a small wave, Charles straightened and scanned the buildings around them. There was one a few streets over that drew his eye, the doors of the building had been boarded over.

The building was too new for it to have happened before the gods changed the world. More than that, though, was what he saw through the windows on the third story. All the windows had been covered, but in one spot it seemed the covering was too thin allowing movement to be seen behind them.

Marking the building in his mind, Charles hurried from the roof and back to the truck.

"I found some people that have holed up in a building." He told Kira, pointing down the street he wanted her to take.

"How many people were there?" She asked, keeping an eye out for monsters as she followed his directions.

"I don't know, the windows are all covered, and the doors have been boarded over. I saw some movement though."

"Wait," Kira said, her foot lifting from the accelerator. "You saw movement in a building with doors boarded over. Doesn't that mean the people are outside and the monsters are inside?"

"Wouldn't the monster have just broken the windows to escape?" Charles asked after a tense second.

Putting her foot back on the pedal Kira glanced at him and then back to the road with a shake of her head. "Whatever, I guess it doesn't really matter. Without Alli here we might as well look at places like this."

More noise drifted towards them, close enough this time for them to realize that it was yells and of people arguing. Perking up they both looked ahead as the building Charles had seen came into view. The sound of people yelling became louder before vanishing entirely.

Charles saw a shadow move behind a second-story window as the truck stopped in front of the building. "Well, if the yelling didn't convince you, I just saw a shadow move on the second story."

Kira glared at him and pocketed the key to the truck as they both stepped out of the now silent cab. The sound of glass breaking in the distance drifted by on the wind as Charles took the chance to knock on the wood covering the door of the building.

"We don't have any food to spare. Go away!" A deep male voice called out from behind the door.

"We're not here for that," Charles called back, trying to keep his voice from carrying farther than it needed to. "We need information on the monsters in the area and on where we might be able to find some people."

Kira stepped closer to him while keeping her eyes constantly moving. "We don't have time for this!" She whispered harshly as her left hand began moving toward her silver bracelet.

"Just hold on, at least give them a chance to think it over first," Charles told her quietly, stopping himself from reaching for her arm.

Kira stiffened and grasped her bracelet as someone stepped into view from around the side of the building.

"If you don't want food, then you might as well come in and talk, maybe you can tell us about what you've seen so far." It was a tall lanky man with slightly graying hair and a lens that had cracked on his glasses.

Chapter 19

C harles took the lead in following the man as Kira continued to look at him warily. He led them to the back of the building where a pair of cargo loading doors were propped open.

The inside of the building was dark, with the only light coming from the open doors. Hidden off to the side in the gloom was the entrance to the stairs that would take them to the next floor. The man they were following stopped and pointed at the stairs as he pulled the doors closed behind them.

"Where are the two of you from? I noticed that you seem to have a working vehicle at least, all the vehicles around here vanished last night without a trace."

Charles waited to see if Kira would respond before he said anything. "I'm originally from here and though it's been a few years, my family still lives here," Kira told the man as they followed him up the stairs.

"I'm from Denver, I'm on my way to Massachusetts where my sister is," Charles said, deciding it couldn't hurt to tell the man that much. His mind was focused on that tidbit about all the vehicles disappearing. Was something like that part of the city being turned into a dungeon? Were other things going to change and vanish as the time of the change got closer?

Stepping from the stairwell and onto the second floor, they could see that it was packed with people. Several people were standing near the covered windows, everything from desks to paper had been used in the effort to block them. Their efforts resulted in a gloomy darkness where people huddled together in fear of what lay outside those very windows.

"We can't spend much time here, so gather whoever is in charge. The things we have to tell you need to be acted on immediately." Charles' voice carried through the room, reaching everyone's ears without issue. Time was of the essence, and they had little time to waste, the next thirty-four and a half hours were going to be packed.

The people were dirty, and the room had the sour smell of old sweat mixed with blood. The edges of the room were lined with bottles of water and packages of food. It was obvious that while they had enough for the people there, it would only last them another couple of days max. Even without the news, they were about to deliver, these people wouldn't have been able to remain holed up like this much longer.

Everyone turned to look at them as the resounding thuds of people running down the stairs echoed through the room. "Where are those two? Where did they get a working truck?" A smooth female voice called down ahead of them.

Kira's eye twitched as she heard the voice, and her expressionless face turned stony. To the side Charles watched this change come over his companion. The man who had led them inside stepped away from them, his own face twisting slightly with apprehension.

Charles twisted to look at the stairs as a group of people thundered into view, not caring about how much noise they were making. The group of four was made up of people from obviously differing walks of life. One of the men wore a police uniform and had a short military haircut. Another was wearing a dirty wife-beater and had bulging muscles. The one that stood out though was the lone female that stood in the middle next to a scholarly-looking man. She had an almost regal bearing and her smooth clear skin and clothes were all sparkling clean.

Her wide blue eyes focused on Charles and Kira, and she tilted her head to the side. "Are you the two with the truck? Tell us how you managed to get it running?"

Kira's eyes darkened, and a scowl appeared on her face at the woman's demands. "You never change, do you?" Kira asked the newcomer.

The woman's eyes flashed as she flipped her blonde hair over her shoulder. "I have no idea what you are talking. Do I know you? You don't look like something I would associate with, there's dirt under your fingernails!"

"I'll give you a hint, it's been sixteen years since the last time I saw you." Her voice was cold enough to make people shiver in the crowded room.

The blonde head straightened as her eyes narrowed. "Hmm, it has indeed been a while then, Kira?"

Kira looked at her for a beat longer and then turned to Charles. "Let's leave, anyone stupid enough to associate with trash like her deserves to die!" Everyone but Charles cringed away from the venom in her voice and words.

Charles shrugged. "That's fine." He cast a quick look around the room. "You should all leave here. Tomorrow night this entire city is going to become a dungeon."

With that last parting piece of advice, he followed Kira as she shouldered people out of her way and headed for the stairs.

"Stop!" The nameless woman screeched at them.

Following her words, a number of people stepped in front of Kira in an effort to stop her. Unfortunately for them with her leveled-up strength, there was nothing they could do to stop her. Without breaking stride, Kira pushed through them.

Charles followed her down the stairs and out of the building as the people in the room began arguing loudly. "Weren't we going to ask them for information about other groups?" He asked somewhat tentatively.

"Not from her, we're not!" She said angrily.

"Who was she?" He dared to ask as Kira stomped angrily towards the front of the building. This was the first time he had seen her act this way like she truly hated someone.

"That," He could hear her grinding her teeth as she spoke. "That was Sierra!"

"Sierra, as in the Sierra from your dreams that you refuse to talk about Sierra?"

Kira glared at him before sighing and looking away. "Yes, that one." The wind blew through the buildings around them, whistling a sad dull tone.

The truck stood waiting for them as they walked past the building. Charles stopped at the edge of the building and cocked his head feeling an odd tingling sensation in the air. "Kira, stop!" He said firmly, his eyes searching.

Kira didn't listen as she continued to stomp angrily away, her mind focused inward on painful memories.

"Kira," He called again, louder this time.

The ground rumbled as Kira took another step forward, the shaking of the ground causing her to stumble and fall to her knee. Her head swiveled as she was forced from her musing. The ground continued to shake as a single large monster came into view heading towards them. The sides of the monster brushed the buildings on both sides of the street, breaking glass and concrete alike.

It was impossibly large and each step it took shook the earth and the buildings around them, making them sway dangerously. It was not only the largest monster they had seen to that point but also the weirdest. It had the shell of a turtle, the horn of a rhino, and the bloated body and legs of a hippo or other equally large animal.

Charles felt his mouth drop open as he analyzed the behemoth monster, 'Shelldragon' Lv. 35. The street was turned into rubble and crushed with each slow swaying step it took. The noise it created was deafening as it trundled towards them and the truck that was in its way.

Kira quickly got to her feet a malicious grin spreading across her face as she looked back at the building. Anything covering was the windows was pulled down or shoved aside as the people inside rushed to see what was coming. Shocked and terrified faces could be seen as everyone began to panic.

Charles followed the path of her gaze and winced as he watched the people scramble all over each other but going nowhere. Just from seeing the expression on her face he could tell that she had no intention of helping the people inside. Not that he could blame her exactly since he himself wasn't exactly inclined to help other people normally. In this case though, with the people about to be killed right in front of him, he was finding it hard to be emotionally removed.

The giant monster continued towards them as they stood frozen in the street until a scream from inside finally shook them free. Shaking her head, Kira turned away from the building and started walking towards the truck again. The malicious hate-filled smile remained plastered across her face as she pulled the key from her pocket.

"Come on, we have more groups to find and help. This one is a lost cause if they can't even get out of a building in time."

With one last look back, Charles hurried after her. She was right; they had already conveyed the message they needed to, anything more than that was up to them. They couldn't be responsible for people that were unwilling to help themselves. There was an entire city worth of people that they somehow needed to find. Taking the time to fight their battles for them would mean that many fewer people that wouldn't know they needed to flee.

Looking at the monster he couldn't help but ask her, "Would we even be able to damage that thing?"

Kira refused to look at him as she slid into the cab of the truck. "Possibly, but it doesn't seem likely. That shell would stop anything I have to throw at it, and I doubt even a blast of your lightning could make it do more than pause."

Charles climbed in next to her as she started the truck and drove past the building. Behind them, they could see people evacuating and running from the endangered building in a flood of bodies. Kira glanced at the rearview mirror and clicked her tongue. "She's like a cockroach!" She said in annoyance as she watched Sierra escape with everyone else.

"Where to next?" Charles asked as they sped away from the monster.

"My family's place, if monsters like that are roaming the city then I don't want to put it off any longer." Her voice was firm and laced with the anger she felt from seeing Sierra again. "Have you heard anything from Alli yet?" She asked changing the subject.

Charles shook his head as he twisted to look behind them. It was useless though as they had already left the people far behind. "No, honestly I'm starting to become a little worried. Usually, she checks in every few minutes, but I haven't heard from her at all." He twisted to look at her. "Are you going to tell me what she did to you?" He asked trying again.

The anger fled from her eyes, leaving them cold and lifeless. "No, now focus. Since we don't have Alli guarding us right now, we need to be extra alert and watching for movement!"

The sun was starting its descent at this point as they sped through the eerily empty streets of the once bustling city. The cars that had been so prevalent in Denver were nowhere to be seen, having vanished the night before. More than just empty streets though the city itself felt empty, few monsters could be seen or even heard, and the people had all hidden themselves.

"Where are all the people? Even in Denver, I saw people wandering the streets and raiding the stores. Here though there is no one, we haven't seen a single person on the streets."

"Isn't that because of the farms?" Kira asked not really caring either way.

"Is it really? I don't think so, not unless they already gathered everyone. Since, there aren't really any monsters to be seen that could be doing the gathering. I don't think monsters would be that organized." Charles said as he felt his attention drift.

Kira shifted into a higher gear and pressed on the accelerator as she thought about what he had said. "My parent's house is just a little farther, keep watch." They were back in the suburbs in an area with older houses that had seen better days. It was likely that once a upon a time, it had been part of an affluent neighborhood. That was in the past and now belonged to those with lower incomes.

Several of them were damaged with part of the houses having fallen down after walls had been destroyed. It looked like cars had run into a couple of them and others were clearly from monster damage.

There was one obvious difference though, and that was in the space next to the house Kira stopped in front of. There was nothing there, just a hole and a driveway that led to nothing. The house and its foundation had both vanished.

Kira barely gave the empty space a second glance as she rushed from the truck. Her booted feet pounded across their grass yard, and she leaped over a grouping of bushes in her rush to reach the front door.

Charles followed behind her slower, taking the time to turn off the truck. Kira was already inside the house by the time his feet hit the pavement. His eyes flickered farther down the street, noting the open doors on some of the houses. Splashes of dark red could be seen in front of each of those houses, marking where something or someone had bled.

Kira had stopped in the doorway of the house with her hand on the open door. Coming up behind her, Charles could see why she hadn't moved inside of the house. It was a wreck, couches and chairs had been slashed and torn apart, a wooden dining table was laying on its side with a crack running down the length of its top.

"Come on," He said as he gently nudged her into the house. "We're not going to learn anything if we don't go inside."

Kira stumbled as she walked on wooden legs past the destroyed living room and farther down into the depths of the house. Behind her, Charles ran his fingers over the rips in the couch and chairs feeling how rough the cuts were. They weren't smooth like one would expect from a knife but dimpled and torn like they had been ravaged by claws.

He didn't see any blood which didn't make sense to him, just from the damage, he could see in this one room it was obvious a monster had been in the house. If that was the case, though where was the blood? Someone had been in here after or during its presence otherwise the door wouldn't have been closed. There were enough houses on the street with open doors that it was unlikely a passing person had closed it after the fact.

Pulling his hand away from the ruined furniture he hurried after Kira finding her looking into what was undoubtedly the room of a teenage girl. Posters of boy bands and colorful animals decorated the walls in what could only be described to his eyes as haphazard fashion.

"This was my sisters' room," Kira said as she heard him stand behind her. "There is no-one in the house, and I didn't see any blood either."

"Where do you think they went then?" Stepping away from her he peeked his head around the corner and saw the orange light of fading sunlight. The entire rear wall of the kitchen lay in pieces across the backyard.

Kira held a light blue pillow in her hands and a pensive expression on her face as she trailed after him. "The only place I can think of is the high school. It was built to double as a storm shelter. Under normal circumstances that is where they would go, unfortunately, this does not count as normal anything."

"Should we move on then or is there something you want to bring with us? Don't forget this entire city is going to become part of a dungeon. After hearing what happened to all the vehicles, I can't help but think that everything will vanish when it is time. If there is anything that contains sentimental value, then now might be the time to take it."

"No, there is nothing like that, it looks like they had time to grab everything before they left," Kira said as she plucked at a loose thread on the pillowcase with an odd look on her face.

"We should go then, we're on a finite time limit here," Charles told her ignoring the pain he felt in his own chest at the thought of his own family.

Kira stored the pillow in her inventory and turned away from the remains of her parent's kitchen. "Let's go. I'm anxious to see them again." She spun on the heel of her boot and ran through the house.

Thoughts of his family occupied his mind as Charles ran after her. He could clearly picture the face of his older sister. The faces of his parents, however, were fuzzy and blurred, remembering faces had never been easy for him and now it was working against him.

Chapter 20

The pavement passed smoothly under the rolling wheels of the old 50s truck. Kira sat behind the steering wheel in the cab, her face belying just how anxious she truly was. She seemed to be trying to hide how scared she was of finding out that her family was gone and failing miserably.

Charles was next to her absorbed in his own contemplations. He had noticed the way she looked and was fairly sure he knew what she was thinking about. It didn't concern him however and didn't affect him either way. There was a part of him that wondered how she would react if they learned her family was dead. He had seen how she reacted to monsters and other people already. If the reason for her to even try acting normal was gone what would she do?

"Your family?" Charles waited for her to nod before continuing. "If they made it out of the house, then I think it is likely they were able to get to the school."

Even though she knew there was no real basis for what he was saying, the words themselves seemed to help. Her face relaxed a little before tightening again as she turned a corner and the school appeared in front of them. A large fence encircling the property lay in tatters on the ground, metal links spread everywhere.

Groups of people were outside the school with weapons in their hands as they stood to watch. Eyes from all around the yard were fixed on the truck as it came closer to them. None of them had seen a working vehicle of any kind within the last week. Many of them had already put cars into the category of a lost technology, even more so after they had all vanished the night before.

Yet right in front of them was a working truck speeding down the street towards the front of the school.

Kira appeared to be done waiting as she barely kept the truck under control as it swung into the parking lot. The truck had barely come to a stop before she was out and running. A group of people that were guarding the front doors scattered as her Warhammer flashed into being. No one wanted to go up against something like that, besides they were there to guard against monsters, not other humans. They were sure someone inside would ask about the truck; it wasn't their concern.

Charles once more slipped the key from the ignition and stored it in his inventory as he followed behind her at a slower pace. Sensing that none of the people gathered were going to stop him, he pushed open the doors to the building and entered the school. The tiled floors were scuffed and dirty and the air was still and slightly sour. The rumble of conversations could be heard all around him as people were packed into each of the classrooms.

Desks and chairs had been removed from the rooms and lined the sides of the halls waiting to be moved to a more permanent location. Ahead of him he could see Kira running from room to room calling out for her family.

"Mom, dad, Kate are you here?" Her voice could be heard echoing down the halls, silencing conversations everywhere.

Charles followed along slower, taking the time to look into several of the rooms. The people in each of them looked tired from stress and worry, they were clean though. Some had bandages on their arms or legs but were otherwise healthy.

Disregarding the people he had seen, Charles moved past the filled rooms. Kira had stopped at one of the rooms and was looking inside with tears falling from her eyes. Coming up behind her, Charles peered over her shoulder and saw a room filled with tables bearing weapons of every kind. Standing in the corner of the room with a clipboard in his hand was a middle-aged man who seemed to be counting everything.

His shoulders were stooped, and he moved slowly like he had a great weight on his mind.

"Dad," Kira said loudly, her voice grabbing the man's attention.

"Kira?" He asked in disbelief as the clipboard and pencil fell from his fingers.

Charles pushed Kira into the room, her feet dragging at the sudden appearance of her father.

"Where's mom? Where's Kate? Are they here, are they alright?" She asked rapidly as her steps steadied.

Tears fell freely from her dads' eyes. "Kira, is that really you? We didn't dare to even hope that you had survived or that we would ever see you again!" His foot crushed the clipboard, breaking the flimsy laminate board in his rush to reach his daughter.

The change that had come over his normally closed lip and angry companion was shocking to Charles. It was to be expected, and yet the change that had come over her was still beyond his expectations. For the first time since he had met her, she looked happy and... warm.

Charles held himself back from their reunion, standing in the doorway, letting them enjoy the moment in peace. Kira had her head tucked into her father's neck as they held each other and cried quietly.

"Where are they?" Someone yelled preceding the sound of booted feet running down the hall. "Where is the owner of that truck?"

"Kira, hurry it up! We have annoyances incoming." Charles stepped into the room and closed the door.

Kira pushed away from her father and swiped at her eyes with the back of her hand. Her silver bracelet gleamed wetly drawing her father's curious eye as he allowed himself to be pushed back and swiped at his own eyes.

"What's this?" He asked lightly touching the bracelet. "I haven't seen you wear this before."

"It's nothing," Kira said is a rush as she pulled her arm away from him. "More importantly where are mom and Kate? Are they safe?"

His face fell at her question. "Your mother is safe. She should be in the gymnasium right now. Kate, however, was injured that first morning. Our neighbor Paul managed to save her in time at the cost of his own life. Your mom hasn't left her side since." His voice was heavy with emotion as he told them of what had happened. "Paul was coming home from his shift at the fire station when the announcement from the gods happened. He was one of the lucky ones in that there were no other cars near his when everything failed. Apparently, he hurried home only to find it had vanished. Around that time a monster had torn through the wall of the kitchen and was attacking Kate."

"Where were you and mom?"

"We were in the basement grabbing supplies, we knew as soon as the power failed that we needed to make our way to the shelter. To here. In any case, he heard her screams and was able to get to her before we could. When we got upstairs, we found them lying in the grass behind the house bleeding. There was nothing we could do for him, but Kate was still breathing. We bandaged her as best we could and carried her here as quickly as we could. Unfortunately, without proper supplies, there is only so much that can be done for her." The light that seeing his daughter again had brought to his eyes slowly faded the more he talked.

A pounding came from the door behind Charles as Kira's father finished talking. "Kory, you still in there counting?" The doorknob twisted, and the door swung open. "We're looking for a couple of people. Have you seen them?"

Kory, Kira's father nudged her to the side and then stood in front of her as the three people entered the room. Charles stayed silent as he moved to Kira's side, avoiding the newcomers. The loud one was a short round looking man who looked to be in his forties. The other two were well-dressed females that stood with authority, leaving no question as to who was actually in charge.

"You!" The taller of the two women pointed a finger at Kira. "Are you the one who owns the truck outside?"

Kira ignored them and grabbed Charles with both hands, gripping his arms. "If you help my sister, then you can have the truck!"

"Hey, we're talking to you!" The three newcomers said loudly when they were ignored. "Give us the key to that truck, we're confiscating it."

Kira's released Charles' arms and turned to face them stepping around her father, who was blocking her partially from view. There was a bright flash of light and the warhammer appeared in her hands, her muscles flexing underneath its weight. "You and what army? You have no authority over me and my possessions. If you try to take it, then I'll kill you." Her cold eyes flicked away from them and nailed her father to the floor. "Take us to mom and Kate right now."

His eyes drifted to the three intruders and back to his daughter. "Uh, alright follow me."

Charles stopped next to the three stunned people. "You need to get everyone out of the city, it's going to turn into a dungeon tomorrow night." Then, having said what he needed to, he left them in the room and hurried after Kory and Kira.

"Is your friend a doctor or something?" Kory was quietly asking Kira.

"No, I actually don't know what it was he did before this." She answered indifferently as there was another flash and her bracelet reformed on her wrist.

Kory looked back at Charles as they hurried through cluttered and dirty halls. "How is he going to be able to help her then?"

Kira pushed him on faster. "Fewer questions more speed, it'll be easier to just see it in person."

Charles watched them interact with a small smile. Kira's eyes were bright and alive at the thought of seeing the rest of her family.

Kory led them to grey metal double doors with a push bar, hitting it open with his hip he led them into the gymnasium. The moans of people in pain and the smell of decaying flesh were stifling inside, with the vaulted ceiling making everything echo and reverberate.

Kira raised a hand to her nose at the smell as they threaded their way through the forest of cots. Small paths had been created where the cots had been pushed together, creating enough room for a single person to step through.

Kory led them to a corner near a set of doors that led outside. It was there in that corner that Kate was lying on a cot, blood soaking her t-shirt and bandages. A woman was sitting on the ground next to her with her head resting on the cot next to Kate's hand.

Kory knelt next to the woman and gently shook her. "Honey, wake up Kira has returned."

There was a small moan as Kates' eyes fluttered and blearily settled on her older sister. Beside the cot, her mother stirred and reached for Kates' hand before looking up at her husband. "What did you say? Who has returned?"

Kira stepped into view and fell to her knees as her arms wrapped around her mother. Kate blinked her eyes and reached for her sisters' hand as her bleary eyes focused. "Sister," She said quietly her voice raspy and dry sounding.

"Kira, is that really you? How did you get here? When you called us last, you said you were working near the state line." Her mothers' eyes were wide and slightly glazed from sleep.

"We can talk about all of that later, right now Charles needs to look at Kate!" Her voice was firm as she twisted to look at Charles while keeping her arms around her mother.

Charles stepped over the occupied cot next to Kate and put a hand on her head. A green glow spread from his hand to cover her body as he cast his healing spell and concentrated. His left hand drifted to her stomach where she had been slashed by a monster's claws. It had been sewn shut and bandaged, but the damage was too deep for anyone to have done anything more.

The acrid smell of necrotizing flesh drifted lightly from her stomach as his hand pressed down on the torn flesh. The smell grew stronger as puss and diseased flesh pushed free of her body. His hand grew slimy as the thick yellowish liquid oozed around his fingers soaking the bandages with something other than blood.

Kira watched him closely as the green glow from his hands spread across her sisters' body. The first time she had seen that glow, it was wrapping around Alli's fluffy body, and she hadn't been able to truly see anything. This time she could see the change coming over her sisters' body, the pale color of her skin vanished, replaced with a healthy pink color.

To Kira's side and in front of her dual gasps could be heard as her parents watched the color come back into their youngest daughters' cheeks. Beneath his hands, Kate blinked and breathed deeply not feeling pain while she did so for the first time in a week.

"Remove the bandage around her stomach, there is something there." Charles ground out concentrating on healing her properly. He did not want to screw this up as he had with Alli.

Kira reached around her mother and pulled the filthy bandage from her stomach, letting it pool at the top of her pants. The slash in her stomach had mostly vanished at that point, but there was a bulge underneath her skin.

"You'll need to reach in and pull it out before the skin closes the rest of the way," Charles told them with a grimace.

Kira gulped and plunged two fingers into her sisters' stomach right next to Charles's hand. The tips of her fingers felt something hard, and she squeezed it between her fingers and pulled it out. A thick black piece of claw covered in blood could be seen as she pulled it free and Charles finished closing the wound.

"There, she'll undoubtedly be tired, but she should be fine now." Charles felt weak and mentally tired from healing her. Removing the bad flesh, the diseased blood, and the puss had required a fine control of his magic that he hadn't even known he possessed.

Kate's breath came easier to her as the pain disappeared, replaced by a feeling of exhaustion. The lids of her eyes fluttered weakly as she looked at her older sister before closing them fully as she succumbed to the irresistible need to sleep.

Seeing her sleeping there for the first time in a week was too much for her parents, as they started crying with relief. Kory grabbed Charles filth covered hand in a firm grip as he looked at his family with watery eyes. "I have no idea how you just did that but thank you for saving my daughter!"

Something inside Kira seemed to relax as she saw her sister healed, and she sagged against the cot, her mother barely catching her in time. "Thanks, Charles," She managed weakly as her mother held her.

Charles pulled his hand free and cast the cleaning spell on himself and Kate, freeing them of the bodily secretions. "We need to be leaving."

Kira stood, backing away from her mother with a shake of her head. "Yeah, mom, dad, you need to take Kate and get out of the city. Tomorrow night this entire city is going to become a dungeon."

"Will we be fine crossing the river, or do we need to go farther?" Her mother asked after a second of thought, deciding to trust her daughter and the man that had saved her other daughter's life.

"I don't know. We got a quest when we got here that just said the city was going to become a dungeon tomorrow night. It didn't mention anything more, crossing the state line into Missouri might work or it might not. What do you think Charles?" Kira told them, taking control of the conversation.

"I think the river is a natural dividing line, but who knows for certain." He had turned away from the family and was looking at the commotion coming from the entrance. The doors had been flung open and the same three people from before were standing there. They were backed by six more people, each carrying a gun or other weapon.

"Time to go!" Kira told them firmly, following the direction of his eyes. "I'll carry Kate. Charles lead them to the truck."

Charles turned away from the people gathering at the entrance to the gymnasium and to the door next to Kates cot. The truck was at the front of the building but if they left from that door they wouldn't have to deal with the cluttered hallways and annoying people. "Follow me."

Kira gently picked up her younger sister, smearing the drying blood from her fingers on her shirt before touching her. "Come on, we need to be going."

There was a yell from the entrance as they spotted Kira and Charles. Charles refused to look at them as he pushed open the door to the outside and walked out into the fresh air. The sky was showing the last vestiges of color as the sun sank over the distant horizon.

Kory looked at the people splitting up, some of them running into the forest of cots while others turned around and ran through the halls. Pushing his wife ahead of him, they followed after Charles and Kira into the fading light of day.

Chapter 21

C harles ran around the side of the building and spotted someone opening the hood of the truck. "Stop right there!" He yelled, stretching out his hand and preparing to light the person on fire. He needed that truck to get to his sister, and he was not going to allow anyone to take it away from him. Kira said he could have the truck if he healed her sister, and he had done it. That meant that the truck was now his and no amount of annoying people were going to stop him.

A bald-headed man with a large bushy beard stepped back from the truck and placed his hands on his hips. "This truck is now our property, so beat it."

Whatever he had tried at least Charles thought with a mental shrug as he released a firebolt towards the man. The ground exploded in front of the man, leaving a small crater in the pavement. The bald-headed thief stumbled backward and fell to the ground in shock as Charles continued running towards him.

"You were saying?" He questioned as he stretched his arm towards the man in an obvious threat. "Did you take anything?"

"No, no not yet," The terrified man stuttered. "I was just inspecting it I swear!" His eyes kept switching from the furrow in the pavement to Charles and his threatening hand.

"Tell everyone they need to leave the city before tomorrow night," Charles told him, lowering his hand. If the man hadn't done anything to the truck, then there was no problem.

Kira appeared around the corner of the school building running towards him with her sleeping sister in her arms. Dismissing the sight in front of her, she skirted the man and the hole and opened the passenger door. Carefully, she slid her sister onto the bench and closed the door before reaching around and closing the opened hood.

"I'll sit in the back of the truck with my parents, so take us across the river," Kira ordered him as he sat next to her sister and closed the door with a bang. In front of the truck, the bald man scrabbled away on his hands and knees heading for the front of the school.

Charles pulled the key out of his inventory and started the truck while ignoring her. Quickly shifting into gear, he drove the truck away from the front of the school and towards the side where her parents had yet to appear. Beside him, Kate shifted and settled on the bench seat her head thunking lightly against the glass of the window.

The truck jumped as the wheels hit the raised sidewalk as he drove the truck onto the grass aiming towards the side of the gymnasium. Kira's parents were running towards them with pursuers right on their tail. Charles spun the wheel and the back of the truck swung towards them, the worn wheels sliding across the grass.

Kira stretched out her arms and reached for her gasping parents. She ignored the yelling people behind them as she grasped their outstretched arms and pulled them into the truck bed. Her parents collapsed, laying down with their hands intertwined. Kira steadied herself against the metal frame as the truck leaped forward.

Inside the cab, Charles pulled his eyes from the mirror he had angled to focus on Kira and pressed down on the gas pedal. The spinning rear wheels kicked up dirt and clumps of grass as they fought for traction on the slick ground.

The truck shuddered and shot forward, as the tires gained traction on something buried in the dirt. The old truck bounced and groaned as it jumped from the grass to the sidewalk and onto the street. Beside him, Kate's sleeping form tilted and then slumped further against the door.

The screech of tires faded away as they sped away from the school and further into the city. Charles kept his eyes peeled for monsters as well as street signs that would guide him in the right direction.

In the back, Kira was relaxing next to her parents while watching the road behind them. Kory was relaxing against his wife, Krystal, trying to get his breathing under control when he felt her stiffen up and reach for Kira's hand.

"Something seems to be bothering you. What happened?" Krystal's voice held all the love she felt for her daughter.

Kira stiffened and looked away.

"Tell us what happened. Did Charles do something to you? Do you want me to beat him up?" Kory asked only half joking, he didn't think his daughter would let anyone hurt her.

Kira laughed relaxing slightly and squeezed her mother's hand before closing her eyes. "I saw Sierra today." That was all she needed to say to them. They understood why that would affect her, they held no love or even affection for the privileged rich girl.

"So, that shameless blonde-haired bit..." Kory elbowed his wife before she could finish that thought. "Err. I mean that twa..." He elbowed her again, Krystal elbowed him in the stomach in response. "Did you leave her alive?" She asked with a click of her tongue.

"Unfortunately, yes," Kira snorted. "It was such a shock to see her again though, I've been trying to put what she did behind me for years. I know I haven't been successful in the slightest, but I'm trying, and then seeing her just standing there, still acting like she was better than anyone else. It was all I could do to just walk out of that building."

Her parents were silent as they looked deeply into each other's eyes before turning back to Kira, having come to some sort of understanding. "How did Charles react to her and you leaving like that?"

Kira finally opened her eyes, letting her parents see the tears clinging to her eyes from the nature of their topic. "I don't really know. He wondered why, of course, but he seemed content to just let it be. He warned the people that they needed to leave and then followed me out of the building."

"Who exactly is he?" Krystal asked, changing the subject for her daughter's sake. "He was using magic. How did he learn something like that so quickly?"

"I'm not exactly sure. We keep going in circles when it comes to personal questions. I'll ask him something and instead of answering right away he'll ask me something in return that I don't want to answer. All I actually know about him is that he used to be a programmer and that he has a sister attending MIT." Kira decided to keep the other things she knew about him to herself for the time being.

Charles rapped his knuckles on the glass window at the back of the cab, jolting them from their conversation. "We might have a problem up here!" He called back to them.

Kira poked her head around the side of the truck cab and squinted her eyes against the wind. The road they had been driving on had joined up with the main road while she had been talking with her parents. The road should have met up with the bridge without any problems, there was a problem though. A rather large and glaringly obvious one, in this case, the road to the bridge was blocked.

In the first case of true destruction they had seen since entering the city, an entire building was laying on its side with blocks of concrete scattered across the road. The glitter of broken glass reflecting the last rays of sunlight twinkled all along the ground in front of them.

Charles brought the truck to a stop and stepped from the vehicle. "Is there another way to the bridge? It looks like the highway is completely blocked."

Kira stood in the back and balancing her feet on the metal sides climbed onto the roof of the cab. "Yeah, we're not going to be able to drive around that from here, we're going to have to backtrack. It shouldn't be a big problem a lot of the roads can take you to the bridge this was simply the fastest."

"You drive then since you know these roads," Charles told her as he switched places with her and climbed in the back next to her parents.

Kira jumped from the top of the cab, crouching as her legs absorbed the impact without an issue.

"So, tell me about Sierra." He said to them as Kira turned the truck around. "The way Kira reacted to her earlier isn't normal. More than that it seems she is having nightmares about her as well, what exactly happened between them all those years ago?"

Kory looked at his wife and then down at his hands, leaving the decision on what to say up to her. Krystal sighed and twisted to look at her daughter through the windowpane. "Sierra and Kira were friends when they were younger, her father wasn't obscenely rich yet, and they lived nearby. When they were ten though, her father made his fortune with the dotcom boom. Shortly after that, they moved into a huge house and Sierra began to change from the sweet little girl we had always known into an entitled princess. Kate hadn't been born yet, and the girls were close enough that we almost thought of Sierra as another daughter, so seeing her change in that way was hard." Her hand reached for her husbands as she spoke, her eyes distant.

"The girls slowly started to drift apart, but Sierra was changing too much too quickly. Then when they were twelve, a group of men tried to kidnap Sierra while she was with Kira. The two of them ran and hid, but they were eventually caught. From there on, we only know bits and pieces

221

as Kira has never told us the entire story. Somehow Sierra managed to escape by herself and left Kira alone that same night. She went home and didn't tell anybody what happened. Kira was missing for two weeks before the police found her. It took her another month to even tell us that Sierra had originally been there with her. Kira changed after that, anyone would. We have some idea of what didn't happen, and the scars on her back give us some idea of what did happen but that's all." Krystal's voice petered out as she finished discussing the serious subject.

"What did they do to her?" Charles asked quietly, his eyes drawn to the woman driving the truck.

Kory took over speaking for his wife in a subdued tone. "They tortured her, they took out their frustration on not getting Sierra out on her. As a result, she didn't speak for a month once she was rescued, and she has never trusted anyone again. She also has anger issues and hates most men, it was surprising that she even stayed with you."

Charles looked away and snorted. "What makes you think she did? This morning, she left me in some small town in the middle of nowhere. Alli, she's my dog, and I found her a while later because the truck had run out of gas, which of course was the reason we had stopped in the first place. After that, we drove to the city and here we are, so yes she did try to get away from me."

Krystal looked closely at Charles before turning to her husband. "That barely counts as trying to get away from someone, especially for her. The last time Kira wanted to get away from someone she broke his leg and dislocated his arm and that was just a coworker that annoyed her."

"You're right." Kory pulled his wife close and whispered into her ear. "Do you think she likes him, or is it something else?"

"It's too soon to say, they only just met. The way Kira is acting is odd, however, let's keep an eye on them." She whispered conspiratorially to her husband as Charles looked on oblivious.

"What's the deal between Kira and her sister?" Charles asked them, keeping his eyes on Kira's back.

"What do you mean? They're just normal sisters." Kory replied perplexed.

Charles tilted his head. "Kira was utterly focused on getting back to Kate like she was the most important thing in the world to her."

Krystal sighed and squeezed her husband's arm. "That's because she is. I had Kate when Kira was thirteen. She had barely spoken to anyone for over a year and was becoming ever more withdrawn. Kate was a lifeline for her, seeing her little sister and taking care of her, brought her back to life. I don't think it's an exaggeration to say that Kate is the most important person in Kira's life."

Charles looked away from the interior of the truck and focused on the married couple. "What are the four of you going to do now? It's obvious Kira won't go anywhere without Kate, and I assume you'll go wherever they go."

"You're right about that, Kira hates to leave Kate's side. Honestly, we know it's unhealthy, but at the same time, we don't want Kira to regress. We tried that once, at the behest of a therapist we kept them separated. It was terrible." Krystal swallowed a sob and continued. "Kira shut down mentally and physically, she refused to eat or drink and barely moved from her bed. We had to take her to the hospital within a week, needless to say, that particular experiment didn't last long. It's taken years but Kira can finally leave for a few days at a time for work."

Charles could appreciate that kind of devotion, being willing to do whatever needed to be done for family.

"Charles, I'm getting close to you. I can smell you on the wind, I'll be with you soon." Alli's voice intruded in Charles' mind before he could say anything to them.

Reaching up, Charles knocked on the glass window getting Kira's attention. "Alli is nearby, slow down and let her catch up to us."

Kira let the truck slow as the bridge appeared in front of them. Alli was running alongside the river, her limping stride carrying her quickly towards the waiting truck.

Chapter 22

Alli's stride shortened as she neared the truck, her limp growing more pronounced the slower she ran. Her silvery fur and hair were covered in blood and gore, and something green was dripping from her muzzle.

"Charles, could you clean me please, the smell is getting to me," Alli asked as she limped over to him, favoring her right foreleg.

"Were you able to save anyone?" Charles asked her as the cleaning spell spun circles of water down her body, leaving everything glistening in its wake.

Alli's head sank as she was reminded of her mission. "I don't know..." She said slowly. "Even after I saved them, it seemed like there was something missing in them. Their eyes were blank and hollow, it's like they were empty shells. I broke their chains and killed the monsters, and they never moved, they just lay there." Her voice was puzzled as she spoke to him.

Charles healed the damage to her leg, and they both climbed into the truck. Kory and Krystal moved to the side, so Alli could lay down.

"Let's go, Kira, keep driving," Charles called out as he settled next to Alli's head.

"I don't understand Charles. What was wrong with those people? I just don't understand humans. Don't they want to live?" She put her large head in his lap and closed her mismatched eyes.

"Not everyone can handle this new world," He told her gently as he stroked her fluffy ears.

Alli let out a huff of air and lifted head to look at the two other occupants with them in the back. "Who are these people, they smell like Kira."

"Give me your hands, please?" He requested of them placing their hands on Alli's head. "Alli these are Kira's parents Kory and Krystal; her sister Kate is in the front with her."

"It's nice to meet the both of you. My name is Alli. I am Charles' companion."

"She can talk?" Kory drew back his hand in shock.

"It's telepathy actually, she can talk to people in their minds as long as they are touching her head," Charles explained, putting Kory's hand back on her head.

The truck rumbled onto the bridge as they left the Kansas side of the city behind and crossed over into Missouri. The usual swaying that could be felt on bridges was absent without the multitude of cars that normally occupied it.

On the other side of the bridge, people could be seen moving about in packs armed and watching the people around them.

Kira stopped the truck at the end of the bridge and stepped out to stand next Charles while reaching for Alli's head. "What are we going to do about our quest? After seeing the people there, I don't even know if there is anything we can do for them."

Charles shook his head as he thought. "Now that Alli is back with us, we might be able to find the groups that are trying to survive like the people at the school or the office building. We could at least warn them and tell them that they need to leave. We have just over twenty-four hours left, we should be able to hit a decent portion of the city in that amount of time."

Kira turned away from him and looked at the sleeping form of her sister. "What about my family?"

Charles looked at her in confusion. "Don't you already have a place for them in mind? I thought that was why we came here in the first place."

Night had fully fallen in the time they had been standing there talking. "Uh, well about that." Kira turned away from him the light from the headlights the only thing that allowed her to be seen at all. "I was planning on just leaving the rest of the city to die."

Her father sighed heavily. "That's a little too cold even for you, Kira." He said in admonishment.

Her voice was utterly devoid of warmth as she answered. "They are not more important than Kate or you guys!"

"Nice to know where we stand with our daughter," Krystal muttered softly to her husband.

"Please, you know Kate is always going to be more important to her." He whispered back just as quietly.

"So, what you are saying is that now that your family is safe, you're willing to think of everyone else?" Charles asked.

"Like you're any different?" Kira shot back with a cold smirk.

"No, I'm not," Charles replied without hesitation. "We're wasting time right now though, what are we going to do?"

Kira brought her hand up to her mouth as she yawned loudly. "I've only gotten a little bit of sleep in the last forty-eight or so hours. I'm tired and need some sleep before I do anything. So right now, we are going to find a place to sleep for the night, and then we'll decide in the morning."

Charles noticed that Alli's head was dragging tiredly as well making the choice easy to make. "Fine, let's do that then." Alli lay her head down in the back of the truck as soon as he finished talking.

"I'll just take us someplace with a garage then," Kira told them as she got behind the wheel of the truck.

Kira kept the river to their left as she drove slowly down the road looking for a suitable place to park for the night.

Noises could be heard in the air above them as the night air began to fill with the monsters that came out at night. Screeches and shrieks mixed with the flapping of wings and the subtle thumping noise of wind and air being displaced.

Charles kept a hand on Alli as he ducked down next to Kira's parents, all of them keeping a wary eye on the clear dark sky above them. The moon had yet to rise, but without the light pollution caused by the countless lights found in cities a week before the stars provided ample light to see by. The light from the stars highlighting the forms flitting through the air above them.

An old warehouse across the road from the river stood open with roller doors partially up. Kira aimed the truck at the entrance and stopped the headlights illuminating the interior. Charles hopped out of the back of the truck and into the building looking to the side of the doors for the chain that would raise them.

A loud clanking noise came from above the doors as he pulled on the chain and it rose slowly into the air. Outside the truck revved and inched inside the building, the sound of the exhaust reverberating into a deep bass inside the metal warehouse.

Kira shut off the truck as Charles began lowering the door, the chain spinning quickly under the weight of the metal door. The interior became pitch black as the bottom of the door met with the concrete flooring.

There was a grunt and a muffled curse in the darkness. "Charles, we need some light!" Kira called out as she grunted again.

Charles focused and cast the light spell with a wave of his hand throwing them into the air. Bright white light shone down revealing an old air conditioning unit laying on a pallet that Kira had walked into. New and old units lined the wall of the building, giving them a hint as to what the warehouse had been used for.

Kira carried Kate from the truck and looked around speculatively, unsure where to set her down.

"Put her down in the office. I have some sleeping bags and pillows everyone can use," Charles told them as he made sure the doors were locked.

Alli leaped from the back and hurried over to Kira as her parents climbed slowly out while holding on to each other for support. "The smell of people in here is still fresh. There have been people in this building several times over the last week," Alli informed Charles as she sniffed the air.

Charles followed everyone into the office at the back of the warehouse and began pulling things out of his inventory. Pillows and other items for sleeping were pulled out first, followed by food and water for everyone.

Krystal took several of the sleeping bags and unfurled them next to each other in the corner. Kira gently settled Kate onto the bag closest to the wall and put a pillow behind her head. Kira flopped down next to her and relaxed.

Kory watched as the lights in the warehouse began to vanish, leaving everything outside the dark once more. "I feel like I should really be asking about the magic, but right now I'm too tired to even think properly."

Kira's parents lay down next to their daughters and closed their eyes, seeming to fall asleep within seconds.

"Thanks for saving my sister," Kira muttered sleepily.

Alli curled up next to Charles as he extinguished the last of the lights as everyone descended into the land of dreams.

Charles focused his mind and started the meditation process, his mind splitting and the partitions appearing. Relaxing the control on his mind Charles let himself sink into the depths of his meditative trance. His awareness of the world faded away as he leaned against the metal wall with his legs outstretched next to Alli.

The subtle tremors in the ground brought him back as Alli stirred and lifted her head. Charles opened his eyes and cocked his head as an ever-brightening light trickled in from the small gaps at the floor. Getting to his feet, he rushed from the room and flung open the door to the outside.

The moon hung high in the night sky as the river directly across from the warehouse reflected the light coming from the bridges. Each bridge stretching across the river whether it was built for cars or trains was glowing with a white light.

Alli came out to stand next to him, her shoulder brushing against his arm. "I have a feeling we're not going to be going back into that city." She sounded conflicted at the thought.

Charles sighed as he continued watching the glowing constructs. "Why do you still care? You tried to help them already, how much more are you going to do for people that have given up?"

"I'm not doing it for the ones that have given up, I'm doing it for those that haven't." Alli looked away from the river and lifted her head to look him in the eye. "Don't worry. I'm not going to put you in danger."

Charles grabbed the scruff of her neck, forcing her eyes to stay on his. "I'm not worried about me getting injured. I'm worried about you getting hurt and me not being there to help."

The tremors in the ground grew into rumbles, distracting them from their conversation. Behind them, Kira appeared at the door with wide eyes already focused on the distant bridges. The light now encompassed them fully, and they had started to shimmer.

Kira squeezed past Alli and stepped into the night air with them. "What's going on?"

Charles let go of Alli and scratched at the dusting of unshaven hair on his jaw. "We're not entirely sure, but I have a feeling that this is the same thing that happened yesterday with the cars."

"You mean you think the bridges are going to vanish?" Kira asked without looking away from the light.

"Yeah," He answered simply. "From what I overheard from the people talking about it, it seems like something similar happened before they all disappeared."

"If they disappear, then there goes our quest." She informed them.

Charles shrugged not particularly disturbed by the idea. "There was no mention of what the reward was, anyway. I only accepted the quest because of Alli and you. Now that we have found your family, and we can't go back into the city, I see no reason to stay."

"Wait," Kira exclaimed, stopping him. "I want to see the city transform. I want to see how it happens."

Charles turned away from the light show and faced her. "That almost makes it sound like you are going to continue traveling with us."

"Why do you think that?" She asked not confirming or denying the thought.

"Because there is no other reason for us to wait for you since we are now done with our business here. The only reason we have to wait for you and not leave is that you intend to keep traveling with us." Next, to him, Alli seemed to perk up at the idea of more traveling companions.

"I admit that the idea has crossed my mind," Kira began, hedging her words. "Now that we found my family there is nothing holding me here any longer. The only thing is, I'd want them to come with us as well. I can't leave Kate alone in this new monster-ridden world."

Charles snorted and spoke before he could stop himself. "This world was always filled with monsters; the only difference is that now people can recognize them."

Kira stilled, her entire body going stiff. "What do you know?" Her voice was low and had a dangerous lilt to it.

Alli backed away from her, her ears lying flat on her head.

"Only what your parents told me earlier, they didn't go into many details," Charles told her gently while reaching for Alli in an effort to comfort her.

Kira's face was screwed up in an expression that Charles couldn't decipher. "My parents don't tell anyone about that time. Why would they tell you? They just met you!"

"I can't answer that, all I can say is that I asked them about Sierra and why you reacted to her so violently. I can't say as to why they decided to trust me with your story, but I'm glad that they did. Before they told it to me, I would never have even considered letting you join us after everything you put us through. Now, I'm at least open to the idea. I know you now and that puts you and your family in a separate category than the faceless people that inhabit that city." He finished with a tilt of his chin towards the city across the river.

"What does that mean?" Kira asked, letting some of the tenseness out of her body.

Charles held onto Alli as he made a split-second decision. "It means that as long as your family is alright with it, then you can join us." What he had told her was true, now that he knew her and her family it wasn't so easy for him to turn away from her like it was everyone else. He had other reasons as well for wanting to bring her with them, they would need more vehicles, eventually. She was the one who was a mechanic and could get them running again, not him.

"Are you sure about this Charles? What if she decides to leave us in the middle of nowhere again?" Alli's voice was unsure as she questioned him.

"It'll be fine, Kira won't leave us like that again," Charles said loud enough for Kira to hear him as he answered her. He wasn't sure where the conviction behind his words came from, but he was certain they were true. She was in many ways similar to him. When they had met, he wasn't family, and she had only remained with them because of Alli. Now though, something had changed that for her, same as it had for him.

The light started to fade noticeably, drawing their eyes back to the river before they could say anything more on the matter.

Alli noticed it first. "The bridges, they're becoming transparent."

She was right, they were. The light was taking the bridges with it. The more the light faded, the more the bridges disappeared as well. Soon enough the light and the bridges were all gone, leaving them standing there underneath the moonlit night sky.

"Let's get some more sleep, there's nothing more we can do for those people," Kira said firmly as she turned her back on the river and faced the dark interior of the warehouse. "Thanks for letting us come with you." She said, softy, as her hand brushed his bicep.

Charles remained still watching the monsters flapping in the sky that they had ignored up till that moment. Next, to him Alli twitched her ears and turned to follow Kira, pausing at the door. "Come on, Charles. She needs light."

Charles shook his head and turned away from the soon to be lost city. His hand made a grab for her fluffy tail as she hurried out of his reach with a shallow yip. A ball of light formed in his hand with a thought and floated ahead of him as he secured the door behind them.

Chapter 23

The rest of the night passed quickly as Charles sank into his meditations for the second time that night. He still could not sleep, but mentally he could feel the effects of staying awake for so long. The strain of staying awake for so long had affected his thoughts on more than one occasion already. People were not meant to go so long without the restful nature of sleep to ground them and organize their thoughts.

Meditation was a poor second to that, but it was the only thing that was keeping him sane. The potion on his hip helped as well, it healed his mind and wiped away the buildup of toxins in his body that came with lack of sleep.

He was growing weary of the potion though. It had other effects on him than just healing his wounds. In the week since the gods had renovated the world, he had gone from a skinny and soft fleshed desk-jockey to someone with muscle. His stomach was flat, his arms and legs were lean from all the exercise he had been getting. His belt was cinched tight around his now loose-fitting pants. He liked these changes, but the fact of the matter was that they were too much too quickly, and that was ignoring the silvery runes that now tattooed the thigh of his left leg.

The outside changes were good, they would undoubtedly help him to stay alive even. What worried him though, as if drinking the potion was changing his physical body this much, then what was it doing to his mind. More than that, what might it be doing to Alli?

He had noticed how smart she was right away, and she had only continued to grow smarter. Could some of it be the potion changing her and not just her leveling-up? Going along with that thought, was it a bad thing, or could it turn into a bad thing? He had been giving her the potion more than to himself, and now he found himself hesitating.

With a shake of his head, Charles dispelled the errant thoughts and decided he would discuss the matter with Alli later. Right now, he had something else to do. Messages that he had been ignoring all night were brought to the fore as he began to read.

Congratulations, the effects of meditation have been increased due to the runes inscribed on your body. As a result, Basics of Mana Usage has been upgraded to Mana Usage. The mana in spells can now be freely felt and changed for greater or even differing effects. New spells may now be learned outside of Meditating.

Congratulations, your animal companion Alli has leveled up. She is now level 15; her status points have been automatically distributed.

Congratulations, your animal companion Alli has become the first being to reach level 15 and unlock the class system. As the first being to reach this milestone, she is allowed to choose from any class, regardless of requirements.

Charles paused as he saw that message his eyes wide with shock. He hadn't even known there was a class system, he could only barely grasp what that might even mean. Beneath those messages was another one at the very end of the list, obviously one that had come in late last night.

Kira Lourne would like to join your party. Do you accept?

She must have sent the request last night after they had talked, with that in mind Charles accepted her into the party.

Across the room, Kira stirred and opened her eyes. "I was wondering when you were going to notice that." She told him softly so as not to awaken the people still sleeping.

"I ignore the messages for the most part and tend to only look at them at night. Reading them during the day is pointless for me. I don't need to know that I leveled-up since it does nothing for me." He explained as Alli stirred at his feet.

Kira climbed carefully to her feet and came to stand next to him. "How does that work exactly? Not being able to level-up, how are you still able to survive?"

Charles looked at her and spoke in a dry voice. "Did I look like I was doing a great job of staying alive when you met me? The only reason I'm still alive is because of Alli and the gifts I was given. The potion is great if I haven't used it recently and the glove allows me to use powerful magic but destroys my arm forcing me to use the potion. Without being able to distribute the points I get from leveling up, I'm barely more than a glass cannon." Charles sighed and closed his eyes. "I'm not even sure how long I can keep this up. My normal magic isn't going to be effective at all soon, which only leaves the glove. What happens to me when even that is no longer useful?"

Kira stood above him with her arms folded thoughtfully. "Have you at least distributed the points, I mean I know that they only take effect when we go to sleep. Maybe they'll increase slowly over time. I mean the way I see it, is that they take effect at night to help us with the change. It might work differently for you if nothing else at least you'll be set for when you do fall asleep or get knocked unconscious or something. It would suck to have let an opportunity like that pass you by."

Charles opened his eyes and stared at the ceiling as he considered her words.

"She is right Charles, you should distribute them all now. You were not expecting to get knocked unconscious last time and look what happened. If something like that happens again it would be a wasted opportunity at the very least." Alli told him firmly as her mismatched eyes flickered open, and she climbed to her feet in front of him.

Kira sighed next to them, "You realize I can't hear you two talking."

Alli's tail twitched, and she stepped closer to Kira offering her head to be touched.

"Fine, whatever," Charles said as he quickly dumped his available points into everything but strength. The bulk of them ending up in his magic and intelligence categories. "There it's done, let's move on."

Kira held firmly to Alli's head as she spoke, her eyes drifting to her sleeping family members. "We should go outside before we wake them on accident."

Charles pushed up to his feet, using the wall for support as his stiff muscles protested against their sudden use. Alli's tail brushed against his face as she walked ahead of him, Kira's hand still resting on her head as they quietly talked.

The sky was a deep cloudless blue as he followed them outside and saw the way the cityscape had changed during the night. Across the river, the large shelldragon's from the day before were slamming their massive bodies into buildings destroying them. Distant buildings had already succumbed to their bashing and had fallen over into a pile of rubble.

Charles stepped away from the warehouse and across the road next to the river. The sides of the river were muddy and strewn with rocks keeping the fast-moving water a distinct muddy brown color. The morning light had brought people out in droves all standing near the river with their gazes fixed on the city they could no longer access.

The subtle murmur of people talking next to the banks of the river reached his ears carried like the current of the river. The line of shelldragon's kept advancing in the distance crashing into buildings with every lumbering step.

Alli came to stand next to him. "It's completely smooth."

"What is?" Charles asked her, turning his head from the city to look at her.

"The road where the bridge was," She told him simply her head turned towards where the bridge had been the day before.

She was right, the section of road that had connected to the bridge was completely smooth. Everything that might have even so much as hinted to the existence of the bridge was gone. Every metal girder, strut, and pylon had vanished.

"Interesting, it's like it was cut from the ground and not ripped out." He said as his eyes drifted over the people crouching next to the smooth ground feeling it.

"We need more gas for the truck," Kira told them as she came to stand behind them.

"I have a little left in my inventory, why don't you use that, and then we'll go around collecting more," Charles told her as he pulled the two containers that still had gas from his inventory.

"Sounds good, now that we're back in the city there is something that I want to find as well. I think most of the boats around here should have a hand crank pump somewhere on board. If we can find one, then we'll be able to take gas from the tanks at the gas stations instead of just from the cars we find." Kira had a hand running through Alli's fur as she spoke to them.

"A hand pump?" Charles questioned.

"It's just a small pump that uses a hand crank to suck gas through a pipe and out the other end. Boats have them for barreled gas, and some people have installed them on their trucks for the same reason." Kira explained as she pointed to a small pier that could be barely seen in the distance.

The vague description she had given was enough for Charles to get an idea of what it looked like. "Alli and I'll go down to that pier and see if we can find gas and that pump. Why don't you fill up the truck with these and look it over? It's been driven a lot since you fixed it. I assume it would be a good idea to make sure everything is in good condition."

Kira picked up the red containers of gas he had set on the ground and turned away. "Keep your eyes open. It doesn't look like the people are overly worried about monsters around here. There may be a reason for that, or it might just be them being stupid. Be careful and pay attention."

Alli rubbed against her as Kira walked passed leaving them alone for the moment. "She's still worried about her sister, she doesn't want to go farther from her than she has to right now," Alli told him as she watched their companion hurry back to the warehouse.

"Let's hurry and find this pump and some more gas. If I have a choice in the matter, I would like to be far away from this place when that city gets turned into a dungeon." Charles wandered down the road, keeping an eye on their surroundings.

The morning light reflected off of the river drew glistening rainbow arcs in the misty air. Alli's tongue lolled out as she enjoyed the cooling moisture and warm rays of the late fall sun.

People stayed away from them as they walked down the road and after a couple of minutes made it to the small pier they had seen. The pier itself was bigger than he had thought it was, but that wasn't saying much as the only things tied to it were rowboats. A couple of them had small motors hanging off the back, but none of them were big enough to need a pump of any kind.

"There are larger boats farther down," Alli told him after seeing the disappointment on his face.

Charles stepped out onto the pier and let his eyes follow the curve of the river. What Alli had said was true, right where the river began to bend there were several large barge type boats tied up next to a small port.

This early in the morning the people that were outside were watching the city across the river and not the boats. Jogging lightly, they hurried to the barges they had spotted and leaped on board as soon as they drew close enough.

The deck of the first barge was slick with dew but otherwise bare as everything on it had already been taken. The second barge, however, had wooden crates stacked in the middle with metal barrels lining the edges.

Alli jumped to the second barge and started sniffing the barrels. "Some of these have the same smell as those containers you gave to Kira."

Charles was surprised as she told him that, he had been sure there would be nothing but barrels of diesel. He had thought that was what most boats used, after all, then again small generators probably used regular gasoline. If that was the case, then it made sense that there would be both on a large boat such as this barge.

Shoved between the barrels and the crates were two separate hand crank pumps that had been painted red. Grabbing both of them he stuck them in his inventory and turned to Alli. "Show me which of these barrels smell like the gas I gave to Kira." He could mark them now, and then they could come back for them later.

Alli led him to the first barrel as he pulled out a knife to mark it. The knife held in his hand as he paused a stray thought flitting through his mind. Instead of marking it, he simply tried to put the barrel in his inventory. Shock was evident on his face as the metal container vanished, he couldn't understand the rules involved with his inventory. He already knew that it was different from other peoples, but it seemed inconsistent in some regards. For instance, he couldn't place a mountain bike inside it, but a fifty-gallon drum full of liquid was not an issue?

With an exasperated sigh, Charles followed after Alli and quickly placed the other four barrels in his inventory. It was enough gas to keep them on the move for the foreseeable future and more than any generator should have required.

Charles took a second to look at the many large wooden crates stacked around the barge before turning away. He didn't feel like spending the time to go through whatever was in them, besides the remaining people in the city probably needed whatever was in them more than him.

"Come on Alli, let's go back to Kira. We found what we needed and have more than enough gas now." Charles told her as he jumped from the deck of the barge and onto the pier that ran next to it.

Alli's paws thumped on the flooring of the deck before she jumped and landed next to Charles. Her muzzle lifted into the air, and she breathed in deeply sniffing the air. "Charles we should hurry, the smell of monsters is growing stronger. A large number are coming this way."

Instantly Charles was running back to the warehouse. He had no reason to doubt Alli. If she said she was smelling a large number of monsters, then that was exactly what she was smelling. He didn't want to get caught in a wave of monsters if he could avoid it, more than that, they needed to warn Kira and her family.

Ahead of them, they saw that the large warehouse doors had been rolled up allowing the morning light to shine in while Kira worked on the truck. Beside him, Alli ran into the warehouse and to Kira's side as Charles wrapped his hands around the chain and began lowering the large door. The loud clicks and clangs of the chain speeding through the contraption at the top of the door filled the open warehouse.

The door closed with a bang as Kate and her parents ran out of the backroom to see what was going on. "Everyone be quiet!" Charles barked before anyone could say anything.

Holding his hand in the air he hurried over to the other door and opened it enough for a sliver of light to shine through. Bringing his head close to the crack, Charles peered out for a second before shaking his head and closing the door.

"Alli smelled a large number of monsters heading our way, we need to be as quiet as we can for now," Charles told the family as he backed away from the door and focused on Kira. "We found two pumps and some barrels full of gas. How is the truck?"

"It needs some oil, but other than that it is looking good. Where are the barrels, how large are we talking here?" Kira informed him as she stepped away from the truck and drifted towards her sister.

"The barrels are about this size," Charles told her with a smirk as he pulled one of the metal containers from his inventory next to the truck. "And this is one of the pumps."

The gathered people all felt their mouths drop open in surprise and shock as the barrel materialized before them. That was not how inventories worked. Kate who had been lying in bed sick for the last week was even more shocked than everyone else.

Kira held her hand out for the pump as Alli sank to the ground and growled at the door. "They're here." She announced to Charles.

Chapter 24

O utside the closed doors of the warehouse, a rumble could be heard growing closer. Charles stepped towards the door and cracked it open as everyone else huddled together with wide fear-filled eyes. As soon as the door cracked open, the noise grew louder and was accompanied by a myriad of other noises. The screech of metal being crushed and scratched alongside heavy breathing made them all cover their ears at the cacophonous noise.

Charles brought his eye to the door before stepping back and waving Alli and Kira forward in puzzlement.

The walls of the building shook as monsters impacted into it, one after another. The reason for his puzzled expression soon became clear as they pressed their eyes against the crack in the door. All of the monsters were running past the buildings and leaping into the water.

Lines of monsters stretching around buildings and filling the roads and alleyways to capacity, all running towards the river.

Everyone was quiet as the horde outside the doors continued to rush past for several minutes. The walls continued to shudder and shriek as the metal stressed and dented inwards. As one Kira and Alli backed away from the door and gently pushed it closed.

Creeping closer to Charles, Kira placed her hand on Alli's head and whispered to him. "What do you think they are all doing?"

"They're going into the city before it becomes a dungeon," Alli told her confidently. "Don't forget all the monsters on the other side were heading to the city as well."

"I didn't forget, but we didn't run into any monsters in the city. If they were all heading there, then where did they go?" Kira whispered back harshly.

"This must be the last group trying to get into the city before it becomes a dungeon." Charles quietly said thoughtfully as he moved back to the door and opened it a crack and peered out. "Well, that explains it." He muttered to himself before waving the others over to look. "Watch what happens when they finish crossing the river."

Kira pushed him away from the door taking his place. Pressing her face against the opening she squinted her eyes as everything came into focus. "They're disappearing like the bridges last night." Her whispered words barely reaching anyone's ears.

Kate clung to her parents as her face scrunched up in confusion, and she had to bite her lip to keep from speaking. Seeing this Kira wandered over to her and explained. "Last night the bridges crossing the river going into the city were encompassed in light and vanished. Right now, something similar is happening to the monsters crossing the river. Each of them is being swallowed up by the light and then vanishing."

"How much gas is in the truck?" Charles asked backing away the door and getting close to them.

Kira tilted her head back as she thought. "It should be around a little less than half the tank. Enough to get away from the city in any case."

"Good, everyone get into the truck. Kira, you drive I'll open the doors as soon as it is clear." He ordered them as he pulled out the key for the truck and stored the barrel and pump.

"What's going on?" Kira whispered to him softly as her family climbed into the back of the truck next to Alli.

"I'm not sure, but the glow isn't just surrounding the monsters anymore. The ground next to the river is starting to glow as well, I'd rather not be near it for whatever is next. As soon as the monsters clear up, we'll leave." Charles whispered back to her before going back to the door.

The number of monsters running through streets had started to dwindle as they talked. Only a few of the slower monsters were still running towards the river. Charles felt his eye drawn to the sight across the river. Each of the monsters that had swum across and made it to the opposite bank had begun to glow and release small motes of light before the light swallowed each of them in turn.

What had him worried though was what was happening about a hundred feet up from the bank of the river. A line of deep blue light that stretched into the distance was emanating from the ground itself. Something about the light and its placement bothered him. Whatever it was, it was connected to the dungeon, and that alone was enough to make him wary of it.

Charles waited for a minute after he saw the last monster run through the street before closing the door with a deep relief filled breath. Everything had quieted down as the monsters had decreased, forcing fewer of them into the sides of buildings.

Reaching out, he grasped the chain connected to the large rolling warehouse door and began to pull on it. Behind him, Kira started the truck and shifted it into reverse, the back-up lights shining on the rising doors.

As soon as the doors were high enough, Charles motioned for Kira to move. The truck backed up slowly, clearing the door with inches to spare. Running to the passenger side of the truck, he flung open the door and pulled himself in next to her.

"Let's go!" He ordered as soon as the door was closed, swiveling in his seat to watch the river behind them.

Kira shifted the truck into first and gunned it as her family held onto the sides in the back. The wheels screeched, and the truck shot forward, speeding back down the roads they had come the night before. There were few cars on the road in this area of the city allowing them to pick up speed as they hurried to the highway.

"I thought the quest said we had until midnight tonight before the city became a dungeon!" Kira said angrily as one of her hands smacked the steering wheel.

"It did," Charles answered turning to face forward. "My guess is that just means when it is finished becoming a dungeon. If that is the case, then we had little time to help the people of the city to begin with."

"Why did they even bother giving us a quest then in the first place?"

Charles grunted, sharing her annoyance. "They probably just thought it would be interesting or something, the gods seem like the type to do something like that."

"Oh, have you met many of them then?" Kira asked with a crooked brow.

"Just one and believe me that is one too many," Charles answered refusing to meet her eyes.

Kira steered the truck up the ramp onto the highway and didn't reply. Meanwhile, Charles took the chance to look back at the river and the city beyond one last time.

"It's a wall!" He exclaimed suddenly sitting up straight. "That line of light on the other side of the river is turning into a wall!"

Kira risked a quick glance over her shoulder and saw the same thing he had. The line that had once been on the ground was now hanging a foot or two in the air and rising slowly. Beneath it, a brown and grey wall of earth and stone that extended into the distance was flowing up from the ground. Turning back towards the front her foot jammed down on the accelerator and a new sense of urgency swept through her.

Next to her, Charles kept his eyes on the wall that was growing ever higher. In the back, Alli met Charles' eyes for a brief moment before she turned away to watch the wall. "Charles, I think I should choose a class now before it is too late. The closer that dungeon gets to completion the more I feel something is about to happen."

Charles rolled the window down slightly, so she could hear him better. "What class are you thinking of choosing?"

"I can't seem to make up my mind, I have access to all of them including the advanced ones. The problem lies in what I am capable of, many of them revolve around certain types of weapons or the ability to use magic. I've already decided against choosing any of the weapon-based classes for obvious reasons. The magic-based ones are a different matter though if I choose one of them, do I gain the ability to use that magic or have I just selected a useless class?"

Charles looked down at the glove on his hand and remembered how he had come to learn magic. "You might be able to learn magic through my glove if the class doesn't allow it automatically." He hesitantly uttered into the wind.

Alli looked back at him. "We'll try that out later then, I think for now it is better to choose something that will be useful right away. I've made up my mind!" She announced to him firmly having made her choice.

The large silver dog in the back of the truck seemed to draw in the light around it. The people next to her flinched away as her massive frame flickered out of focus and turned incorporeal. Then just like that, it was over. The shadows took their normal places and her body stopped drinking in the surrounding light. She became solid again and let out a shaky breath.

"That was most uncomfortable." Was all she managed to get out before she slumped down unconscious.

Kate reached out a shaking hand to make sure that Alli was real before looking at Charles with wide eyes.

Charles noticed the presence of a new message in the corner of his vision and focused on it bringing it to the fore where he could read it.

Congratulations, your animal companion 'Alli' has chosen a class. As the first of her kind and the first entity in over a millennium to gain a class, all abilities related to the chosen class have been unlocked and can now be learned.

Congratulations, Alli has become a 'Shadow Walker'.

They would have to see what she was capable of later, for now, he felt his eyes drawn back to the growing wall. Kira had been speeding down the highway dodging parked and destroyed cars for several minutes and still, he could see the wall. It had grown to over a hundred feet and was still growing.

Vaguely he was aware of other people watching the wall on the roads around them, many of them beginning to run. Kira ignored them all and kept her foot pressed to the floor. The truck began to shake as she pushed it to the limits as the road cleared up for the moment.

The city could no longer be seen behind the walls as they continued to grow. The shelldragon's had continued to destroy each building they came across and many of the larger buildings had already been destroyed.

"Charles," Kira said through gritted teeth, getting his attention. "Look at the information on the quest!"

He didn't bother to question her as he brought up the quest and immediately saw what had her so tense. The information had changed since the last time he had looked at it over a day before.

The gods have issued you a quest, rescue the people of Kansas City from the clutches of the monsters. This is a timed quest, as the Kansas City location will be converted into a free-spawning dungeon in 3 minutes. Due to the abundance of people left in the city when the creation of the dungeon began, you have failed the quest. All remaining people left without the bounds of the city and dungeon have been absorbed as material and energy, shortening the time required for completion. No rewards will be given for this quest.

"Haha," Charles laughed hollowly after reading the information. "It really was a quest that we could never complete from the very beginning it was rigged against us. There is no way we could have gotten everyone out in time, and anyone left inside would have just shortened the time-limit."

Kira slammed on the brakes and shifted the truck into neutral as she opened her door and turned to face the wall that now rose above the city. "I want to watch what happens next. I want to watch what we couldn't prevent... I want to watch what the gods have in store for us." Her voice had started out strong until it petered out at the end.

In the back of the truck Kory, Krystal and Kate climbed out and stood next to her in their vigil of what was to come.

Charles quickly climbed into the back and shook Alli waking her from her class choosing induced slumber. "Watch, the creation of the dungeon is about to commence." He told her as her unfocused eyes flickered open.

Charles kept one eye on the quest details, watching as the time began to countdown to zero.

"5"

"4"

"3"

"2" The light at the top of the wall grew brighter, casting shadows everywhere.

"1"

"0" The light at the top of the wall vanished and a great gust of air was expelled from the walls.

"It's complete, I guess that's what a dungeon looks like from the outside," Kira said aloud, feeling somewhat let down that it hadn't been more impressive. "Let's go."

Kira got back into the truck as Charles jumped from the truck bed and turned away from the wall. He stumbled on the pavement as his eyes were drawn back to the wall at the last second while he was in the air.

"Oh, that's not good!" Charles muttered looking at the monsters clinging to the top of the wall surrounding the dungeon. With a distant roar that could only just be heard, they began to leap from the top of the wall and down into the river far below.

Epilogue

"With this, the creation of the first dungeon is now complete. The game will begin in one week's time. Has anyone else decided on who they want to choose as their hero?" The cloaked leader of the game informed the gods gathered around the table.

"Whatever you say 'Bob'!" Zeus yelled laughingly.

"I can't believe he decided to call me that." The shadowy DM sitting at the head of the table muttered darkly. "Absolutely no respect, you'd think he'd be happy to gain the favor of a god, but no he does something like this. In fact, I don't think I'm going to tell him the real reason he was chosen just yet!"

The gathered gods began to talk and laugh at his expense for a few minutes before he could calm them down.

"I've made my selection," Odin announced, firmly silencing everyone.

"And who have you chosen?" Bob asked, grateful for the change in the topic.

"I have chosen the girl Sierra!"

The table was silent for a second before exploding into conversation in the wake of the unexpected announcement.

Brigit slammed her hands into the table and glared at the one-eyed man before turning and stomping away from everyone.

Book 1 End

Afterword

First, I would like to THANK YOU! for reading this book. I hope you have enjoyed reading them as much as I'm enjoying writing them.

Book two is on hold until I finish the first book in my new Dungeon Core with a twist Fantasy series. If you enjoyed either this book or any of my others, then I would really appreciate it if you took the time to rate and review it on Amazon and Goodreads. Amazon rewards writers when we get four or five-star reviews, so please take the time and leave a review.

I have heard many complaints from people that Amazon is making it harder for them to leave a review, so if you can't, I understand, but if you can, a brief short review is as useful as a full-on, in-depth analysis.

Thanks for reading and until next time,

Joshua Kern

Acknowledgements

I would like to thank my alpha readers, my family, who spend endless hours reading and re-reading everything I write as well as seeking out any plot holes and typos. It has taken me a long time to get to the point in my life where I can actually sit down and write like I have wanted to for so very long, to all the people that have encouraged me over the years and helped make this possible, I thank you!

About the Author

Joshua Kern was born in a little town situated somewhere in Ohio and raised in an even smaller town someplace in Colorado. He attended University for a time, where he discovered that while he enjoyed Electrical Engineering and Computer Science his true passion lay in writing. He lives primarily in Colorado but has been known to move around as the need arises. When not writing Joshua enjoys riding motorcycles, reading anything he can get his hands on, and anime.

Other Books by Joshua Kern

Refton & Thomas

Forgotten Spies

Forgotten Child

The Game of Gods

Arc 1 – Human

The Beginning

The Death of Champions

Arc 2 – Demi-God

Fragments

A Tower Novella

Pieces of Divinity

Arc 3 – God

The Dungeon Alaria

Arc 1 – Integration

The Dungeon Alaria

The Creators Daughter

Arc 2 – ??

The Well Within

The Well Within: Part 1

Stand Alone

The Ridden

Duologies & Box Sets

The Game of Gods: Arc 1 Duology Box Set

The Dungeon Alaria: The World of Alaria Arc 1 Duology Box Set